IF ONLY FOR ONE NIGHT

by
Victoria Christopher Murray
and
ReShonda Tate Billingsley

BROWN GIRLS BOOKS

Houston, Texas * Washington, D.C.

If Only For One Night © 2018 by
ReShonda Tate Billingsley, Victoria Christopher Murray

Brown Girls Books LLC
www.BrownGirlsBooks.com

ISBN: 978-978-1-944359-72-0 (ebook)
ISBN: 978-1944359-73-7 (print)

CHAPTER 1

Angelique Mason

I snapped the band of my thong onto my waist, then shimmied until everything was in place. As I twisted from the left to the right, checking out my image in the antique leaning mirror, the price of these ten inches of satin and lace once again skipped through my mind.

"Two hundred and twenty-eight dollars," I whispered, but then, I shook my head and tossed that thought aside.

Really, it just didn't matter. This little teddy and thong was so worth every one of those dollars that I'd charged to my American Express. If there was anything that was going to make Preston walk in the door and drop all that he was doing and all that he was thinking, these little strips of red material would do it.

Turning back to the dresser, I faced the array of fragrant creams that were lined inside my vanity tray and finally selected the Jimmy Choo lotion. I hadn't opened it, had actually tossed it into the trash when Preston came home with this gift-wrapped inside a huge basket — my consolation prize after he missed the Chamber of Commerce dinner where I was honored for my foundation, Black Girl Magic.

It was ironic that Preston had missed that night when he'd been the one to bring the good news home to me about six months ago. Even now remembering it, all I could do was smile:

I couldn't imagine who was banging on the front door like that. It had to be the police.

Rushing from the kitchen, I peeked through the side window and frowned.

"Preston," I began when I opened the door. "What are you...."

Before I could finish my thought or my words, my husband swept me off my feet and into his arms, swinging me around.

"Goodness!" I gasped, and then giggled. "What...Preston...what..." It wasn't until he put me down that I was able to string together a full sentence. "Oh, my." I pressed my hand against my chest. "What are you doing?"

"I'm just so proud of you."

"Me?" I frowned, trying to figure out what my husband was talking about.

"Yes. You. My beautiful wife." He pulled me into his arms again. "You are the two-thousand-seventeen recipient of Houston's Woman on the Move Award."

"What?" He had to be kidding. This was Houston's most prestigious community service award. Why would I be given this honor? I glanced up at my husband and I couldn't remember a time when Preston's grin had been wider. "You're serious."

"I wouldn't kid about something like this."

Indeed! These kinds of accolades were so important to my husband and the pride he had for me beamed right through at that moment....

I sighed. He'd been proud then, but there wasn't enough pride inside of him to put his own work aside to be there for me.

So last Monday, I'd donned my off-the-shoulder crepe evening gown and strolled that red carpet alone, sat on the dais alone, and accepted the award, then had taken hundreds of media photos — all standing alone.

I'd had to force every smile and force back every tear, but I'd done it...because practice had made me the perfect pretender. In the last three years, there were so many times when I'd cried while wearing a smile. All because of Preston.

"Stop it," I scolded myself. Why was I thinking of all of this negativity? Wasn't I always talking to the girls in my foundation about the law of attraction? Wasn't I always telling them that you become what you think about?

So, I turned off those memories and in my mind created a new one — of tonight.

Picking up the lotion, I sat on the bed, then squeezed a quarter-size dab onto my palm. As I raised my leg and massaged the lotion into my skin, I closed my eyes and imagined that my fingertips were no longer mine...my fingers belonged to Preston. And now, his tongue followed the trail set by his fingers.

I sat up and shuddered.

I could almost feel it, I could almost imagine it.

Almost.

That was the problem. It was hard for me to imagine because it was hard to remember all the way back to the last time when his hands had touched me that way, since his lips had made me shudder. Yes, we'd had quickies, once or maybe twice a week when Preston just needed a release....

"Stop it!"

Why did I keep going back to how it used to be? Why couldn't I just focus on what would happen once Preston came home? Tonight was going to be one for the ages after my husband saw me in this lingerie and these…I pushed myself from the bed and slipped into my six-inch Louboutins, another consolation gift from my husband, although I couldn't remember what his apology was for that time.

Turning back to the full-length mirror, I finger-fluffed my curls that were still fresh from my appointment today. I didn't like wearing my shoulder-length hair out this way, preferring my signature ponytail when causal, chignon when professional.

But Preston loved my hair curled and he loved my legs in stilettos, and he loved me wearing more skin than clothes. So tonight…Preston would love me.

The chime of the downstairs door opening shocked me, and made me freeze for just a moment. Of course, I expected Preston home — it was just after nine. But still, my heart fluttered.

"Alexa," I spoke to my wireless speaker, "play *Adore* by Prince."

"*Adore*, explicit by Prince," Alexa told me.

Explicit! That was exactly what Preston and I needed.

I jumped onto the bed (not so sexily), but by the time I plumped up the pillows and leaned back, I was nothing but sexy. I was sitting in the middle of a memory — our wedding night, *Adore* (our favorite song) playing on a CD as we made love, over and over and over….

I sighed and then, I smiled. Mentally, I was finally in the right place.

Until the end of time
I'll be there for you….

My heart beat to the rhythm of the song as I listened for Preston. I heard his faint steps on our parquet floor in the foyer, but then, I heard something else…his voice.

Please, God, let this night be perfect.

His steps were coming closer, he was on the stairs. But his voice came with him. He was still in the hallway, but now, I heard him clearly.

"I told you that's not the way to go. You're too young, your company is too young for such a conservative approach. You have the luxury of waiting out the stock market."

I closed my eyes as there was a moment of silence.

Then, Preston started up again, "Yeah, there will be some bear markets, but the bull is always charging. Trust me on this. High risk equals high rewards."

Of course he would be on the phone, no matter the time.

In a second, I decided to change my approach. I'd thought laying back on the bed would remind him of our wedding night. But now, I scooted to the edge and crossed my — what Preston still referred to as my gold medal gymnast's — legs. Yes, we'd been married for eight years, but I'd been blessed to be one of those women who looked better now than on the day we'd married. I'd been a girl in 2009. Back then, even at twenty-six, I still had my competitive gymnast's body, hardly gaining a pound after college. I was a tall gymnast, at five-five, but I was as svelte as any who had ever glided through the air.

But marriage had filled me out and Preston always told me he loved the new bends and curves of my body — all one-hundred and thirty pounds of me.

So I sat, tugged at my teddy to reveal even more (of the little) cleavage that I had and crossed my best assets, my legs. Once Preston walked into our bedroom, he would drop the phone (and the call) and focus only on me.

"I don't know why you don't want to trust me on this," he said as he stepped over the threshold.

He looked up.

I smiled.

He didn't, though he did pause long enough to walk over, lean down and kiss me on my forehead.

Then, "Yeah, it's your money, but you've hired me to help you make the big bucks." He kept talking...all the way into the master bathroom.

It took a moment for me to close my mouth, but the shock hadn't worn off. It was like he didn't even notice.

He didn't close the door, so his voice was still clear. He said, "Look, I have to go. I have something important to tend to...."

He did notice me!

"We'll pick up on this tomorrow, but stay off the Internet. Anybody can post anything. You need to talk to people who've made this money and who can help you make more."

I scooted back on the bed, thinking that I should resume the wedding-night pose.   "All right, man. Let's touch base first thing in the morning."

There was not a time when Preston had ever shut off a call for me. That was a good sign. This was going to be epic.

There was nothing but silence for a few moments and I waited for Preston to come strolling out of the bathroom. But when he didn't, I called out, "Hey, baby. How was your...."

"Kelvin, it's Preston. I just got off the phone with Brad and you're not going to believe what he's talking about doing."

Wait! What had just happened? Hadn't he just told the other guy that he had something important to tend to? Wasn't I that important something that needed tending?

I scooted off the bed, all thoughts of being sexy gone! I wobbled a bit as I tried to stomp across the room; clearly stilettos weren't meant for this kind of mood.

In the bathroom doorway, I stood there wearing ten inches of satin and lace and a whole lotta attitude. With my arms folded, I glared at my husband.

He paced across the space between the double sink and the Jacuzzi tub, not even looking my way.

His head was bowed as words poured from him. He was so deep into his conversation that he didn't even pause. Not until I cleared my throat and said, "Ummm, hello."

When he glanced up, his eyes roamed over me and the way he paused at certain parts of my body, I knew he'd finally seen me. But then, what was his reaction?

He held up his forefinger.

His forefinger.

I had a finger for him. "No," I said, my tone filled with my demands. "I will not give you a minute."

"Babe, come on," he whispered, though his eyes did travel the length of my body again. But then, he returned to his call. "This is our reputation and yeah, it's his money, but he came to us because we know what's best."

I stood, seething and Preston must have felt the heat. Now, he had something else for me — this time, when he gave me his glance, his eyes stayed for a moment and then, he gave me…a thumbs up.

A. Thumbs. Up? I knew what I looked like in this get-up. There wasn't a Victoria Secret's model nor a Playboy bunny who'd want to stand next to me right now.

"That's what I told him." The phone was still pressed to his ear when Preston strolled toward me. He pulled the phone away, whispered, "You look hot, babe," then gave me another peck, this time, I was rewarded with a graze on my lips.

He moved past me, out of the bathroom and out of our bedroom, still talking, his hand moving, punctuating his words.

It took moments for me to turn, to move, to stumble to the edge of the bed. I wouldn't have even been able to explain how I felt — pissed, angry…no, it was more that I was hurt.

"*When we be making love…*"

"Alexa, shut up," I snapped, then bounced onto the bed. Inside, I growled, trying to figure out what I was going to do.

But before I could wrap my mind around a plan-of-attack, my cell phone chimed with a notification. Reaching over to the nightstand, I snatched it up.

Your play.

Really? Right in the middle of what was supposed to be a loving night with my husband, this notification from *Words With Friends* comes in?

I shook my head — until I saw that TruBlu had scored sixty-seven points.

My smile was automatic. "Go 'head," I said, my thoughts, at least, for the moment, turned from my husband.

I loved this game. My best friend, Sheryl said I was addicted. But that wasn't it at all — it was more like I was trying to recapture a time, when my dad and I sat at the kitchen table every night after I finished my homework, and played Scrabble for hours, until my mom made us stop for dinner. Or maybe it was just that playing this game made me feel like I always had friends. How could I be lonely as I sat up at night waiting for Preston to come home when there were at least ten friends (I always had ten games going) waiting anxiously for me…even if they were only inside an app on my cell.

TruBlu was one of my newest friends. We'd only been playing for about two weeks, but he was rising to the top of my list of favorites. Because he was that good — almost as good as me.

I clicked into the game and checked out the move my friend had made.

"Oh, yeah. Nice, Mr. TrueBlu." I kicked off my shoes, and with my heels, scooted back until I leaned against the pillows. I stared at the letters I had, then studied the board, before I moved a couple of tiles in place. I checked out several options — this was serious, this was strategic. And after about ten minutes, I found my best move — one hundred and twelve points.

Beat that!

I turned my phone off, returned it to the nightstand, but when I did that, my forgotten-for-a-moment feelings rushed back to me. I was pissed, I was angry…and I was hurt.

Pushing myself from the bed, my image stared back at me. Walking closer to the mirror, I tried to see myself as my husband saw me. I was a toned size six, thanks to not only my genetics, but my dedication to the five-times-a-week, ninety-minute workouts that did my body good. I worked hard because I'd been trained that way; I was an athlete. But so much of what I did now was for my husband. I wanted him to be proud always, just as I was proud of him.

Shaking my head, I turned toward my closet. It was time to get out of this. One of my old sorority T-shirts would do.

"Whew."

I turned around at the sound of my husband's deep sigh. I didn't even hear him return to our bedroom.

He said, "I thought I'd never get off the phone."

I pressed my lips together. Not need for me to spout out what I'd been thinking. Preston had heard this all before.

He loosened his tie and tossed it onto the chaise. "Babe, you wouldn't believe the day from hell I had."

I folded my arms, said nothing, as he unbuttoned his shirt.

"The merger that we're handling for Citibank...."

He stepped into his closet.

"It's our biggest project. And then, Brad...."

I heard the zipper on his pants.

"We did his annual review and I think his earnings scared him. Can you imagine? Tripling a six-figure investment and you're afraid?"

He stepped from his closet wearing just his boxers.

"I've got to be up early. At five for a meeting at six, so I'm gonna turn in early." He folded back the duvet, then climbed between the sheets. Resting his head on the pillow, he exhaled again. "Whew! I'm exhausted."

For the first time since he came into our bedroom, he turned and made eye contact with me. "Damn, you look good, babe." He paused. "You should wear that to bed more often."

I tried. I tried my best to hold back and not say a word. I tried. I tried to just roll my eyes and go into my own closet. But, no! I had to say it. "Wear this to bed? For what?"

I saw the sigh in his eyes. "Come on, don't be like that."

"Like what?" I shrugged. "No need for me to wear anything like this when no one notices."

"I noticed," he almost whined. "You know I think you are so sexy. It's just that the work on this merger, and we still have all of our other clients." He shook his head. "And remember, it's just me and Kelvin as the major partners. We've been blessed, but with this blessing comes long hours. You know that. I've just been preoccupied."

"As always," I mumbled.

"No. Just until we get past this merger."

"This time it's the merger. Last time it was a new client. Next time...what will it be?"

"Angelique, you know I'm working hard. Working hard to give you everything. And it's paying off, babe. You've just got to be patient."

Be patient.

That's what he always said.

"I promise, I will make it up to you."

Another thing he always said. And he did make it up to me — with all kinds of gifts. I had a closet full of designer bags and shoes and fragrances.

"Okay," I said, though I didn't move.

My arms were still folded, even as Preston studied me. "Okay?" he repeated as if my word surprised him.

I shrugged.

"I love you," he said as he reached for my hand.

It was with reluctance that I moved toward him, then took his hand.

"I love you," he repeated, and then he squeezed my hand as if that would seal his words.

"I know you do," I said what I knew to be true. "I love you, too."

He tugged at my hand and I leaned over to receive his kiss before he released me. When I stepped away from the bed, he snuggled into his pillow. By the time I made my way to my closet, I was sure that I'd heard his first snore.

I blinked and blinked and blinked because no matter what, I was not going to cry. I'd shed too many tears already, not ever really sure what I was crying about. Why should I be crying when my husband gave me everything: a custom-built, five-thousand square foot home with all the amenities I wanted, a double sized closet with all the fashions and accoutrements that I desired. Truly, there was nothing that I longed for that I didn't already have.

Except for the attention of my husband.

Inside my closet, I slipped out of the lingerie, leaving it right on the floor when I stepped out of it. Then, I slid the T-shirt that I'd slept in last night over my head. By the time I returned to our bed, Preston was deep into his sleep.

I rolled my eyes, but then, I thought, this could be worse. My husband could be somewhere with a mistress. At least I didn't have to compete with that. No, my husband's paramour was Wake Forest Investments, the investment firm he'd started just four years ago.

The business was an instant blessing for him, and an instant curse for me.

I sat up in the bed, but I was certainly not sleepy. It was barely nine-thirty and I didn't have to be up at five. Picking up my phone, I turned it back on and right away, a *Words with Friends* notification chimed.

Your play.

Really? TruBlu had come back that quickly?

Then, I opened the app, and my mouth opened wide. "You've got to be kidding me," I whispered. "One hundred and forty points?"

I thought I was doing something with my one hundred and twelve. He'd never scored like this before. What was he doing — using one of those cheating sites?

I leaned into the pillows, determined that I was going to come up with something that would shut Mr. TruBlu down. But before I could begin moving my tiles, an alert blinked to let me know I had a new message. I clicked on the notification app.

You like that? 😄 *Your move.*

I laughed, then covered my mouth as I glanced over at Preston. But it seemed like he couldn't hear me above the sounds that he made.

TruBlu had never messaged me before, so this was cool.

Snuggling back, I sent this man my own message:

Oh, it's on, now.

Dots appeared on my screen, indicating that TruBlu was responding:

I'm not from Missouri, but show me!

There was no way my smile could have spread wider. I didn't get it, though. It was just a couple of little messages. So why did I have that butterfly feeling?

Snuggling back even deeper into the pillows, I began to type:

I can show u....

CHAPTER 2

Blu Logan

There were three reasons why I couldn't jump up and give myself a high-five the way I wanted to over those one-hundred-and-forty points I just scored. First, I was already in bed, second, I was lying butt-naked in the dark, and third...

"Ugh! Will you get off that game?"

And reason number three: I was in my bed, butt-naked...next to my wife.

"Please," Monica whined.

The end of my lips turned down just a little, but I wasn't going to let Monica steal my joy. Because Lord knows, she wasn't the one who'd given it to me. All of this joy that filled me right now was because of DivineDiva. Damn, she was a challenge.

"That light is too much."

And then, there was the woman next to me who didn't challenge me at all. Although, Monica had once — six years ago.

I turned my attention back to the game, so wanting to stay in this place. It wasn't often that I got a chance to one-up DivineDiva. Two weeks, and I hadn't beaten her once. But this move right here, it had been calculated, it had been strategic, and there wasn't anything that she could do.

"Did you hear what I said?" Monica said.

Monica was that thief in the night. Because all of my joy — stolen! "How is the light from my phone bothering you?"

She pushed herself up in the bed, and leaned back on her elbows. The light from the television was what made the room so bright and I easily saw her glare.

She said, "You have a six-plus. That thing is dang-near the size of an iPad. And I'm trying to sleep." Then, she sat up and adjusted the pink hair roller that was falling into her face.

I sighed, remembering the days when she would have never worn those things to bed. Remembering the days when she told me that she wanted to be sexy twenty-four-seven just for me.

It was those memories that made me snap, "You're always trying to sleep, Monica. Five o'clock in the morning, you're sleep. Five o'clock in the evening, you're sleep."

"You know I can't help it." She folded her arms and her bottom lip trembled. "You know what I'm suffering from. You know how it's affected me."

This was where I was supposed to have empathy. Maybe pull Monica into my arms, give her a hug, assure her that everything was going to be okay. But even though I wanted to, sometimes I couldn't. Because I felt like I didn't have any more understanding inside of me.

It had started years ago, right after our daughter, Raven, had been born. As soon as I brought Monica and Raven home, I'd noticed the change in my wife: she was moody, had trouble sleeping, couldn't eat. In the beginning, we'd just thought she was just suffering from baby blues because she hadn't gone through that with our son who was ten when Raven was born.

But after a few weeks, she'd been diagnosed with postpartum depression.

Of course, I wanted my wife to have the best care and her ob-gyn was on it. Her doctor gave her medication, taught her relaxation methods, and suggested a support group. Well, Monica never attended a single meeting and only took about two deep breaths to relax herself. But the medication — Monica rode that one for as long as the doctor gave her prescriptions.

When Raven was a year old, Monica's gynecologist had referred her to a psychologist...and even though she'd been seeing Dr. Nichols ever since, it felt like we were in the same place.

"I don't care what you say," she broke through my memories of when this all began. "I'm still suffering from PPD."

She'd become so familiar with the term that she only spoke of it through its acronym. But postpartum depression wasn't her problem at all.

"Raven is six, so it's not postpartum depression," I said, refusing to call such a serious disorder by a nickname. "You're suffering from a lot of things, but that's not one of them."

Her glare became harsher. "Whatever," she said, snatching the covers away from me. She turned her back and snuggled deep under the duvet.

I shook my head. Maybe I should have tried one of my old approaches. But then the chime of my phone turned my attention away from my wife.

A message:

I can show u better than I can tell u.

Okay, so why did that make me smile?

My response: *That's what most ppl who lose say.*

Then, I waited. The seconds ticked by, time passing so slowly. But the digital numbers on my cell only changed from 9:32 to 9:33 before DivineDiva responded:

Payback isn't going to be pretty.

I couldn't get my fingers to move fast enough.

Bring it.

I paused. Because I was just talking about the game, wasn't I? I'd been playing this chick for the past two weeks. That was it. And tonight was the first time that I'd ever messaged…well, that I'd ever messaged her. I mean, I did chat with women, though I kept it friendly and not too flirty.

But this connection with DivineDiva…it was instant and it felt real.

Maybe it was just the game. I spent hours playing *Words With Friends*; it was the half-analytical, half-creative break that I needed from the hours I spent pushing numbers over at PricewaterhouseCoopers. I mean, I loved my job and I was well on my way to being a partner. But this…this game relaxed me. And now, I had someone who really challenged me.

I stared at my screen, waiting for another response and feeling that joy rise back up in me, until I heard, "So, the game. Off please."

"Go to sleep," I said to the thief.

In another language those three words must have translated into four new ones: sit up and argue.

Because that was what Monica did. She sprang up, leaned forward, and spat, "Why are you so nasty to me?"

I wondered if she saw the irony in her question. She was the one with spittle flying from her mouth. That was when I knew for sure she hadn't taken her meds and I would have to call Dr. Nichols in the morning.

I inhaled, then exhaled calm. "How am I being nasty to you when all I said was go to sleep?"

"It's the way you said it. And it's the way you kept your phone on even when I told you that I couldn't sleep with the light."

"But the TV is on, Monica." My inhale hadn't helped because now, my voice was raised. "You have the TV on every night. You fall asleep with the TV and that light — from a forty-two-inch TV — that light should bother you."

"It's not the same. It's the light from your phone and the tapping on the screen that's so distracting."

She said that like it made sense and that was it for me. "Fine." I threw back the covers and swung my feet onto the floor. Traipsing across the floor wearing nothing but the skin I'd been born in, I tried not to stomp, but I was pissed. It was like at every turn, Monica wanted to fight. I didn't want that, I didn't need that. I'd had six years of it and wasn't sure how many more years were in me.

I grabbed my robe from the hook on the bathroom door and wrapped myself inside the Turkish Terry before I stepped back in the bedroom. I moved to the bed, only to retrieve my phone. Monica was still sitting up, her eyes following my moves, but I made sure not to make eye contact with her.

"Oh, now you're going to ignore me?"

I grabbed my phone.

"You're going to just walk away like I did something wrong?"

I walked toward the door.

"Why do you have such an attitude?"

I was about five feet away from freedom, so why did I turn around? Why did I have to respond? "I don't have an attitude, I just don't want to fight."

"This isn't a fight, it's a discussion."

"I'm not fighting, I'm not discussing, I'm just leaving."

I turned, took five steps, and she yelled out five words, "Do you want a divorce?"

I stopped so suddenly, I almost toppled over. This time, I spun around slowly. "Where is that coming from? Did I say I wanted a divorce?"

There were tears in her voice when she said, "Well the way you act, I can't tell. You're always acting like I've done something to you. You're always charging out of here. You're always...."

"I'm always?" I had tried to hold back, but we were ending the day the same way it had started. With a fight. "Do you hear yourself? I'm always doing something to you? You know what I'm always doing, Monica? I'm always walking on eggshells because I don't want to set you off."

Tears trailed down her cheeks. "I cannot help the way I feel."

It was the way she said it that made me soften. Made me remember that my wife really did have an illness. I took slow steps back to the bed. I didn't know why I was doing this. Talking to Monica never ended well. But I'd left her this morning, standing in the kitchen crying. Because I had to get Raven to her school bus and then I had to get to work.

I didn't have that excuse tonight. And really, I did want to help Monica because I believed in our vows. I just prayed that one day, we could get back to the 'for better' part because we were drowning in all of this for worse.

Sitting on the edge of the bed, I reached for her hand, but she kept her arms folded. "Monica, have you taken your meds?" I prayed that my calmness would calm her. "What is

Doctor Nichols saying?" This was a question that I asked her often.

"That quack?"

That was the answer that Monica always gave me even though Dr. Nichols was far from being a quack. And Monica knew it. That was why I challenged her. "Well, if she's a quack, why do you keep going to her?"

Everything on Monica tightened, she pinched her lips, pressed her arms closer to her chest, and squinted. But she didn't answer.

So, I answered for her, "If you don't like her, you don't have to go to her anymore. We can try...you can try... maybe to work on it without the medication."

I'd done enough research to know that while medication definitely helped some people, for others, it sent them on a destructive emotional roller coaster. That was my fear for my wife and after six years, I wanted for us to try something different. Maybe a life without meds.

With the back of her hand, she wiped away a tear. "You always say that, but I need those drugs. You don't know what it's like for me."

"You're right, I don't. But I wonder what would happen if you tried to work at it a little harder." I glanced around the room that had become my wife's stockade. She hardly left this space and it showed. Her nightstand was covered with empty packages and tossed aside wrappers that once held cookies and cakes and chips. They were piled high next to a line-up of empty soda cans. She even had a loaf of bread pushed behind her lamp. "I really think if you were to try, you'd see positive results. Sometimes leave this room for more than just your doctor's appointment, leave this house and hang out with the kids. They miss you, I miss you. All I'm saying is try."

"Oh, what are you? A doctor now?"

I felt my impatience rising, rising, rising. Monica wanted to fight. But I swallowed my agitation and said, "Of course I'm not a doctor. I'm just trying to...."

"You're just trying to do what you always do. You're trying to say that there is nothing wrong with me."

"No, I'm not saying that," I popped off, my impatience bursting out of me. "Clearly there's something wrong. You're on depression meds. You don't go to work anymore. You stay home all day and eat bonbons and Oreos and potato chips." I slowed down. This would not end well. I needed to be the bigger person. So, I calmly said, "There is something wrong, I just wonder if we should try a different approach."

Now, her top lip quivered like her bottom one. "I'm doing the best I can, but you always...."

"I *always* go to work, I *always* come home, I *always* pay the bills, I *always* take care of the kids...."

"But you don't support me. You never do."

It was her 'always' and her 'never' that made me just hold up my hands. "You know what? We don't need to talk about this right now."

I turned toward the door, moving the way I should have kept doing a couple of minutes before.

"See! That's what I'm talking about. You always...."

I was out of the room before she berated me about something else that I always did.

But I guess my silence was too much for her, a soda can followed me into the hallway. I turned around and paused. She'd actually thrown an empty can of Sprite at me. Yeah, I needed to call Dr. Nichols in the morning. Even though she never discussed Monica's illness with me, I told her when I had concerns.

I picked up the can, then turned toward Raven's room. My hope was that our daughter was asleep and hadn't heard a thing. That was something that always worried me — our children being drawn into this dysfunction that I was still trying to call a marriage. I'd never wanted Raven and our sixteen-year-old, Tanner, to hear what I called arguments and Monica called discussions.

It was an impossible feat, though. Because I never knew when Monica would go off.

Inside Raven's room, I picked up the blanket she'd kicked off the bed, and covered her again, knowing that it would be back on the floor in minutes. For a moment, I stood over our daughter. Whenever I looked at our children, I remembered they were the gifts that Monica had given to me. So I had to try, I had to remember the sacrifice she'd made so that we could have a family.

That was why I had to find a way to be patient.

"But it's been six years of this," I whispered before I tiptoed out of her room. For a moment, I paused outside of Tanner's room, but I wasn't worried about our son hearing a thing — he never took his Beats off his head.

I trotted down the stairs and didn't even bother to turn on the lights. I just settled on the leather sofa in our family room, a space that had become far too familiar for my slumber. But tonight, I didn't feel any kind of anger toward Monica. I wasn't restless at all.

Tapping the home button on my phone to awaken my screen, the first thing I did was check to see if DivineDiva had made her move. She hadn't. But, she had sent a message:

You're really good at this.

"Yeah," I whispered as I swiped her profile picture. I had looked at her photo before, two weeks ago when we'd first started playing. But now I studied her like she was an amoeba underneath a microscope. It was amazing how everyone had two eyes, a nose and a mouth, but sometimes God put the features together in the right proportion, so perfectly, that all you could do was stare. DivineDiva was one of those perfectly proportional women. From her light brown eyes, to her not-too-narrow, not-too-wide nose, and then, those lips that looked like they were made for kissing....

I shook my head. Why was I thinking about that?

Turning my focus back to her eyes, I squinted. She reminded me of someone, and after a few seconds, I got it — Meagan Good. Yeah, that was who she looked like. Meagan Good and those lips.

I just stared and stared before I typed back:

U are too....

But I didn't hit send. I hesitated, wanting to add a little bit more, wondering if I should. And then, before I changed my mind, I added:

I bet you're good at a lot of things.

This time, I didn't have to wait at all for her reply. Within seconds, it came back:

I am.

Oh, yeah. She was confident. I liked that. Again, I hesitated, then typed:

I find that very sexy.

I pressed 'Send', then right away wanted to take that back. Suppose I'd gone too far? Suppose she thought I was a pervert?

When my phone chimed, I was almost afraid to look at her response. But then, I peeked at my screen. And then, I smiled.

She hadn't written a word. Only a smiley emoji.

That was good enough for me. But then, I started thinking: what did that really mean? Did that smiley face mean that she liked my flirting? Or was she saying, 'No this fool didn't?'

Another chime:

Calling it a night. Don't play any more big words on me. Sweet dreams.

This time, my reply was safer:

Good night.

I closed out the game, then tossed my phone onto one of the side tables. As I leaned my head back on the sofa, I tried to remember the last time Monica had said something so kind before she went to sleep. I couldn't even remember the last time she'd said good night.

And that thought made me sad. Made me wonder what my life would look like a year from now.

CHAPTER 3

Angelique

There was chatter and clatter all around me, I was sure. But I heard not a bit of it. I guess the hearts in my eyes were like buds in my ears.

I woke up thinking about u and you're still on my mind.

My sigh was long and deep as I read the message in my *Words With Friends* app again.

"Well, dang."

Looking up, I had to blink a couple of times, just to get my eyes to focus on my best friend, Sheryl. If she hadn't been sitting across from me, if she hadn't spoken a word, I might have just sat here in this restaurant without ordering or eating a thing, even though we were at Houston's on Kirby, one of my favorite spots.

She said, "Either I'm just awful company or your man is putting it down, even through texts and I'm so glad to finally hear that. Damn!" She laughed. "You got pics? Wanna share?"

I laughed with her as I set my phone on the table. "You're wonderful company and no, "I sighed, "my man is not," I paused long enough to make air quotes, "putting it down. And

I certainly don't have pictures. Can you imagine? Preston sending me nude shots?"

I shuddered, and so did Sheryl.

"Ewww. Why did I even kid around about something like that? I mean, your husband is fine, but it would be like looking at my brother. Ewww." She shook her shoulders as if the idea of that appalled her. Then, after taking what I assumed to be a cleansing breath, she said, "But if I'm wrong, then you need to explain why you're acting like you never got any home training from Marie and Kelly," she said referring to my parents.

That made me chuckle, and once again glance down at my phone. I stuffed my fingers beneath my legs. That was the only way I wouldn't reach for my cell just to check to see if Blu (that was his real name) had sent me another message...on top of the hundreds we'd exchanged in the last week.

I needed to keep my attention on my best friend because though we spoke on the phone and texted all the time, two months had passed since she, and the third spoke of our three-wheels, Cassidy, and I had gathered together.

These get togethers fulfilled a promise we'd made when we graduated from The University of Texas at Austin — me with my double degree in French and Italian and Sheryl and Cassidy both majoring in psychology — we would have lunch or dinner at least once a month, every month, till the day we died.

Of course, we meant that vow at the time. But in the years since graduation, life had stepped in and one month had turned to two. And today, Cassidy wasn't even here. While Sheryl had turned her psychology degree into becoming one of Houston's most prominent psychologists with not only a thriving practice but with weekly TV appearances on various news shows, Cassidy had used her educational training to help her handle the hundreds of passengers she had to service in the friendly skies as a lead flight attendant.

She had planned to join us for this early dinner, but it seemed that one of her many 'friends' had swept her up for a quick getaway to Dubai. So, it was just me and Sheryl. And with the way she was looking at me right now, I so wished Cassidy was here to give Sheryl and her inquiring-mind-that-always-wanted-to-know, someone else to focus on.

"Ahem!" She cleared her throat. "So you want to tell me why you were so rude and why now, you're just staring at me with this goofy grin like you're a teenager in love."

"My bad." I waved my hand in the air, like it was nothing. My hope was that the subject would change to something that didn't have to do with me. Because then, Sheryl wouldn't press.

Usually, I didn't falter under my friend's scrutiny. Of the three, I was the most private...not on purpose. That was just the way I'd been raised. To endure all things and to remain silent. To be private to the point of almost being secretive — the way my mother had lived.

But this...this was something that I wanted to share. Especially since over the past four years I'd opened up (especially to Sheryl) about Preston. So, since she'd listened to hours of my distress, I wanted to tell her about what was going on with Blu and how a few innocent messages between us had morphed to a couple hundred of very flirtatious ones.

"So, what's going on?" Sheryl asked, right as the waiter stepped to our table.

I sighed with relief. A reprieve. Time enough for me to figure out what I wanted to share.

"Ladies." The young man, who looked like Terrance Howard's son, gave us a smile that had made some orthodontist a lot of money. "Can I start you off with drinks?"

"Just water for me," I said.

"No," Sheryl interjected. "Two martinis. A dirty one for me and one of those girly pomegranate lemonade ones for her." When my mouth opened wide, she said to me, "I'm a doctor. That's my prescription to get you to tell me the truth." To the waiter, she directed, "Bring our drinks and by the time you come back, we'll be ready to order."

He nodded, chuckled and then, turned to do as he'd been told.

Bringing her attention back to me, she said, "Close your mouth." She held up her hand. "No, not all the way. I want you to start talking. What's going on?"

I shook my head and laughed. "I told you, nothing."

"I'm not going to play twenty questions with you. So here are the facts," she said, sounding more like a psychologist than my friend. "The last time I talked to you, you were complaining about how Preston had missed the Women on the Move event. But he must've made it up to you 'cause the way you're grinning, he must have your kitty cat purring."

I blew out a long breath. "I wish."

Sheryl's eyes narrowed. "Keep talking."

Once again, I wished for Cassidy's presence and wondered why I was so reluctant to share with Sheryl. Maybe it was because of what I was doing with Blu.

In the last week, Blu and I chatted constantly. He messaged me in the morning, mid-morning, noon, afternoon, evening and night. And then, there was that one special message that he sent right before I closed my eyes:

I hope I'll join you in your dreams because you are always in mine.

Sigh. Swoon.

There was no longer any pretense with our flirting. It was straight out and straight up — for both of us. He told me how

30

he couldn't get me off his mind and I told him that I couldn't stop thinking about him either. He told me that he was sure he'd never met anyone like me and I told him that even though we hadn't officially met, I felt the same.

It had been ten days of back and forth exchanges, it had been ten days that was almost beginning to feel...like a relationship.

"Angelique." Sheryl drew out my name.

But just like a few minutes before, the waiter returned with our drinks and I once again breathed at the time I was being given to figure this out. In the couple of seconds that it took for Sheryl to ask about the dinner specials, then order her usual barbecued ribs with mashed potatoes and a salad, I again contemplated how much I wanted to confess.

It wasn't that I didn't trust Sheryl or thought that she'd judge me in any way. She'd been by my side through any of the traumas and tragedies that I had been willing to tell her about: trifling boyfriends, drama with girlfriends, issues with Preston...and then, the ultimate — the death of my mom. She'd been the first one at our house (arriving even before Preston had come home) to give me a hug, then take over whatever I needed. There was no risk, only an upside in telling Sheryl.

It was just that I truly didn't know what to say to my best friend: *Hey, I met this guy in this app and I think I've got a thing for him. And ummm...no, we've never met...we've never even spoken on the phone.*

"Angelique?"

"Huh?"

"Aren't you going to order?"

I blinked and looked up. "Oh, I'm sorry." I shook my head, then ordered the house smoked salmon and Cajun trout.

The moment the waiter stepped away, Sheryl said, "Okay, drink up."

I took a sip of my martini only because it bought me a few more seconds.

After she'd taken two sips of her own, she said, "Okay, talk up."

"I keep telling you, it's nothing."

She wagged her finger. "No ma'am." Now, her head shook back and forth, too. "You're gonna have to come up with a new word because 'nothin'' ain't what's going on. That smile on your lips," she pointed to my face, "that ain't nothing."

I chuckled at the way Sheryl, who was by far the most successful one of us professionally, could always bring it down back to the language of South Park, the hood where she grew up.

She kept on, "That's the smile that you had only for Preston when he used to take care of his business. So if you're telling me that Preston ain't putting it down and isn't responsible for the smile on your face, then I need to know what...or who is."

She leaned back in her chair, crossed her arms, rolled her neck, and the way she pursed her lips, I knew nothing else was going to happen until I started talking. I sighed. This was the reason why Dr. Sheryl Roberts from South Park got paid the big bucks. Because inside her office, she got people to talk. Inside her office, she solved problems.

So, I opened my mouth...and my cell phone chimed. It was more than a habit that made me look down and pick it up — it was the anticipation and the excitement.

I clicked on the notification so that I could see Blue's entire message:

Are you finished with dinner yet? I miss you.

"Oh," I whispered and pressed my hand across my chest. And then, I remembered…I wasn't alone.

Dang!

Raising my eyes slowly, my glance settled right on Sheryl's glare. It was easy to see her because she was no longer sitting back. Now, she leaned forward, her head almost half-way across the table.

I knew I had to start talking now.

"Okay," I said. "I met someone." Then, I held up one hand. "But he's just a friend."

"Friends don't make friends smile like that." And then with a quickness that I didn't expect, she snatched the phone from my hand.

"Hey," I said. But it was too late. She had full possession.

My screen had darkened, but that didn't stop Sheryl. She pressed the home button, then tapped a few keys.

"You really need to stop using your birthday as your passcode," she said without looking up.

"And you really need to stop acting like you just stopped picking locks yesterday."

My words didn't faze her. She kept her eyes on the screen and my heart pounded.

She finally looked up with a frown. "Okay, so are you deleting the texts right after you look at them?" She turned my phone around to show me the empty text message screen. "If you are, that's smart. But damn, that was quick."

"Would you get out of my phone?" I snatched it back. "And I'm not deleting any texts. We're not texting."

She took another sip of her drink, but I knew that was just to give her a moment to think. Sheryl was sure that she could figure out everything. She put her glass down. "I saw you sitting there, grinning like you just had your first kiss or your

33

first...whatever. So what are y'all doing? Tweeting? Facebooking? You know that's how thirty-seven percent of marriages are now ending - behind social media."

"My marriage isn't ending because I'm not doing anything wrong," I said, shaking my head with every word. "And we're not on social media. It's a game."

She frowned, then blinked. "A what?"

"A game."

She held up her glass and side-eyed her martini as if she'd had too much to drink.

I laughed. "We play a game. *Words with Friends.*"

Now, Sheryl really looked confused with the way her eyebrows furrowed. "So, playing a game brings a smile on your face like that? What did you do? Score one thousand points?"

"I wish. No. We chat while we play."

"In a game? In an app?"

"Yeah."

"Damn. This world of technology." Then, after another sip, a smile spread across her face. "So you...sneaking around...."

"No."

"Doing sneaky stuff."

"No...just communicating."

She laughed. "That's a new word for it."

"Come on, Sheryl," I said, feeling like maybe I shouldn't have said anything.

"I'm just sayin' you can call it what you want, but it is what it is. And I ain't mad at you. I told you before Preston needed to get himself together because what he won't do, another man will." She raised her glass as if she were toasting me and I wondered if that was her professional opinion.

I shifted my hips, suddenly not so comfortable in my seat. "I'm really not doing anything. No man is doing anything for me. Preston has nothing to worry about."

"Ummm," Sheryl hummed. "Preston has nothing to worry about...yet."

"Stop saying that, don't even think it. I haven't even met this man. I've never spoken to him on the phone. Only messengering in the app."

Her martini glass was right on the edge of her lips and she froze. Then, a couple of seconds later, she returned her glass slowly to the table. "So wait. Your smile, this glow," she moved her hand in a circle in front of my face, "and you ain't even met the ninja?" She leaned back. "Damn."

I was getting ready to explain it to her, but then that sound that made me smile. I didn't even try to hide it since I'd just told Sheryl everything. I knew I had to look like a kid at Christmas with the way I grabbed my cell and then tapped onto the app:

Did you get my message? I miss you.

I typed back:

I got it. Still at dinner.

Not even three seconds seemed to pass:

One day I'd ♥ to take you to dinner.

I gave myself a moment to swoon. I'd been thinking about asking Blu for his number, just so we could chat since we enjoyed each other so much through the messages. But I'd been afraid to ask, especially after he'd told me he was married. That meant that he'd just wanted to keep this a virtual thing.

But now...he was practically saying that he wanted to see me. I closed my eyes for a second, then, responded:

Maybe one day we can make that happen.

I smiled, pressed 'Send' — and then, the chatter and the clatter started up again around me. That quickly, for those few — what were they? Seconds? Minutes? — I'd forgotten that I was in this restaurant…with my best friend.

Dang!

Slowly, I put my phone down and Sheryl just stared at me. And then, the waiter saved me again. For the third time. This time, he placed my meal in front of me before he served Sheryl her plate.

When he stepped away, I said, "I'll bless the food," giving myself a few more seconds before I'd have to face Dr. Roberts.

And that's just what happened. The moment I said, "Amen," Sheryl piped in, "Aww hell no!"

"Really, Sheryl. Cursing like that? I just said grace."

"Don't try to change the subject. You can try to tell yourself, you can try to tell me that that," she pointed to my phone, "ain't nothin'. But I'll tell you this, if it's nothing now, it'll be something soon." She paused. "And that's my professional opinion. I ain't even gonna charge you." She sat back, did another one of those neck rolls, and pursed her lips as if she dared me to challenge her.

All I could do was look down at my salmon. And since my head was bowed, I decided to say another little prayer. *Please God….* And then, I paused. What did I want? What did I want to ask God to help me to do?

My heart started pounding. Because if I couldn't answer those questions, if I couldn't pray to God, I had a feeling that this could lead me down a road that had been traveled by too many. A journey that I was not sure that I wanted to take.

CHAPTER 4

Angelique

*I*t's *just coffee.*

That was what I'd told myself when Blu sent the message last night:

Let's do it. Let's have coffee tomorrow.

My hands couldn't stop shaking when I'd read that message and it was the same now as I speed-walked toward Starbucks. I'd driven downtown the exact same way, over the speed-limit when traffic allowed. As if speed would stop me from changing my mind.

It worked. Because speeding (while driving and now walking) had kept me focused on moving and not on the single thought in my mind: *Turn back!*

There was no need to turn back when this was just coffee.

Stepping inside, I glanced at my watch, then my eyes roamed through the coffee shop. It was filled with patrons, even though it was about an hour before noon. But there was no one in here who even resembled Blu.

Once we'd started messengering each other so seriously, I'd taken to Google to do my homework on Barry — his real name — Logan. But still, Catfishing was real and who knew if the pictures on his Facebook page were current or even his?

I was pretty confident, though because I'd found other photos that he couldn't have manipulated — one in the *Defender* of him accepting an award from Houston's Urban League, and the other was on his firm's website. So, I was sure that I would know him the moment he walked through this door.

Now, my decision was whether I should order coffee or wait for him. It didn't take me more than a couple of seconds to figure that out. I grabbed the table in the back, in the corner, almost in the dark. My hands were shaking too much for me to even carry a cup across the room and I needed to get settled before Blu arrived or he would think I was some kind of nutcase.

And then, my choice of tables...it looked the most comfortable.

That was what I told myself.

But sitting down didn't help at all. Those butterflies in my stomach that had been fluttering around, now started doing cartwheels. I remembered feeling this way once — on my first date with Preston.

Why was I thinking about my husband when I was about to meet this man?

Because it's just coffee.

"Angelique?"

The richness of his voice brought me from the memories of my past into this very present moment. I blinked, I gasped, I prayed that I would find my voice. That was going to be difficult because truly, the man who stood before me was a vision of loveliness. I knew that wasn't a normal description for a man, but I had no other words.

As a gymnast, I was astute, taught to use every one of my senses. So, I kinda knew that right now, all eyes in this shop were on me. No, that was a lie — the eyes were on him. Because Blu made heads turn, women and men alike.

I wasn't sure where to begin. Should I start with the sexiness and silkiness of his skin? Oh, my goodness. He'd told me that he'd gotten the nickname Blu because the bullies in school used to say he was so black, he was almost blue. So, even his friends started calling him that and Blu hated it. But his mother had turned that insult into the greatest compliment. She'd convinced him to embrace the beauty God had given to him and then, she'd had him do some modeling in the JC Penney catalogue. Blu said even at the age of ten he knew that wasn't going to be his thing. But it had accomplished what his mother had hoped — given him confidence and helped him to not only accept, but come to love the skin he was in...and his nickname.

It was a wonderful story, but his mother had been wrong. She should have changed the name from Blu to Black Silk — that would have been more appropriate. And by the time he was a teen, they should have added 'sexy' to that name. Yes, Black Sexy Silk. Or maybe they should have dropped his skin color altogether and called him Smooth Sexy Silk because that was who Barry Logan was now. There was not a blemish on his skin, and that smile that was illuminated by his perfect teeth was only made better by the dimple in his left cheek.

Oh, and then there was the sexy part...this man had swagger even though he was standing still. Part of it was the suit that he wore, clearly tailored, no Men's Warehouse end-of-the-year sale. The suit that showed broad shoulders that gave way to a slim waist. I stopped my eyes right there because...whew!

"Angelique?"

He said my name like he'd called me more than a couple of times. And when I took my eyes back to his, he smiled, only it was like half a smile. With just his left cheek and that dimple.

I had to inhale before I said, "Yes," and then held out my hand for him to shake. I wasn't even sure how I had the composure to do that, but I guess it came from the poise I'd learned as a gymnast. "Nice to meet you," I had to pause because I had twisted his name so much I had to pull his real name from my memory, "Blu. Nice to meet you, Blu."

He glanced at my hand for a moment, and then he took it, but not the way I expected. He pulled me up and into his arms in an embrace that hardly let me breathe. Not that he held me too tightly. It was just being that close to him was an assault on my senses. He'd already given me so much to see. But now, the way he felt — I relished the hardness of his chest. The way he smelled — I loved Issey Miyake.

Then he pulled back, looked into my eyes, and said, "So, we finally meet."   And he had that voice, too? He'd told me he was a music buff who loved to sing — Luther was his favorite. Now the way he spoke, I had no doubt that he could rival one of my favorite singers.

I was glad when he released me because I wasn't sure how much longer my knees would be able to take it. And how embarrassing would it be if my wobbly knees gave way?

So, I sat down and he did the same, taking the seat right across from me. That was good because if he'd taken the one next to me, it would have sent ripples through my blood stream and I would have been done.

"You just walked right up to me," I said. "How did you even know you had the right woman?"

He laughed, a chuckle that had been designed by God. And those ripples….they went right through me.

"Oh, trust me. I know DivineDiva." He glanced down at the table. "You want some coffee?"

"Yes, I was going to order a cup."

"I'll get it for you." Then, he stared and studied me, and all of my blood rushed right to the center of my body. He said, "You look like a dark chocolate mocha type of woman."

I grinned and hoped that I didn't look giddy. "No, what I am is all-black. No cream."

He gave me that chuckle again and this time, I was rewarded with a wink before he stood and headed to give our orders to the barista. The moment he turned his back, I exhaled and almost collapsed. It took effort to be in his presence.

My goodness!

I watched him for a moment, then turned my glance to others in the shop, especially the women who watched him move (with that swagger) to the counter. Most were respectful with their stares. They looked up, then down, then back up again.

Well, all except one woman who sat at the table closest to the counter. She might as well have worn a flashing sign around her neck: *I want you, right here, right now, right on this table.*

I understood.

If Blu were fazed, he showed no signs. He took care of his business, glanced back at me, winked again, then brought over our coffee and set mine in front of me.

He wasn't even fully in his seat when he said, "You're even more beautiful in person."

"That's original." I smiled.

He shrugged. "I'm a lover, not a writer."

I laughed.

He said, "And it's the truth. I mean, I expected you to be beautiful. I knew that, even before I checked out all of your pictures." When I raised an eyebrow, he did the same and said, "Don't trip. You know you did your homework on me, too."

Again, I laughed.

He leaned forward on the table. "And after all of your research, I guess you liked what you saw."

Then, I did something that was so out of my comfort zone, so out of my character, but then, just being in this Starbucks was so different from who I thought myself to be. But since I was here, I decided to play along. I placed my arms on the table, leaned forward and mimicked his pose. "I guess you liked what you saw, too, or else you wouldn't be here."

He didn't even blink. "I liked it before I saw it."

That made me sit back and frown a bit. I couldn't play the game if I didn't understand the language. "What do you mean?"

He shrugged, but with only one shoulder. "I liked it, you, before I even walked into this place. I liked your personality. I liked our online connection."

This time, I stayed back when I said with more boldness than I'd ever had, "Is that what we have? A connection?"

Now, he mimicked me. He sat back, though the way he leaned into the chair, he was far more comfortable than me. Or maybe it was just his swagger that he had even sitting down. "What would you call it if not a connection?"

Oh, it was a connection all right. It was an electric connection.

"Are you gonna answer me, or just leave me hanging? What would you call this?" He pointed at his chest, then at me.

A dangerous connection. That was what I would call it, but not what I said. "I call it friends getting together."

He said, "Friends with a connection."

I smiled, then sipped my coffee.

"Friends with a connection…who are married."

His words dimmed my smile. "Wow!" I put my cup down. "Just put it out there."

"It's already out." He held up his hand, showing his wedding band. Then, he glanced down at the four-carat diamond that shined from my finger, an upgrade from my two-carat engagement one. The upgrade — a gift for our fifth anniversary.

My eyes glanced downward.

"The reason I mentioned our marriages," his voice made me lift my chin, "is that I want it out there. And I want you to know that I've never done anything like this before."

I spoke without thinking, just told him what was in my heart. "Yeah, right. That's what they all say."

"Well," he paused long enough to sip his coffee, "I could say the same thing about you."

Touché.

He held up his hands. "Just sayin' that I could. But I wouldn't because I have a feeling that you've never been in a place like this."

"A Starbucks?"

He grinned.

But then, I got serious. Shaking my head, I said, "No, I really haven't. And to be honest, I don't know what I'm doing here now."

"You know why you're here." When I looked at him blankly, he said, "It's because…we have that connection."

We laughed together.

"No, seriously," he said. "We have all these things in common. You're a gymnast."

"And you like watching gymnastics on TV."

He nodded. "See? And then, there's the fact that you majored in French and Italian."

I frowned. "Wait. I thought you majored in accounting."

"I did, but I speak a language. I speak English."

Another shared laugh before I said, "And I went to UT and…."

"I went to Texas A&M."

"Boooo!"

More laughter and Blu said, "And don't forget the music."

"Yeah, you love Luther, and while he's a fave, Prince will always reign."

"But, we both have the same favorite Luther song," he said.

"Yup."

Then, together we said, "*If Only For One Night.*"

Now, we laughed together…again.

He said, "And then, there's this. This connection. Where we laugh all the time."

That was true. In all of our conversations inside the app, we laughed. I guess that really was why I was here. Because there was nothing sexier to me than a man with a sense of humor.

"Seriously, though, Angelique." He paused and reached across the table for my hand.

I hesitated. I'd agreed to this meeting because it was just coffee and anyone who might have seen me, wouldn't think anything about it. I was the creator and founder of *Black Girl Magic.* I was always out, holding meetings, but not holding hands. How would I ever explain that?

That was my question, but my action — I gave my hand to him.

44

He was silent for a moment and then, squeezed my fingers. "This is nothing more than two friends who connected, getting together and talking. So, there is no guilt, just honesty, okay?"

I nodded.

He said, "I don't ever want it to be awkward with us. That's what's so special about us now. We hadn't even talked on the phone, but we could talk about everything. I want it to stay that way. Let's talk about anything and everything, anytime."

His words made me think that he'd want to get together again. And not just one more time. He was talking like this was a long-term...friendship with a connection. I wondered if that was what he meant.

But I asked no questions. I just let him hold my hand for another moment before I reluctantly pulled away. Still, I said, "Another thing we have in common, we like to talk about any and everything."

"And where I'm from that's the basis for an amazing friendship," he added with a smile.

A friendship, I thought, and my stomach did one of those triple backflips, double twirl in the air that had been my signature move on the floor exercises in my gymnastics competitions.

Coffee. Just coffee, a little voice reminded me and I quickly pushed aside that desire to know this man as more than just a friend. That was never going to happen. I was going to work hard to make sure it never did.

CHAPTER 5

Blu

I *had a great time today. It was so nice meeting you in person.* The grin that had been on my face since I'd met up with Angelique this morning was still in place, even as I read her message.

I typed back: *Ditto. Looking forward to doing it again soon.*

She had to be at home (or wherever) just waiting for me because her response came in seconds: *Can't wait.*

"What's so funny?"

Before I could even look up, Monica leaned over to get a glimpse of my phone. We were sitting close together, each on one of the bar stools at the kitchen counter, but I twisted just enough so she couldn't see my phone's screen.

"I just read something on Facebook," I told her. "It's no big deal."

She shifted back to sitting up straight, but frowned her disapproval as she shuffled through mail that had been piling up for days. "Why do you spend so much time on that mindless thing?"

"What? Facebook?"

She nodded. "They call it social media, but I think it makes people less social. It shocks me that you're sucked into that."

I was about to respond, but then paused. What I wasn't going to get sucked into was another fight. In fact, what we should have been doing was celebrating. This was the first time that Monica had ventured out of our bedroom in over a week.

So, I put down my phone — even though I couldn't wait to talk to Angelique — and I talked to my wife.

"I'm glad to see you're up."

She shrugged, then looked at me. "And I'm just pleasantly surprised, that's all." She glanced up at the clock that hung above the sink. A Boy Scout project that Tanner had made when he was twelve. "It's not even five and you're home."

I nodded. "Yeah. I...got finished early and thought I'd come home so we could all have dinner together."

She shrugged again and I wasn't sure what that meant. Was she telling me that she didn't care?

It was true; I hardly came home before seven or eight in the evening. Not because I was a workaholic, though my position as a Senior Associate in the Auditing department was important to me. It was just that I preferred working to arguing.

But after my meet-up with Angelique, I was no good in the office. It was hard to concentrate when all I could think about was that woman. That face, those lips. And then, there was that shape. It had been my pleasure to walk behind her as we left the coffee shop together. She was lean, but shapely. Those legs, that butt....

"Did you hear me?"

I blinked myself back to our kitchen. "Huh?"

Monica sighed. "I don't know why I bother."

I shook my head, hoping that would get me back into this conversation. "I'm sorry. I was thinking about...something that happened today...." That was true. "At work...." I sighed with that lie. "What did you say?"

"I asked, since you're home, are you cooking?"

I just stared at her. From the moment I came home and found her downstairs (though she was stretched out on the couch in the family room, using the remote to flip from channel to channel to channel), I'd been hopeful that the fact that she'd gotten out of bed, had showered and dressed, then had made her way downstairs meant that my wife was trying to make her way back to herself.

I didn't want to make a big deal out of it, so I'd just kissed her, then come into the kitchen. When she followed me, my hope expanded. Maybe she would do something — like cook dinner. That would be another step.

Finally, I said, "What if we cooked dinner together?"

She looked at me and then did something she hadn't done in weeks, maybe even months — she smiled. But then, she said, "Nope," and went right back to the pile of mail.

"Awww, come on." I was encouraged by her smile. "This is something we can do side-by-side like we used to."

She didn't even bother to look up. "You like to cook. I don't."

"Well, what about if I bake some chicken and you put together a salad. That's not really cooking."

When she kept sifting through the mail, I said, "What are you looking for?"

"The decision letter for my disability appeal."

I pushed back the words that wanted to come out. Monica's disability had run out last year, and she was on her third appeal. She found the letter she was looking for it, then tore it open in anticipation. The way her shoulders shrank told me she'd been denied. Again.

I did what I'd done on the last two denials, I took a step forward and rubbed her back. Just like I rubbed Raven's back when she was upset. "It's okay, Sweetie. We're gonna be fine."

Tears had filled her eyes. It's not like we were hurting for money, so I'm not even sure why she desperately wanted this approval. I almost think it served as some kind of validation that she really was sick.

I didn't need the state to confirm that.

I didn't want to upset her any more than she already was, so I kept my voice low and calm as if I were talking to our six-year-old rather than to my wife. "I'm going to go out and pick up something to eat. For all of us. For dinner."

Her shoulders rose, then sunk again. "Okay."

Okay? I waited, but that was it. Just okay. Nothing more.

She slid down from her barstool, then stepped toward me. When she reached her arms forward, I almost stepped back. Not because she'd ever hit me or anything. We'd never gone to that place. It was just that her reaching for me was something that was almost foreign now.

But then, I embraced her. Held her for longer than I could remember doing for very long time. When we stepped back, I looked at her and she looked at the floor. I shifted to the left and she did the same to the right.

"Um...." she said.

"Ah...." I said.

Then after a couple of more awkward moments that should never happen between a couple who'd been married for seventeen years, I said, "I'm thinking about Chinese."

She nodded. "That will be good."

I waited. She said nothing else. I asked, "Anything that you want in particular?"

She smiled. "Moo goo ga pan?"

The way she stood there in front of me without any of the drama that accompanied her disease or medicine, gave me a little glimpse of the woman I used to know. The most beautiful and smartest woman who two years out of law school could negotiate multi-million dollar real estate deals over the phone, while she balanced our six-month old son on her hip and fried up bacon at the same time.

She'd been my Wonder Woman then, earning far more than I did, but never making me feel less of a man. We stood together as equals, planning our future, the children we would have, the trips we would take, the business we hoped to one day open together.

It had been that way for ten wonderful years.

"You're gonna get the usual for the kids?" she asked through my memories.

I nodded. "And an egg roll for Raven."

"Make that two for her."

Now, she grinned and I almost…laughed. But I certainly smiled. And leaned over and kissed her before I grabbed my keys, wallet, phone and almost danced out the door.

There were all kinds of thoughts spinning in my head, but they were all captured with this one thought: I didn't know what had just happened, but whatever it was, it was a great thing.

I slipped into the car and tried to remember the last time Monica and I had chatted like that, like husband and wife making dinner plans, without any arguing, without any tears, without any sadness. Pulling out of the driveway, I couldn't remember the last time I'd left my home, not wanting to floor the accelerator out of frustration.

Maybe Dr. Nichol's had given Monica a new prescription. And maybe this meant that all of my prayers for her were being answered.

At the corner of our street, I held my foot on the brake, plugged in my phone, hit my second favorite Luther song and then, turned the ballad that Monica and I had danced to at our wedding into a duet:

My love, there's only you in my life…
The only thing that's right.

Luther and I sang *Endless Love* a couple of times until I rolled my Tahoe to a stop in front of QQ's Chinese Palace. I jumped out of the car, my mind still on Monica and my spirit so hopeful, until I saw the name of the restaurant written in English…and Chinese.

"So, why did you major in French and Italian? I mean, it's hard enough for me to speak the king's English."

Angelique laughed, a soft sound that made its way to my soul. "I would have majored in every language, even Chinese, if I could have. I always wanted to be a child of the world. I wanted to visit every continent, get to know all the people, speak as many languages as I could."

I was impressed with the expansiveness of her desire. "Wow! That's me, too, kinda. I mean, I only want to speak English, but I want to travel everywhere." I paused, thinking about how Monica, with all of her sophistication, never wanted to travel past the Galleria Mall. "How many continents have you visited?"

The entire time that we'd been sitting in this Starbucks, every part of her body seemed to smile at me. From her eyes to her lips; I even imagined that her fingers curled around her cup and made some kind of smiley face.

But now, she cried. There were no tears, but it was like sorrow engulfed her.

"If you don't count North America...." She shook her head. *"I haven't been anywhere."*

I *didn't even have to ask her the next question; intuitively, I knew why her desire to travel had been held in check. Her husband was choking her the way Monica was stifling me....*

"You ready with your order?"

I blinked, not even realizing that I'd walked into the restaurant. Even though this young Asian woman had seen me several times a month over the past few years, she stared at me like this was my first visit and my presence at best annoyed her or at worst, (even still wearing my navy suit and white shirt) made her suspicious.

I gave my normal order: kao pao shrimp, moo goo ga pan, shrimp fried rice, chicken wings and two egg rolls — a dish for each one of us. When I sat on the bench to wait for my family's dinner, my thoughts returned to my coffee date with Angelique.   I'd suggested that we meet at Starbucks because I hadn't been sure. After we 'talked' that first night, I knew that I wanted to meet her, but what I couldn't figure out was why? Was I just looking for a new friend? Was it because I wanted a friend with a connection? And what did friends with a connection really mean?

I sighed. I wasn't that cat. From the moment I asked Monica to marry me and she'd said yes, I'd been faithful and knew that I would always be. My vows were serious — for better for worse, for richer for poorer, in sickness and in health....

Sickness and health. This was where I was being tested.

I had no problem with my wife being sick — I was willing to stand by her and with her until she got better. My challenge was I could never tell if Monica wanted the same. Did she want to get better, too?

"Number forty-four!"

I glanced up at the woman shouting from the counter like we weren't cooped in this tiny restaurant and couldn't hear each other thinking. Jumping up, I gathered the bags and hopped back into my car. As I drove, this time I didn't turn on my music. I wanted the silence so that I could just think about home. I was so encouraged by the way I'd left Monica — with a smile, with a hug. Some would look at that as nothing, but to me, it was a small victory. It gave me hope for tonight — a pleasant dinner with the kids and then, dessert…in our bedroom.

For the first time, I could see it and I could say it: Monica was trying. And that meant there was something that I had to do.

At a stoplight, I grabbed my cell phone, and opened the *Words With Friends* app. Monica had made her move, and now, I would make mine.

I sighed as I looked at the current game that I was playing with Angelique. All I had to do was resign, then block her — and that would be it because she didn't have my phone number, she didn't know where I lived. It had been real, it had been fun, but this would be the end.

When a horn blared from behind me, I jumped and glanced up. The light had turned green. I tossed my cell back into the cup holder on the console and hit the gas. I'd take care of this later — I'd delete Angelique from my life when I got home.

CHAPTER 6

Angelique

"Just do it," I whispered, looking down at my cell phone. Sitting at my desk, I had the *Words With Friends* app open and was really surprised that I didn't have a message from Blu. We'd messaged back and forth for hours yesterday after we'd left the coffee shop. But then all of a sudden, it stopped last night.

I wasn't sure if it had stopped because of him or me. I had sent the last message, but then, I'd turned my phone off because it was getting to be too much. Just reading Blu's messages made me want to see him again. If I didn't stop, my next message was going to be: *Let's meet at the gas station.*

And since that was just ridiculous, I had turned off the phone to stop myself from acting like a fool.

After that, my Foundation became my distraction. I'd worked and waited in my office for Preston to come home. And hoped that my husband could take my mind away from my friend-with-a-connection.

It was after nine when Preston finally found his way to the house we shared, but by that point, my annoyance level was at its apex. My plan had been to just stay in my office until I thought Preston was asleep; I was sure he'd never notice that I wasn't beside him in bed.

But then, Preston had come looking for me. Leaning back in the chair where I'd been sitting last night, I closed my eyes and remembered:

I felt him standing in the door jamb, but I kept my eyes on my computer screen, tapping away as if I were writing the next great memo. But all I was doing was an old typing exercise that I'd learned back in high school, the home row: a;sldkfjgh — I typed that over and over until Preston said, "Hey babe."

"Oh," I said as if I were surprised by his presence. The way Preston looked at me made me think that one day I might want to consider taking acting lessons. But I played it off. "I didn't even hear you come in."

I wanted that to be an insult. As if he were so insignificant in my life that I wasn't listening for him because surely, I hadn't been waiting for him. I wanted him to feel as irrelevant as I felt that I was to him.

"I understand." He paused and I wondered if he really understood what I'd just said and what my words meant. He said, "You look busy. Working on something big?"

When he craned his neck to get a peek at the computer, I hit the F1 button, darkening the screen. "Nope," I said and spun my chair to face him. "Nothing big. Nothing important."

His eyes were sad as he nodded. "I'm really sorry, babe."

"For what?"

"For all of this," he said. "We haven't had dinner together in a couple of weeks."

"Ummm...your timetable is off."

"Has it been longer?"

I nodded. "Way longer and I didn't think you noticed."

His eyes widened as if my words surprised him. "Are you kidding me? I always notice when I don't get to spend enough time with my beautiful wife."

My hard heart melted — just a little.

He said, "I'm really tired...."

I kept my expression the same even though I wanted to roll my eyes and ask what else was new.

But then, he reached for me. "But, will you come to bed with me?"

There was no way for me to keep a straight face now. Not with the way my heart pounded with anticipation. He wanted to go to bed with me? I mean, yeah, we slept in the same bed every night, but this was an invitation, though a bit formal.

He pulled me up and into his arms. I inhaled his fragrance and felt his hardness, then exhaled. It had been too long, I was so ready.

He said, "I have to get up early, but I just want to hold you."

Maybe I wouldn't need those acting lessons after all because my body was like plaster — I held back my disappointment as he took my hand and led me into our bedroom. We undressed in silence, and then, he gave me what he promised — he laid on his back, opened his arms, then folded me inside his embrace.

I wanted so much more, but this was a huge start. Because Preston had come home tonight and searched for me. He saw me. He hadn't been on the phone, he hadn't been checking his calendar, he hadn't been reading proposals or plans. All he wanted was me......

Opening my eyes, I looked down at my phone again. That move by Preston meant that he was trying. And that meant that I needed to do the same.

I tapped on the app. The score was 232 to 209, my favor and it was my move.

My move needed to be to resign and then block Blu. I needed to end our connection so that I could plug-in to my husband once again.

"Just do it," I told myself again. "Resign. Block."

I sat there for a few more moments, then sighed before I tossed the phone back onto my desk. Why didn't I want to just unfriend Blu? It wasn't like I really knew him. It wasn't like we were really even friends.

Sitting there, I massaged my temples, thinking once again, about last night. And how Preston had made that effort and how I needed to do that same. Then...I got an idea. I sat for a few moments more, thinking it through.

Yes! This would work. This would be wonderful. This would help me to unconnect from Blu and reconnect with Preston.

I glanced at my watch, then calculated the time in my head. If I got started now, the timing would be perfect. I jumped up and dashed into our bedroom.

*****

This was a big move, I knew it. But it was a winning move. It was a bit out of character for me. Perhaps Sheryl's, definitely Cassidy's style. But that was part of the excitement. I was a desperate housewife ready to be bold.

I swung my car around the curve, pulling into the downtown parking structure for the building where Wake Forest Investments had their offices. It was Friday, just about noon, so it wasn't difficult to find a spot. I stuffed the bottle of wine into my tote before I jumped out of my SUV. Then before I took a step, I tightened the belt on my trench coat, making sure everything was in place.

The heels of my stilettos clicked against the concrete of the parking lot and with each step, I got more excited. By the time I strode into the main elevator, I was giggling.

This reminded me of the old days. When we'd first gotten married. On so many Fridays, I'd stop by Preston's office and we'd sneak away for a quiet lunch...or a nooner in his car. My hope was that this would jog Preston's memory all the way back to our olden days.

I pushed the bottle of wine down further into my bag before I stepped off the elevators on the seventh floor. I was still smiling wide as I looked at the huge gold letters — WAKE FOREST INVESTMENTS — and the cheery receptionist chirped, "Hi. May I help you?"

My smiled dimmed a bit. I didn't remember her name, but I at least remembered the receptionist's face from the Christmas extravaganza that Preston and his partners held last year. Clearly, though, as Preston Mason's wife, I wasn't memorable at all. That might have something to do with the fact that I never visited Preston here at the office. I didn't like this place. What wife celebrated her husband's mistress?

"I'm here for Preston Mason ," I said, deciding not to reintroduce myself to the woman. There was no need; I wasn't here to bond with her.

"Do you have an appointment?"

Okay, let me back up. I didn't reintroduce myself because I was sure that once I said Preston's name, she'd remember that I was his wife. Did she even remember that he had a wife?

"No, I don't have an appointment." My fake grin was so wide, my cheeks were already aching. "But since I'm his wife, I don't think I need one."

My words, my tone were sharper than they should have been. It wasn't this young lady's fault that I wasn't part of the Wake Forest Family.

"Oh," she exclaimed. "I'm so sorry."

"No worries. I'll just go back," I said, hoping that Preston's office was in the same place. I'd only taken a couple of steps when she called out.

"Wait." She sounded as if she were really trying to stop me. When I swiveled just a bit to face her, she said, "Maybe I should call him first?"

Since she was asking, I said, "No, I'm good. I'm sure he'll be happy to see me," and tugged on the belt to my trench.

I'd wanted to approach his door with a kind of saunter, a walk so sexy that by the time I sashayed into his office, my intentions would be so obvious. But I'd been a bit distracted by the receptionist and my thoughts returned to how removed I was from Preston's life as I tapped on his door.

I pushed the door open at the same time that I heard a giggle. I frowned, until I stepped inside. His secretary, Ashley, sat opposite him and they both looked up as I walked in.

It was a good thing that I hadn't opened my coat.

"Angelique," Preston said, popping up from his chair. "What's wrong? What are you doing here?"

"Uh...." I glanced at Ashley.

I knew my husband, so these were the words I expected from him. And I had my answers ready. But I couldn't answer the way I wanted to with Ashley sitting right there. And she made no moves to get up and get out.

"Angelique?" Preston called my name.

"Uh...." My eyes darted from my husband to his assistant. "Uh....."

Ashley said, "Maybe I should leave."

You think?

Still, she stayed in place for a few moments before she gathered a couple of files, smiled at me, and then walked out, closing the door behind her.

Preston stepped from his chair and rounded his desk. "So, what's wrong? What are you doing here?"

With a breath, I put down my tote, then, yanked the belt of my coat.

"Angelique?"

Wait! The trench was supposed to snap open. I had practiced it at home. But instead, the belt did just the opposite. It tightened around my waist. "Uh…." Looking down, I had somehow knotted it. Ugh! How had I done that?

"Angelique, you're worrying me." He took a step closer.

I fumbled with the belt, thinking that now, instead of the acting lessons I thought I needed last night, I really needed to find a stripper as a mentor instead.

With a couple of more tugs, yanks, pushes and pulls, I snapped the coat open.

Preston blinked. "Oh!" He stepped back and my hope was that he did that so he could get a better view.

I sucked in my stomach, brought my leg forward in a pose, and then wondered if I could find stripper lessons on-line.

"Oh!"

"You like?"

He said, "Uh…yeah…but."

Moving toward him, I shook my head. "No buts. Unless…." I grabbed his hand. "You're touching mine."

He smiled. "What's gotten into you?"

I wrapped my arms around Preston's neck. "I miss you, baby," I purred.

He raised his arms into what I expected to be an embrace. But instead, with his hands, he pushed my arms away. "Uh…"

I guess it was his turn to stumble.

He held my arms at my side.

"What's wrong?" Now, I was the one asking that question.

"Uh…you look good, babe."

I grinned.

"But," he said.

"No, buts."

"Yes. But. Because I have to work."

I frowned. I stepped back. I looked down at my body that was covered only with that two-hundred and twenty-eight dollar teddy and thong that I'd bought for the other night. These ten inches of satin and lace were supposed to get me something better than, 'Uh'. These ten inches of satin and lace should have gotten me at least ten minutes with his ten inches.

He said, "Babe, I'm sorry, but I can't even take lunch today."

I shook my head. "I'm not asking for lunch."

His eyes glossed over my body. "I know, but...."

I held up my hand. "Don't say 'but' anymore."

"Baby, I really wish I could take the time, b— and, I can't do it today. I have a big meeting at two, a new client and that's what Ashley and I were doing. I was reviewing the portfolio."

"Really? It didn't sound like you were working. When I walked in, you were laughing. So, you have time to have a laugh with your assistant, but no time to take care of your wife."

He dipped his head a little. "Oh, come on, babe. I didn't expect you."

"That was the point."

"And if I'd known, if you had called...."

"You would have shut me down."

"Only because...."

"I know." I sighed. There was no point to my trying to continue this. "You have to work."

He nodded. "Please understand."

"I. Understand."

He moved toward me and hesitated a moment before he wrapped his arms around my waist making me shiver. "Do you?" I lowered my head, but with his fingertips, he lifted my chin. "This was a really good idea, and I so wish...that I could, but...."

I said nothing.

"It's just that today. It's not a good day."

I opened my mouth to tell him that no day was good. But then, I pressed my lips together. There was no need to say more, my words weren't going to change anything."

So, all I did was step back, and pull the lapels of my raincoat together.

"Wait," he said. "Let me do that for you." He pulled the coat open and stared at my body for a moment, before he sighed, then closed it and wrapped me up inside. Once he tied the belt so that it was really secure, he hugged me again. "You are such a beautiful woman. And as soon as all of this is behind me, I'm going to make this up to you."

I almost asked him for a timetable, but changed my mind. I already knew when he was going to make this up to me — my husband and I had a date for 'never'.

A tap on the door made me and Preston take a step away from each other.

Ashley peeked her head in. "I don't mean to interrupt, but...."

There was that word again.

"No, come on in." Preston walked away from me and around his desk. "We have to get back to work."

I turned, picked up my tote, and then, without saying goodbye, I moved toward the door. Right before I stepped into the hall, my husband called out.

"Get home safely."

I didn't turn around because if I had, I would've embarrassed him. I would have told him that the least he could have given me were three other words. Instead of saying, 'get home safely', he would have done much better with, 'I love you'. But he didn't even think about it and I didn't even bother.

My steps were quick, and I kept my eyes away from the receptionist so grateful that the elevator came within seconds. Inside the chamber, I blinked and blinked and blinked.

I blinked until I jumped back into my SUV and only then, did I allow that first tear to fall.

Grabbing my cell from my purse, I opened the *Words With Friends* app. I clicked on the game with Blu and sent him a message:

What are you doing?

But I couldn't see if he replied because a tear rolled from my eye and dropped right into the center of my screen, blurring everything.

CHAPTER 7

Blu

I grabbed the six-pack that I had set in the passenger seat, but then I turned off my car, silenced my music and just leaned back inside my Tahoe. Did I really want to do this? Glancing at the two-story, modest house across the street, I knew Lamar was home; the garage door was up. I couldn't see inside, but if I knew my boy, he was in there working out, or he had just finished since it was already after ten. He always got his workouts in before noon. It helped that he didn't have to drive twenty minutes to do that...he had put together a serious home gym inside the garage of the home that his parents had left him when they passed away in a car accident the year we graduated from college.

But still, did I want to do this? Did I really want to have this conversation?

Lamar had been my boy from way back, since we were both the new kids on the block in the seventh grade. We'd bonded over being the outsiders since the other kids in the neighborhood had known each other forever. And even though we'd eventually made friends with the other guys (especially once we joined the basketball team) Lamar was still my bruh.

For the last thirty or so years, we had shared everything — from how our parents just didn't get it, to deciding to go to Texas A & M University together, to choosing our careers. But what we talked about the most — the girls (and later, the women) in our lives.

But we had never talked like this. Because there was never a need for this conversation.

Before.

I rested my hand on the car door knob and then paused again. On Thursday, when Monica and I had connected, I never thought I'd be in a place like this. In those few moments, she'd given me so much hope and even now, I couldn't figure out how that hope had just floated away:

Grabbing the bags of food, I hopped out of the car with all kinds of expectations. I knew Monica would have to take it slow, she had been down for a long time. But if she just got active around the house and in the children's lives again, that would be enough. I was sure she'd want to go back to work eventually, now that she was feeling better, but I was going to advise her to take it slow. I didn't want any kind of stress that would send her back into a depression. I didn't want any chance of any kind of a relapse.

The moment I opened the door from the garage, Raven dashed to me. "Daddy!"

"What's up, Munchkin?"

"You're home early."

"I know. And look what I have." I held up the bags.

"Yay," Raven said, jumping up and down. "Did you get me an egg roll?"

"I did." I chuckled. I didn't even have to tell her what was in the bags. Chinese food was her favorite and she probably smelled it before I'd come into the house. "I got you two."

"Two? Yay!"

"It was your mom's idea to give you two." Stepping into the kitchen, I dumped the bags onto the counter.

"Can we use paper plates?"

I shook my head. Raven thought eating off of paper plates was the coolest thing. I guessed it reminded her of the picnics I took her on sometimes, just to get her out of the house. I nodded, then asked, "Where's your mom?"

My daughter's smile slipped away. "She's upstairs." She sighed. "She's in bed."

"What?"

"She's always in bed."

I wanted to tell my daughter no. I wanted to tell her that less than an hour ago, her mother was up and out and back. "I'll be back, sweetheart," I told Raven before I ran out of the kitchen, then took the stairs two at a time.

I busted into our bedroom as if the house was on fire...and then, I stopped. Raven was right; Monica was in bed, the covers pulled to her chin, as if she'd never been downstairs.

She lay on her side, her back to me and I walked slowly toward the bed. When I stood over her, I whispered, "Monica."

"What?" she asked, her voice monotone.

"What...what happened?"

She rolled over, faced me, and that look in her eyes, the glossy vacancy was back.

"What are you talking about?"

I kept my voice low, calm, hoping that alone would remind her of the conversation, the connection we'd just had. "I bought Chinese...for dinner."

66

Her stare was blank, almost as if she weren't seeing me.

I said, "Remember...moo goo gai pan for you and...."

"Blu, I'm tired. Can you please just leave me alone?" She rolled over.
"Please." She turned her back on me and the hope that I'd allowed to
build up inside.

I'd walked out of our bedroom just stunned, thinking that my wife
had been lucid less than an hour before. Thinking that maybe it was my
fault — I shouldn't have left her.

That was my thought as I made sure Raven and Tanner had their
dinner, and that was my thought when I finally joined Monica in bed and
tried to talk to her again. But she had returned to her pattern: she snapped,
she complained, and then, she cried....

By yesterday morning, I'd let the guilt go — whatever had
sent Monica back to her state wasn't my fault, this was all
Monica's illness.

And by the time Monica got through with me yesterday
morning, I was ready to move out of our house. And I was
certainly ready to talk to Angelique.

But even though I'd spent half of my time at work staring
at my phone, I hadn't sent Angelique a message at all. Not even
when she'd sent me one yesterday afternoon. Because I was
trying, trying hard to stay away. I just had a feeling that if we
connected again, it wouldn't be good for her, it wouldn't be
good for me.

But the more estranged I felt from Monica, the more
engaged I wanted to be with Angelique.

That was why I needed to talk to someone. Someone who
could talk me out of this trap that I was about to stick my neck
into.

This time when I grabbed the knob, I pulled the Tahoe's
door open and jumped out, not talking myself out of it this

time. I trotted across the street, up the slanted driveway and then, peeked inside.

My friend was laid back on his weight bench, holding a sixty-pound dumbbell in each hand, doing double bicep curls.

"What up, Lamar?"

Without looking up, he did one last curl, then dropped both weights heavily onto the garage floor.

He sat up, straddling the bench, his biceps still bulging and on display with the white wife beater he wore. He leaned forward, gave me some dap, then cocked his head. "What's up with you?"

I plopped down on the LazyBoy recliner in the corner.

"Let me guess," Lamar said, shaking his do-rag covered head. "Monica."

I didn't have to say a word, Lamar knew. He'd been by my side through this struggle, so my body language spoke before my mouth did. My only spoken answer was, "I brought beer."

"Man, it's just ten o'clock in the morning. I haven't even had my orange juice." He laughed.

I chuckled with him. "Look, it's noon somewhere."

"Oh, and that's your start-up time now?"

I nodded, twisted the cap off a bottle, and took a long swig of the cold beer.

Lamar kept his eyes on me. "Wow. It must be bad."

I took another swig, then nodded. "It is."

"What's up?"

Shaking my head, I didn't even know where to begin because Lamar had heard it all before. Still I needed to get it out. So, I told him about Thursday and how I'd seen some semblance of my wife.

"Dang," he said when I finished the story. "What happened? Why'd she revert?"

"I have no idea and that's the frustrating part. I'd gotten my hopes up...."

"And she dropped them, lower than you'd been before."

Lamar had summed it up. That was what years of friendship did, I guess. Or maybe it was his engineering education and it was some kind of law of physics.

"What does her doc say?"

I shook my head. Lamar always asked that question, even though he knew I didn't have the answers. Because of the law, Monica had to grant me access to her doctors and her medical information — and she didn't. "I talked to Doctor Nichols, told her what happened, but that was it. She couldn't tell me anything."

"So, what you gonna do?"

"What are my choices?" I didn't wait for him to answer. "I can't leave."

He locked his eyes with mine for a moment, and then looked away.

"What?" I said, my forehead creasing with my frown.

He shrugged. "Nothing."

"Nah, bruh, we been too close for all these years for you to...."

"Okay, okay." He swung one leg over the bench, so that his whole body faced me. "Man, you are one committed brother, but I'm just thinkin', how much longer can you go through this? How much longer can you expose the kids to this?"

"She's not doing anything to the kids."

"She's not doing anything *with* the kids either. When was the last time she interacted with her own children?" He didn't give me room to respond. "Man, I feel sorry for Tanner, but I'm not worried about him 'cause he's too old to want all those motherly hugs and stuff. But what about Raven? At least Tanner can remember the way she used to be, but Raven?" He shook his head. "I worry about her."

I didn't tell my friend that I worried about Raven...and Tanner, too. I just defended my wife. "She's sick, man, you know that. She's doing the best she can."

He waited a moment before he said, "Okay, if you say so."

"Nah, you're not gonna do that," I said, shaking my head and raising my voice at the same time. "Keep talking. Just say what you feel."

"I just did." He waved his hands as if his gestures would make his point, too. "I just told you. You've put up with a lot."

"So, what am I supposed to do? Just leave her?" I asked him that question because I knew what his answer would be.

But he shocked me with, "Yes."

My eyes widened.

"Look," he lowered and softened his voice, "you know how much I love Monica." He held his hand over his heart. "But this, what you're going through, it's just too much."

"What about for better for worse, in sickness and in health?" I paused. "Would you be saying the same thing if she had cancer?"

"Nah, that's different."

I shook my head. "See, that's the difference between us. Cancer, mental illness, it's not different to me. Mental illness is as real as any other disease."

"But she's not getting better."

"And there are people who never go into remission, who have terminal illnesses and we don't blame that fact on them."

He nodded, though I wasn't sure if he did that because he wanted me to calm down or if he really agreed. Finally, he said,

"So, what you're telling me is that you're willing to hang in there for the long haul…forever."

My answer: I took another swig of beer.

He paused for a moment, then said, "I gotta ask you this." He let a couple of beats of time go by. "Now, don't get mad about it 'cause it's just a question."

His hesitation made me shift a bit in this recliner. "Would you just say what you gotta say or ask what you wanna ask?"

He nodded, still paused, then said, "Are you staying with Monica because of her money?"

I didn't hesitate at all. "Monica doesn't have any money."

He chuckled as he spoke, "You know what I mean, bruh. Her family." Then, he stopped again. "You're not staying because her family is related to Jed Clampett on the black side."

He'd made that joke to take the edge off of his question, but I stayed serious because there was nothing to laugh about when it came to this. "I got my own money. I don't need her family's."

"I know that, I'm just asking."

I looked straight into his eyes when I said, "And I just answered."

"Asked and answered, then."

"Done."

Lamar leaned forward, resting his arms on his legs. "Look, bruh, you know me. That wasn't meant as any kind of an insult. All I can say is that I've got nothing but respect," he banged his fist against his chest, "for you. But I keep wondering why you're being the martyr? Man, I know you got needs. What you gonna do about *that* if Monica doesn't get better?"

My needs.

It was true, I needed some serious healing of the sexual kind.

But I didn't say that to Lamar. I didn't say anything. I just took another swig, though this time, I took a long, long, long one. So long that I emptied my bottle.

Lamar's eyes narrowed. "Wait...a...minute...." He paused. "What's up with you? Talk to me. What's going on?"

And there it was. The opening. The reason I'd come over here. To talk to my best friend.

So, I did. "Now, I'm not saying that I would ever step out on Monica...."

"No one could fault you if you did."

I shook my head. "You and me. We always said we were going to be the most faithful men this side of the Mississippi."

"We've tried to be."

I nodded and thought about the fact that it had always been so important to me to be faithful. Because I'd heard too many sisters talk about men and dogs as if they were the same breed. And Lamar and I didn't want to be *those* black men.

But still, I told Lamar what I'd come to talk about. Still, I told him the truth. "I've met someone."

Lamar let out a long breath.

I held up my hand. "Not in that way."

"Well, in what kind of way? How long have you known her?"

I calculated the time in my head. "A couple of weeks, but I only met her Thursday."

Lamar frowned. "Where'd y'all meet? Work?"

I shook my head. "I met her...playing *Words With Friends*."

He waited a moment and then, he laughed. One of those man-get-out-of-here chuckles until he saw that I didn't join him. And then, he straightened up real quick. "Wait...a...minute. You're not kidding."

While shaking my head, I went on to tell Lamar about how I'd met Angelique....

"I love her name," he said.

And how we'd finally agreed to meet.

"Hooking up at Starbucks, that was good. No pressure," he said.

And how I'd known we had a connection before we met, but after sitting together for two hours, I was so certain of it, I didn't even want to leave her.

I finished up by saying, "She's beautiful, intelligent, she stimulates my mind."

His eyebrows rose. "And that's what you need right now, right? Your mind stimulated?"

"Man, whatever." I chuckled. "Seriously, though, by the time I walked her to her car and watched her drive away, I was already strategizing how I would see her again."

He glanced at the clock on the wall. "So today is Saturday. What are you waiting for?"

"Because after Thursday night with Monica...."

"Oh." He dragged out the word, letting me know he understood.

I said, "I thought things were going to be right with my wife."

"But now you know...."

"I don't know anything. I just know that...I'm lonely, man. And Angelique, she listened to me."

"And she probably laughed at your corny jokes, too."

I grinned. "Every time."

We laughed, but then we both got serious. "Blu, man, I'm not gonna come right out and tell you what I think about this situation because you know where I stand."

"I know." I paused, letting a few beats pass. "There's something I haven't told you about Angelique." I figured the best thing to do was to just come out and say it. "She's married."

"Whoa."

"Yup. She's been married for awhile. She and her husband have eight years in."

"So what's she doing creepin' with you?"

"She's not creepin'. We were just playing a game."

"And hooking up."

"At Starbucks, not the Sheraton."

"For now."

"Forever."

He gave me one of those raised eyebrow yeah-sure-bruh looks.

I said, "I think her being married is another thing that makes her so attractive to me."

His question was in his eyes.

"I know nothing will happen because I'm married…she's married."

I'd said that with every bit of seriousness in me. But for some reason, that sent my boy into buckled-over-laughter. I just sat there, staring at him, having a good laugh over my bad life. And when he finally sat up straight, he said, "Man, hand me one of those beers."

I almost wanted to crack him over the head with it, but instead, I just tossed him the bottle.

"Can't believe you got me out here drinking so early in the morning like we back in college or something." He twisted off the cap, took a swallow and then said, "I guess you never heard, an unhappy wife makes the best mistress."

"You know you just made that up. And I never said she was unhappy."

"Then, what is she doing creepin' with you?"

I shook my head; I wasn't going around in that circle anymore.

"I'm just kiddin'," Lamar said. "Look, you've got to do what makes you happy."

I bobbed my head up and down, not sure if I was really nodding to agree with him.

He said, "You've tried, man. You've done everything that you could with Monica. And now...." He held his hands up as if he were surrendering to something. Or maybe that was his signal to me.

"Just be happy," he said.

Be happy. I repeated his words in my head. That really was all that I wanted. Which was why, I pulled out my phone and with Lamar's eyes on me, I opened the app and made a move that had nothing to do with the tiles.

I sent Angelique a message:

I've missed you. What you doing?

I almost put the phone away, expecting having to wait, if not a couple of hours, at least a few minutes. But the notification came to my phone before I could move.

I thought you forgot about me.

My fingers couldn't move fast enough:

Never! I was just busy....

I hesitated and then, added to my message:

At work. I was busy at work. But not busy anymore.

Her response: ☺

I wanted to send my own emoji — the one with the hearts for eyes. But instead, I did the one thing I knew would just make me happy. I typed:

When can I see you again?

And then, I looked up, gave Lamar dap, and I grabbed another bottle of beer.

CHAPTER 8

Angelique

It wasn't often that I got to hang out with my girls. But when the three of us got together - we did it up big, especially if Cassidy was in charge of our meet-up.

And today, since it had been a couple of months since the three of us had gathered, Cassidy had arranged a Saturday of pampering. She'd booked the whole afternoon at The Woodlands Spa and for five hours, we had a team of people showering us with the works —an olive oil manicure and pedicure, an oxygen infusion facial, and then a hot stone massage. The best part of all of this — we weren't paying a dime for this three-hundred dollar (each) afternoon. Cassidy had done what Cassidy was great at doing — she'd convinced some rich guy she'd met on one of her many travel adventures to foot her bill.

"So, Dubai is a place where everyone must go," Cassidy said.

We were chillin' in-between treatments in one of the private rooms. The butter-soft leather recliner felt like it had molded itself to my body and after that pedicure with that foot massage that hit every pressure point and sent shivers everywhere, I was so relaxed, I was almost floating in the eucalyptus and spearmint infused air. Floating in air that was colored Blu.

When will I see you again?

That was where our conversation had ended; I hadn't answered that question.

"I'm telling you, everyone's rich in Dubai."

Cassidy's words barely penetrated my semi-consciousness.

"Well, when I can travel the way you do — for free, I'll go." That was Sheryl's answer, which was the same answer she gave to everything.

"You are the cheapest doctor I know." Those words and Cassidy's laughter brought my mind and my body all the way back down and into the room. And, I laughed, too.

If I could have seen Sheryl's eyes under the cucumber patches that she wore (she was so extra sometimes), I was sure she hadn't even blinked at what some might consider an insult. "I prefer the term frugal," she said. "Don't hate me because I save more money than you."

"You save more money than God," Cassidy told her before she turned to face me. "Since Frugal Fran has given me her update, tell me what's been going on with you?"

Sheryl removed her eye patches and brought her lounger up from its semi-reclined position. "Yeah, I gotta sit up to see this reply." Then, she stared at me, making it totally obvious that something was going on in my life. I couldn't deny anything, even if I wanted to. I made a note to myself (and not for the first time): never rob a bank and tell Sheryl. Because the police would surely be at my door.

In the silence, Cassidy (who sat in between us) looked back and forth between me and Sheryl. I knew what she saw: Me, with my expression of guilt and Sheryl, with her stare that told the world I was guilty.

"Well?" Cassidy said. "Is somebody gonna say something?"

What I wanted to do was lean back and return to the floating that I was doing a moment ago. But my best friends would never allow me to ignore them that way.

Sheryl raised an eyebrow and all I could get out was, "Ummmm."

I guess that little hum wasn't all I did because Cassidy's eyebrows perched.

"Oh no." Now, she sat at attention, too. "Somebody better start talking because that smile you're wearing...that's the smile of a woman who's been getting her back blown out."

Was I smiling? And if I were, did she have to be so crude about it? Oh, to be floating again.

"So," Cassidy began. "I guess Preston got himself back in the game. Heyyyy!" She lifted her hands in a raise-the-roof gesture.

The mention of my husband's name ripped away any kind of smile that had been on my face. And once again, all I could get out was, "Ummmm...."

"Well, I'm glad to hear that you and Preston are working it out," Cassidy said, filling in her own blanks because I'd stayed silent. She'd written her own end to my story. "'Cause if he can make you smile like that after all the years you guys have been married, then, I need...."

"It's not Preston!" I shouted.

"What?" Cassidy said with confusion in her voice.

"It's not Preston," I repeated. "He's not the one who's been blowing my back out. I mean," I waved my hands because that was not what I meant to say, "it's not Preston, it's someone else."

Her eyes widened. "It's not Preston," she whispered. "Who's blowing your back out?"

I glanced at Sheryl for help. But she just sat there, her elbow perched on the arm of the chair, her chin in the palm of her hand. She said nothing — if you didn't count the expression on her face.

Taking a deep breath, I said, "Let me start over. If I were smiling — and I said 'if' — it's not Preston."

"I got that part," Cassidy said.

"It's someone else. I met another guy."

"I got that part, too."

"Well, the part you didn't get is that nothing is going on with us. I mean, I'm a married woman...."

"You're a neglected woman," Sheryl said.

She could have kept her first contribution to our conversation to herself.

"Look, Cassidy," I leaned forward in my chair, "it's not even like that. I just met a guy."

Sheryl said, "Through an app."

"And we've been talking to each other."

"Through an app."

"And we finally got together for coffee....only!"

"But ask her if she's still talking to him...through an app!"

The way Cassidy's head moved from side-to-side, from me to Sheryl, back to me, then back to Sheryl, I was sure she was getting some kind of whiplash.

"Do not listen to that woman," I said, pointing to Sheryl and rolling my eyes.

Sheryl sat unfazed, still with her elbow perched, still with her chin in her hand, still with that expression on her face.

I said, "Sheryl's making more out of this than there is."

Cassidy wagged her finger in my face. "No, she isn't. What got this started was your smile."

Sheryl stuck her tongue out at me as if she thought we were in the third grade. And what did I do? With all the maturity in my thirty-four-year-old body, I returned the gesture.

Cassidy was silent for a moment. "So, why do I feel like this is a bigger deal than what you're saying?"

Before I could respond, Sheryl piped in, "Because it is, and I say go for it."

"What?" Cassidy said as if Sheryl's words offended her. "How can you tell her that?"

Sheryl shrugged. "Because she's been neglected for too long. Preston has taken advantage of her."

"But there's a Preston in her life. She's. Married."

Sheryl leaned kinda to the side, kinda to the back in her chair as if she were trying to get a better look at Cassidy. "Says the woman who flies all over the world with all kinds of men."

"And I'm not married."

"Still, you're being taken care of."

"Because I'm single...on purpose. Because I respect the sanctity of marriage and I can't believe that you don't, too."

"I do, when both people are putting in the work. Color me cynical, but there's a reason why I'm not the greatest believer. I deal with people and relationships and I see this all day long. Preston acts like Angelique doesn't even exist. He takes her for granted and being married doesn't give him license to neglect her with no consequences."

"I agree." Cassidy nodded. "And that's why she needs to work this out with her husband."

I held up my hand. "Hello! I'm sitting right here."

"I'm sorry." Cassidy rolled her eyes at Sheryl before she turned back to me. "I'm just shocked by all of this. We don't see each other for a few months, I come back and you're involved with another man?"

"That's not what's going on. I met a guy, I really like him, we've connected, but we're just friends."

"For now," Sheryl huffed.

"Forever," I told my friends. "Look, as much as I'd love to daydream and imagine what it would be like to be with Blu, there will always be the fact that I'm married...."

"Oh, and don't leave out the fact that he's married, too," Sheryl just had to say, making me regret all the phone calls we'd had since our lunch last week. I'd filled Sheryl in on everything — including that fact.

Cassidy bounced back in her seat. "Oh, Lord!"

"Why are you calling out to Him?" Sheryl asked. "Shoot, if you ask me, everything is lining up for our girl. Because the key to this is to make sure you have an affair with someone who has as much to lose as you do."

Cassidy's eyes were wide when she said to Sheryl, "You're actually giving Angelique advice on the methodology of cheating?" She shook her head. "Or, this dude could be a stone-cold dog who cheats on his wife perpetually and Angelique will be just another one of his conquests." She turned to me with fear in her eyes. "Don't do it, girl. I don't want you to be hurt."

Sheryl said, "And I say, go into this like a grown woman, with your legs...and eyes wide open and your heart closed. And then, you'll never be hurt. Because if this man can do for you what Preston won't," she snapped her fingers, "just lay back, kick it and enjoy the ride."

"Angelique is your best friend, Sheryl," the one who was supposed to be carefree said with horror in her voice. "How can you say that to her?"

"I told you, every day..."

Cassidy held up her hand, stopping Sheryl. "I hope this isn't the kind of advice you're giving your patients."

"No, they pay me to work it out, even when it's not work-out-able. Angelique isn't paying me, so I'm telling her the truth."

"Would you both just stop it?" My hands cut through the air with my words. "I'm going to say this one last time and then we're ending this here...I have a new friend." I paused and almost asked them to repeat after me. "Friend. That's it. He's married, I'm married, which is the ultimate barrier to either one of us doing anything that we shouldn't. End of the freakin' story."

Because I was the calmest of the three and never used words like 'freakin', I guess I'd tripped them out and shut them up.

And to put a period on the whole thing, I said, "Okay?"

"Okay," Cassidy said.

It took me staring down Sheryl to get her to say, "Whatever." But then, my glare made her add, "Okay."

"Okay," I sealed it and closed the conversation.

We all sat back, eyes closed, our skin and nostrils soaking in the eucalyptus and the peace. And I was trying to float right back up to the place where I could only see Blu.

But then, the silence was cracked wide open. "But just know there ain't nothin' wrong with a little bump and grind."

I opened my eyes to see Sheryl raising her champagne glass in a toast to me.

I tried hard not to smile (though I didn't succeed). I pretended to shake my head in disgust. But then, I leaned back, closed my eyes, and all I could do was think of Blu.

CHAPTER 9

Angelique

Surely, this wasn't what God had in mind when He gave us the ability to think, to remember, to wonder. Surely, God didn't want one person to take up so much space in another person's head. But that was what Blu Logan had done to me. He'd taken up residence in my thoughts, in my memories, in my imagination and he refused to leave.

For the just about three weeks now that I'd been talking to Blu, I'd had it bad. But my bad had reached new heights on Saturday when Blu and I had chatted through the app and then he'd asked that ultimate question:

When can I see you again?

Blu's constant assault on my mind had started with those six words. I'd thought about them while I was at the spa with my girls, I thought about them when I went home, then waited for Preston to return from his long afternoon of golf, I thought about them as I ate, when I was at church, and when I laid down to close my eyes to sleep.

I thought about his question from Saturday to now, as I sat behind my desk, trying to get ready for an important week in the office. But it was hard for me to focus on anything else when I was trying to decide — how *should* I answer his question which was different from how *would* I answer it?

When will I see you again?

I wondered what Blu thought of the fact that I hadn't responded to him. I certainly wondered why he hadn't sent a follow-up. We were in this strange place right now. Where instead of reacting to Blu's question on Saturday, I just made my next move — in the game, pretending as if there wasn't an unanswered message between us. And he did the same. We played the rest of the weekend, until I defeated him last night 347 to 320.

And now, here I sat, my wondering continuing, although now my wonder had been upgraded — I wondered what would it be like to answer Blu's question with: *you can see me anytime, anywhere, to do anything....*

The knock on my office door sent me at least four feet into the air from the executive chair where I'd been sitting.

"Hello!"

I pressed my hand against my chest because I'd been so deep into my thoughts that knock startled me.

"Uh...." Camille peeked her head into my office. "Are you even here mentally because I've been knocking and knocking...."

"Oh, sorry." I motioned for her to come in. "I'm here - physically and mentally," I said as I tried to shake all thoughts of Blu and my answer to his question away.

"Well, you might say that you're here," Camille said as she stepped inside, then sat down in one of the two over-sized chairs in front of my desk. "But your mind is definitely someplace else."

I sighed, thinking once again of the response that I truly wanted to give to Blu, the response that was opposite what I planned to give to him.

"Angelique!"

I blinked.

"The way you're zoning out, I almost hate to ask you — what's going on?"

This time when I shook my head, I hoped that my brain would rattle around and knock some sense into me. Because the last thing I needed to be doing at work today was thinking of Blu. I couldn't afford this time — not when I had to finalize the details for the Black Girl Magic weekend that was coming up in two weeks.

I said to Camille, "I'm really sorry. I do have a lot going on right now, including wrapping up everything for the big weekend."

"Well, before you do anything else," Camille paused for just a moment, "I hate to be the bearer of this bad news...."

My professional antenna shot right up and everything I should have seen before, I saw now. I saw the way Camille sat on the edge of her seat instead of leaning in her usual laid-back fashion. I saw the way her lips were pinched and her body sat so stiff and her eyes — what was that in her eyes? Worry? No, it was more than worry, it was kinda sorta like a low-grade fear.

Taking all of that in, I tensed because I knew my assistant was not prone to any kind of dramatics. Whatever was going on was serious. "What is it?"

I wasn't sure if Camille was moving in slow motion or if it was my brain. Her arm edged up, up, up until the folder that she held finally made it into my hand. It took everything within me to hold back from snatching it from her and tearing it open myself. But before I could rip the pages out, Camille belted,

"JT Financials…they won't be funding the Black Girl Magic Weekend."

The only reason I hesitated was because I couldn't get my brain to make sense of the words Camille had just spoken. But then, her expression explained what her words had not made totally clear, and I fell back in my seat feeling like I'd been bludgeoned with a sledgehammer to my stomach. "Are you kidding me?"

"I wish." Worry lines consumed her face.

"How can they do this?"

She shook her head as my eyes scanned the two page letter. She said, "And my question is how can they do this and say that it is effective immediately."

"I know! They can't drop our funding now. We have two hundred girls coming to the Westin in eleven days. They're staying at the hotel, we're taking them shopping in the Galleria, we have all these workshops set up for them. And oh, they have to eat, especially at the gala." I went through the itinerary as if Camille hadn't been the key person to help me put this program together. "It's next weekend," I said as though telling her what she already knew would make a difference.

She let me go on and on before she said, "I know."

"Without this funding, I won't be able to make the final payments…and then, I'll lose all the deposits. What am I supposed to do now?"

She shook her head. "I'm so sorry, but like the letter said, JT Financials is bankrupt. Or at least, they've filed for bankruptcy and so…."

She left it there but she didn't need to say anymore. I wanted my modest office to be quiet anyway, so that I could figure out what to do. Our budget was small (compared to other foundations) for what I wanted to do with these teenagers that I referred to as 'my girls'. There were two hundred of them who were part of my foundation, chosen from my church and six different high schools.

I'd come up with the idea of Black Girl Magic after working with my pastor at Wheeler Avenue. Preston and I had been married for just a month when Hurricane Katrina sent almost a quarter of a million people to Houston and our pastor had asked members of Wheeler to open up their hearts, their homes, their wallets to help the evacuees. There wasn't much that Preston and I could do at the time, but I suggested to Pastor Lawson that I could lead a church group for any teens who'd been displaced and missed being home in New Orleans. I was thinking about the many times I'd felt out of place as I traveled around the country for gymnastics, training away from home during the summers and competing during the school year. It was my personal experience that let me know there was a need for a support group like that.

The church group was small, only seven teens. When I met those young girls, and they spoke openly about the life that they'd left behind — friends, family, their school and church — my heart broke for them. Their pain was in their voices as they talked about how it felt to be starting over and because of their displacement most sounded as if they couldn't imagine much of a future, as if they didn't want to put their hopes in something that, once again, wind or rain could sweep away. They suffered from a psychological trauma that for many would never be addressed and I didn't want that to happen to these young ladies.

That was when I decided that instead of sitting back, I would step up and mentor these girls beyond the one or two sessions I had first imagined. I wanted to show them how they were the master of the lives that God had given to them and their future could be anything they wanted it to be, not based upon their circumstances.

Sheryl came in to work with me and the girls and together we were able to raise their spirits and give them hope.

Over time, the seven girls grew to twenty, and that was when I knew I had a program. There were so many organizations who focused on at-risk teens, and then, of course, the upper-middle and upper class teens had Jack and Jill and programs within the national sororities. But I wanted to start a foundation for the forgotten girls in between — the ones whose parents worked two and three jobs so they weren't on any kind of public assistance, but who would never receive the personal invitation into some of the other programs.

It was four years later when I started the foundation to help expose teens to the opportunities before them in the world. I wanted to let them know college was an option and they didn't need to rule it out because as so many of them felt, they 'didn't want to put an extra burden on their parents.'

The program (which I named before Black Girl Magic became a trending thing) was a once-a-month Saturday and Sunday gathering. On the Saturday, I took them to four-star restaurants for the experience of sitting down in that environment, to upscale spas, art fairs and the Shakespeare festival. And then on Sunday, we came together for workshops and to discuss their experiences. We ended the day with a rap-session where the girls talked about whatever was going on in their lives — from parental issues to boyfriend challenges and all the teen angst in between.

I had such dreams for these girls because ninety-four percent of them who graduated out of Black Girl Magic went on to college. My desire was to take that percentage to one hundred and provide all the financial and emotional support the girls needed through their college years, too.

But before I could achieve that goal, I had to get through next weekend, which was the first time we were making our weekend meetings a full-blown conference. For a year, the girls had looked forward to this. I'd secured the funding, made the plans and was as excited as the girls.

And now it looked like this was coming to a crashing, disappointing end. I'd had three sponsors and I'd done something that I never had before: I made the final arrangements without having all of the committed funds in the bank. Now, I had to find alternative funding. Someone else would have to give me the twenty-five thousand dollars that JT Financials had committed to us.

I held my head in my hands as if that would be enough to stave off the headache that was sure to come. And not just a physical one. Cancelling this event was sure to cause pain to so many.

"I can't believe this is happening." I fought to hold back the moistness struggling to break free from my eyes.

For the eight years that I'd had this program, I worked hard to manage it well. I kept the operational budget low: only Camille and I were full-time staffers, and we shared an office suite with another company, not in the high-rent downtown district, but near Kirby because I wanted to be professional, but keep my overhead low. I held fundraisers for the day-to-day expenses for Black Girl Magic, but enlisted the support of sponsors for special events. We hadn't done anything as special as this for so many of the girls and it had to be my excitement that encouraged me to move forward without having the money in the bank. It wasn't like I was reckless — JT Financials had been on board for a year and this wasn't their first time sponsoring an event. They hadn't expressed any kind of concern to me about being able to deliver and I'd certainly heard no rumblings of their demise.

Camille broke through my reflections. "Is there any other way?"

I shook my head. "Where can I get that kind of money, especially on this short notice?" I just sat there, my mind a complete blank except for the words that kept rolling around in my head — *I cannot cancel this event.*

"Is there anything I can do for you?" Camille asked as she stood. "Anyone I can call? Anything you can think of?"

I wanted to ask her to please be quiet. She was asking questions that I was already struggling to answer. But there was no reason to be upset with her. So all I did was shake my head, thank her and then, with my silence, I dismissed her.

Blinking was my defense, until I was alone. And then, I just let the tears roll out. I knew that wasn't a professional response. Usually when something like this happened, I sprang into action — I believed in turning my fear into my fight. But I was overwhelmed by the amount of money I needed and in such a short period of time. If I didn't fix this, I would have two hundred very disappointed young girls who already had enough of that in their lives.

So I had to come up with a plan — who else? What else? I didn't have the money — I had put so much of my own into Black Girls Magic, which was fine because I believed in this so much. And as it was, even with the twenty-five thousand, I was going to have to put in a couple of thousand, probably close to five, because of the updated budget I did last week. So my bank account wasn't an option.

I could probably ask Sheryl, and even maybe Cassidy. Both were members of my board and I was sure that both had at least that much money saved. But the problem was, even if they did, neither of them were in the position to *give* twenty-five thousand dollars. Because that was what they would be doing. This wouldn't be a loan, the foundation had no way of repaying that money.

Leaning back in my chair, I closed my eyes for what I hoped would be no longer than a minute. There had to be something that I could do, something that I was missing. Then, when I opened my eyes, my glance settled on the single photo on my desk — me and Preston on our wedding day, facing each other, holding both hands just moments before the pastor told Preston that he could kiss his bride. That was the day when Preston promised to love, honor and, most of all, cherish me.

I grabbed my phone and before I could change my mind, I tapped on Preston's name. I wasn't surprised when he didn't answer. But I figured if I called right back, he'd see the urgency in my reaching out to him. But even my second attempt ended up with my call going to voicemail.

I had no doubt that he was at work — that's where he always was. So I blocked my number and called the direct line to his office. This time, the phone rang only once.

"Preston Mason."

I resisted the urge to snap at him and instead said, "Honey, did I catch you at a bad time?"

"Hey, babe," Preston said, though there was no sweetness in his tone. His words were short, choppy, full of urgency, but not for me. "In the middle of something. What's up?"

But that didn't deter me because right now, I really needed my husband. "I just...um...I just needed to talk to you. I'm really in a bad place right now."

"Why?" The urgency in his tone was gone, replaced with the concern that no matter what, Preston seemed to have for me. "What's wrong?"

"It's my foundation and the upcoming weekend that I have planned. One of the sponsors bailed on us. Bankruptcy. And now, we're short twenty-five thousand dollars."

"Whoa. Who?"

"JT Financials."

He sighed as if my words were no surprise.

"What?" I asked.

"I'd heard that they were having challenges."

"And you didn't tell me?" That snapping reflex that I was trying to hold back came out. "You're on the board, Preston. This is something that you should have told me."

"Uh…no. Because I don't make moves on rumors. And secondly, I didn't know they were one of your sponsors."

"You would have known if you came to board meetings," I said. "You would have known if you listened when I tried to tell you about the weekend any number of…."

"Look, babe, I'm really sorry about you losing them, but I really have to…."

"Wait!" I slowed my roll. Why was I talking to Preston about missing board meetings and never listening to me when I needed something else from him. "I'm sorry," I spoke quickly. "I know you're busy, so I'll just come right out — do you think Wake Forest could…."

He cut me off, already knowing my question and already having his answer. "Babe, I can't make that kind of decision. I couldn't give you the money even if I wanted to. This is a partnership. The money we have doesn't belong to me."

"I understand. But this is an emergency and you told me that Wake Forest wanted to do some charity st—"

"Can we talk about this tonight?" His words were back to being short, choppy, filled with urgency, not for me. "I really have to go."

I gripped my cell phone tighter as if that would keep Preston on the phone longer. "What time will you be home?"

"Not sure. Pretty late. Don't wait up for me tonight, but we can definitely brainstorm about this sometime this week."

Had he listened to me at all? Didn't he realize that I didn't have any time? By the time I said, "Fine, Preston," he had already hung up.

I held my phone, just staring at the screen until it faded to black. A slow sob built in my chest and rose up, through my throat. But right before it escaped through my lips, my phone chimed.

I glanced at it, hoping it was a text from Preston, hoping that he had changed his mind.

But it was a *Word With Friends* notification: *Your move.*

I tapped the open and saw the bubble alerting me that I had a message from Blue:

Beat that. 😄

At any other time, I would've rushed to the game board, to see what kind of move Blu made, to see how many points he'd scored. But today, all I could do was shake my head.

Of course, it would be Blu. Of course, he would reach out to me when I needed a listening ear. Except his ears weren't the ones that I needed. There was no reason nor any need to talk to him when there was nothing that he could do.

I tapped reply and wrote:

I'll play later. Not in a good mood.

What I needed to do was turn off my phone so that I could focus, but before I could do that, another message came back:

What's wrong? Mind if I call you?

For a moment, my thoughts took a left turn…from my challenges to Blu's new question. In all of this time, even with meeting in person, Blu and I had never spoken on the phone. We'd done all of this communicating, but had stayed away from that mode with good reason. Because to me, a telephone call could be more invasive. If he had my number, Blu could call while I was with Preston…or I could reach out when he was with his wife.

But maybe talking to Blu right now was just what I needed. Maybe talking would help with my thinking; with Blue, I could come up with Plan B. He wasn't the first person I wanted to talk to about this, but since my husband was unavailable.….I sent a message to Blu…with my number.

Then, I gently laid the phone back onto the desk. And stared at it like it was a snake. But when my phone vibrated, I grabbed it like it was my savior.

"Hello?" There was a question mark in my voice even though I knew who was on the other end.

"Angelique, what's wrong?"

There was that voice that I'd only been able to savor over coffee. That voice that was now filled with so much care, so much concern — all of it for me.

"Talk to me," he whispered.

And that sob that I'd forgotten about, that sob that was supposed to settle down, it rose again. This time at a speed that gave me no warning. I sobbed into the phone…and it wasn't a single sob. I cried.

"Where are you?" There was an insistence in his tone. As if the only answer he wanted from me was an address.

"No," I said. "I'm okay."

"Really?" he said with sarcasm. "You're crying and I'm supposed to believe you're okay?"

I sighed back the rest of my tears and with my fingertips, wiped my cheeks. "I'm sorry. And really, I'm okay. It's just that I was holding everything inside and when you asked...I'm sorry."

"There's no need for apologies, but what you need to do is tell me what's wrong."

If there wasn't so much angst inside of me, if I didn't feel so much pressure, I would have smiled. "I'm not having a good day."

"You think?" He sighed. "Come on, Angelique. Please tell me. I'm really concerned."

This time, I did smile. And I told him what he wanted to know. "You know my foundation, Black Girl Magic?"

"Yeah."

I could almost see him nodding. I went on to tell him everything, all the details that Preston didn't have time to hear. I told him what happened from the moment Camille walked into my office to now.

"Wow! That's a lot to handle."

"It is. And not for me. It's because of the girls. Some of them already have so much disappointment in their lives and this is just another one of those things."

"I'm sorry, Angelique. Just listening to you, I can hear your passion."

"I think it's because I haven't been blessed with children yet and I've been fine because these girls are my daughters. But unless I hit the lottery this week...." I stopped. "You know what, that's it. I can't do anything about this and I need to stop crying and complaining and make plans to salvage something for next weekend. Just work with what I have."

He was so quiet for a moment, I thought the call had dropped. "Hello?"

"Yeah, I'm here. I'm sorry, I was just…."

"You know what. You're at work and I didn't mean to disturb you."

"I called you, remember?"

"Yes, and I appreciate it. But still, I know you have to get back to work."

"I do," he said as if those were not the words he wanted to say. "But I need to make sure you're all right before I hang up this phone."

I smiled. "I am."

"I need to see it for myself."

My smile turned into a chuckle. "Really? And how are you going to do that? Facetime?"

"No, nothing virtual will be good enough. I'm going to see when we meet for a drink after work."

When will I see you again?

He said, "So, is that okay?"

I hadn't answered his question in the game, but I was going to do it now because this was real life.

"Yes, that's okay," I said. "It's more than okay."

"Perfect. Lock my number in. Then just text me or call around four-thirty or so, and we'll figure out where we want to go. And try not to worry. We'll sit down and brainstorm some alternatives so that you'll be able to keep the conference. Don't cancel it yet."

My smile was so broad when I said, "Okay," and then, "I'll see you later."

When I clicked off the phone, I couldn't believe it. I'd answered his call in tears, and now I was hanging up with the biggest smile.

My eyes rose and settled once again on my wedding photo and for a moment, I wondered if I'd given Blu the right answer.

But I was just getting together with Blu for drinks and really, this was a business meeting. He was going to help me since Preston had no time. And why would I want to go home after work today? I would just be sitting there alone, wallowing in worry.

Nope…I was going to go out and have drinks.

Just the thought pumped energy into my veins. I sprang up from my chair and marched from my office, in search of Camille. I wasn't sure what it was, but we had some work to do.

CHAPTER 10

Blu

I needed a special place because this meeting with Angelique was going to be just that — special. Yeah, it was all about business, but for me, that had just been an excuse. I'd wanted to see her again and I felt like she wanted to get together, too, but she was afraid for some reason. That was why she hadn't answered me when I asked when could I see her? Well, the perfect reason had been given to us.

So when I hung up from Angelique this morning, I hit up Lamar, right away, told him that I was hooking up with Angelique, but that I needed the perfect spot.

"Dawg, you gotta check out B's Wine Bar. I told you about that place."

"Oh, yeah." Then, I rushed my friend off the phone to check it out on the Internet.

Lamar was right. B's Wine Bar was this hip, new spot in Missouri City, that had nothing but four-star reviews. But what was best was that it was on the other side of town. Angelique lived in Cypress and I was in Kingwood, which meant it was a good forty-five minute drive for both of us. So the risk of running into someone we knew was minimized. Not that we wouldn't be able to explain it since this *was* a business meeting. But we wouldn't have to worry about how this meeting looked — we could both lean back and chill…and talk business.

Those were all of my thoughts as I stepped up to the door of B's Wine Bar and walked inside. I paused at the door and took in the atmosphere. The candle-laden tables were perfect whether you were just hanging with friends, or wanted something more close up, intimate. The soft sounds of jazz, the slight scent of lavender — yeah, this place was the set up for the hook up. It was definitely grown and sexy.

It took me two seconds to spot Angelique because even though the place was packed with people, she stood out as if a halo glowed above her. Seriously, when I waved and then, she waved back, I thought I heard harps playing. For real. It was a good thing I wasn't with Lamar or any of my other boys right now because I would have lost all my testosterone points.

I strolled toward the bar where Angelique was sitting, my stride slow, to match the atmosphere and to not give away how much I wanted to just run up and hug this chick.

She stood before I reached her and I almost stumbled. She was wearing a business suit. Just a straight-up skirt with a jacket. But that skirt (I think women called it a pencil skirt) fit her right. Showed her slender, toned gymnast body. As I was checking her out, she opened her arms to me.

"What's up?" I whispered as I held her, and wanted to inhale more than just her fragrance. But I pushed that thought aside. This was all business.

Leaning back, I said, "Wow, you got here early. I thought I was going to beat you. That was my plan."

"Yeah, but after the day I had, I guess I really needed that drink." A smile crossed her face that warmed me like a thousand suns.

I motioned for her to sit back down, and then I slid into the seat next to her. "I'm so sorry about what you're going through, but before we talk about that, have you ordered?"

"Yeah." She nodded. "I ordered a Moscato."

At that right moment, a waitress walked up and asked what I wanted. "Can I have a house wine?" I took out my wallet and handed her my credit card. "And please, put her wine on my tab and keep it open."

The waitress nodded and when I turned back to Angelique, she said, "Thank you."

I waved my hand letting her know paying for her drink was nothing. I said, "For real, are you okay? I couldn't stop thinking about you all day." I didn't tell her that wasn't a new phenomena in my life. She'd consumed my mind from our first *Words With Friends* game when she'd whipped me by sixty-four points.

She shook her head. "I wish I could say that I was okay." She sighed. "But I've been working the phones all day, talking to our current sponsors and people who've sponsored us before. But...." She didn't finish, she didn't have to. "I guess tomorrow I'll figure out how to pare it back. One decision I'll have to make is whether I'll email the girls now or just wait until we get closer to next weekend so they have fewer days of disappointment. I just don't know." This time, when she shook her head, she massaged her temples and I almost had to sit on my hands so I didn't jump up and pull her into my arms. I just wanted to comfort her.

She said, "No matter when I tell them, I just hate breaking this news."

"So, let's talk about this." I leaned back and unbuttoned my suit jacket. "Let's see if there's anything you didn't think about. First, though, tell me about your foundation and what you're doing next weekend."

When I'd sat down in front of Angelique at Starbucks, I couldn't tell what I loved most about her. Was it the way she wore her hair in a curly bob (I only knew that because one of my coworkers wore her hair like that and I loved it)? Or her nose that upturned, a bit at the tip? Or her lips that made me want to suck them before I kissed them?

I hadn't been sure then, but I was certainly sure now — it was her eyes. I asked about her foundation and her brown eyes danced and asked me to dance with her.   She told me all about Black Girls Magic — I told her I loved that name — and why she started her foundation. She told me about the big conference she had planned - from the Friday night social, to the Saturday workshops, to the gala to wrap the weekend up, and where she planned to present ten girls with money (a little pocket change she called it) for college. It wasn't her words that convinced me of her conviction. It was the way her heart beat for them, right there, in front of me.

She talked through almost two glasses of wine, giving me details that I noted in my mind because I had my own plan formulating. It had come to me from the moment I spoke to her this morning. But first, I had to get a feel of what she wanted to do and where she was going.

I'd researched Black Girl Magic, so she wasn't telling me anything new. I didn't tell her that, though. Because I needed to get this from her perspective.

"Something will work out," I said. "I'm sure of it because you can't have your kind of passion and not have it pay off for these young ladies."

"I don't know. To be honest, even if I had the twenty-five thousand, it was going to be tight; I would have had to put in about five-thousand of my own money, but that would've been cool because I believe in this so much." She sighed. "Maybe this was just too ambitious of a project."

"Are you kidding me? You've been in business eight years. I'm surprised you haven't had weekend programs like this already."

"I do a lot of fundraisers, but now that we have girls in college, I don't want to drop them. So that's kinda stretched our finances thin."

"Well, it may be time for you to think about expanding."

She laughed, that soft chuckle that was her weapon. I swore she was trying to do me in. She said, "I'm just trying to make it through the next weekend and you're talking about expanding."

Leaning forward so that I could be closer to her, I said, "You may have to expand your thinking because that will expand your finances." When she opened her mouth to protest, I held up my hands. "But, that's something we'll talk about later."

"Good, because this is what I've been talking about all day and now, I'd like a break," she held up her empty glass, "and I'd like some more wine."

I chuckled, motioned toward the waitress, ordered another glass for both of us and then scooted my chair a little closer. Because business was over. She'd just adjourned the meeting. I said, "So no more talk about work."

"Nope." She smiled and I knew that I was right. This girl was going to slay me with her charm. "Anything but work."

"I agree. So let's talk about you." I paused because I wasn't sure how deep she was ready to go in this friendship, but still, I presented the question that I'd wanted to know. I said, "Can I ask you something?"

At that moment, the waitress returned with our second glasses of wine. But that little interruption didn't deter Angelique from answering my question. When the waitress left us alone, she raised her glass to her lips and said, "Sure, ask me whatever you want. We're friends, right?"

I nodded. "Friends with a connection."

She warmed me with that laugh again. But I stayed focused and asked what I wanted to know. "Is your husband one of those philanderers?"

Her smile left quickly, and in its place, her words spilled out, "No, he's not," she said with such certainty. "Though no one ever knows for sure, but if I had to bet, I'd say no. Preston has been totally faithful to me."

I nodded. Not sure why I wanted to go deeper. I mean, it was clear something was wrong at home because I mentioned her husband and her smile dipped. But I wasn't sure how I could ask without sounding like I was trying to get all up in her business.

She said, "But he does something far worse than cheating."

I released a deep breath. I guess I didn't have to ask the question at all. Whether it was the wine or Angelique just talking, she told me everything — and more — that I wanted to know. She explained how her husband had started his own financial services and investments firm. I'd known that from the research I'd done on her. But what I didn't discover through the Internet was that once her husband and his partners opened that company, it became all about the company and less about his wife.

"It's so frustrating because Preston and I…." She paused and her eyes were glassy. I wasn't sure if that was the wine or her memories. "We used to be…." Another pause, and this time, she shook her head. "But now…."

She hadn't completed a sentence, but she'd told the whole story.

I lifted my glass to my lips and took a long sip that allowed my eyes to roam. My glance went on its own adventure, starting at the shoes she wore (I loved a woman in heels), to the skirt that rose right above her knees (those legs), and I kept going up and up and up, taking in her tapered waist and pausing for a moment (but not long enough to be disrespectful) at the way her breasts rounded out her white tailored shirt.

By the time I placed my glass on the table, I was the one shaking my head. "Just goes to show you that just because you have gold doesn't mean that you're smart enough to know that you're rich."

She giggled, then said, "Huh?"

"That's something my grandmother used to say."

"Translation, please."

"Your husband is a fool."

That sent her into another fit of giggles. "I would agree."

"No, I'm serious. I mean, I don't mean any kind of disrespect, but you're fine."

"Thank you," she said, fighting to hold her laughter inside.

"So, I don't get it. I don't understand how a man could come home to all of that," I made a round motion with the palm of my hand over her face, "and not want to...can I be frank?"

She nodded and giggled some more.

I said, "Come home to all of that fineness and not want to jump your bones."

She did that laugh thing again and my body responded. But this time, I wasn't thinking about how she made me feel. I was thinking about Angelique and how this morning, she'd been in tears. But with me, she could laugh.

She said, "I guess my husband doesn't think I'm fine."

I wiped my smile from my face, and turned my tone serious. "Oh, I'm so sorry."

She blinked, confused. "Sorry about what?"

"You didn't tell me your husband was blind."

This time, her giggles were so loud a few people turned our way. But I didn't mind. None of them knew what I knew. This woman was fighting on all fronts in her life, it seemed. She was fighting for her foundation and she was fighting for her husband's attention. If she wanted to laugh all night, I was going to help her do it.

She said, "That was a good one."

I shrugged. "I was only trying to be half-funny. Because on the serious tip, I don't understand your husband because if I had a woman like you waiting for me at home every night…."

That was all I had to say and I meant that. Sitting here with Angelique chatting, laughing like this — this was something I used to do with Monica. This used to be the reason why I had to race to the office in the morning (because I didn't want to leave my wife) and then, I had to race home in the evening (because I couldn't wait to get to my wife.) Sitting here with Angelique — this was the life I had, the one I wanted.

But this wasn't my wife.

That was the last time I thought about Monica. When the waitress came back, I ordered a table full of food: the smoked salmon crostini, Cajun molasses meatballs, then a spinach salad for us to share and finally, a cheese board. And for the next two hours, I filled Angelique with more food than wine.

And we just talked.

Not about our spouses, not about our work.

For two hours, it was just about us.

We talked about her dreams and my desires and then, we commiserated on how we both couldn't stand that fool in the Oval Office and how America just had to find a way to do better.

But the best part was when we talked about music. She was in her thirties and I'd just hit the big four-oh, but we were both connoisseurs of eighties rhythm and blues. We talked a little about rap, but then we sang together as we remembered Luther, Prince, and Freddie Jackson. And then, she went way back to the seventies and proved to me that she was my kinda girl when she asked me about the Stylistics.

"What you know about them?" I asked, leaning back in my chair.

"*Betcha by golly wow,*" she serenaded me and I almost fell on the floor. "*You're the one that I've been waiting for forever....*"

When she sang that whole song to me, every word, every verse, I wanted to ask her to marry me. I could have stayed there with Angelique all night, but right before midnight, I knew we had to go. As I walked her to her car, I couldn't believe we'd spent almost six hours together — that almost equaled the hours that I'd spent in the office today.

When we stopped at her car, I asked, "Are you sure you're okay to drive?"

"I am," she nodded, and there was no hint of slurring in her words. "It was that food. That was smart. It soaked up that wine."

I nodded. "That was the plan."

Then, she leaned against her Lexus and looked up at me. "Thank you and not for the food, not for the wine."

I frowned. "For what, then?"

"For being you. For giving me a reason to laugh. For helping me to remember that I'm someone special. That I am a prize."

"You're more than a prize, Angelique. You're the whole damn lottery."

That made her lower her eyes, but still I could see her smile.

She kept her head down for more than just a moment and my hands were shaking when I reached for her. With the tips of my fingers, I lifted her chin and I saw that she was trembling, too.

Looking into her eyes, I thought about the fun we'd had, I thought about the way we laughed. But then, she raised her hand to touch mine where I was holding her and I saw the glint of the diamond in her ring. The ring on her left hand. It sparkled, almost like it wanted to blind me.

I stepped back, then reached for the knob on her door and opened it for her. She hesitated for just a moment, then slid inside. And I was sure that I heard her release a sigh. What I wasn't sure about was — was it one of relief? Or had she been there with me...when I came so close to kissing her.

But when she was buckled in, I leaned over and said, "Good night," then closed the door. I stood there, until she started the ignition, and then, I waved and trotted to my truck.

I didn't breathe until I got inside and then, I blew out a long breath. What had I been thinking?

Since before we even exchanged vows, I'd been faithful to Monica. Once we were engaged, that was it for me. And I was good with that. I wasn't one of those guys who thought being with one woman for the rest of my life was a prison sentence. I was just the opposite. I was thrilled that for the rest of my life Monica would be the only woman I'd be with and I'd be her only man.

If I had to put any kind of bet on this, I would have put all of my money on Angelique being just as faithful, as I'd been, too.

So what was this about? Where did I want it to go?

"No," I said as I started the ignition. "We're just friends. With a connection. That's all I want this to be."

And I told myself that lie, all the way to my home.

CHAPTER 11

Angelique

Day three. And just like on Tuesday and Wednesday, it was
so hard for me to roll out of bed. Tuesday, I'd had a bit
of a hangover, not just from all the wine I'd shared with Blu,
but also from not getting home until almost one in the
morning. It wasn't until I'd been driving home that I realized I
was going to have to give Preston some kind of explanation —
not that he ever gave me one. He just always said, "I was
working," and that was what I'd decided I'd tell him when I
strolled into our home well after midnight after hanging out
with another man.

But it turned out that Preston didn't need an explanation
because he wasn't home. He didn't do his own strolling
through the door until after I'd undressed and had been in bed
for at least an hour. He'd tiptoed into our bedroom, sighing
with exhaustion, but I didn't turn over. I'd pretended to be
asleep and he pretended to believe that I was asleep.

Then, he'd awakened and left before the sun even thought
about rising, so I never got the chance to say anything else to
him about what was going on. I didn't feel as bad as I usually

did. When Preston ignored me this way, I'd get Sheryl and Cassidy on a three-way call.

But there was no need for a girlfriend intervention because I had Blu. Our time at the wine bar had been exhilarating. And since then, he hadn't stopped calling.

I wasn't sure that I would have been able to drag myself out of bed on Tuesday morning if Blu hadn't called. From that first moment when I heard his voice, I thanked God that I had given him my number:

At first, I thought it was the alarm, but even when I slapped the button on the radio, the ringing continued. I moaned as, with only one eye open, I patted around the nightstand for my cell, thinking that I really needed to change my ringtone to something more obscure in the mornings.

I pressed the phone to my ear. "Hello?" And then right away, I wondered if I looked as bad as I sounded.

A whisper came through the phone, "I'm sorry to be calling you...."

My eyes popped open.

The voice continued, "But I sent you a message and texted and when you didn't respond, I was worried."

Blu? It was a question in my mind so, I said his name into the phone.

"Yeah," he said. "Again, I apologize...."

I pushed myself up in the bed. "Why are you whispering?"

"Oh." His voice returned to normal. "I'm sorry."

"Why do you keep apologizing?"

I heard him take a breath. "First, are you alone?"

I nodded, even though he couldn't see me and I was so grateful for that. "Yes."

"Okay." He exhaled. "I didn't want to call you while you were with your husband."

I almost rolled my eyes. "There's little chance of that."

He didn't acknowledge my sarcasm. "I just wanted to make sure you were fine. I texted you last night; I should have told you to text me when you got home."

"Oh, I was fine. I just feel a bit hungover now."

"Really?"

"Not from the wine. Just from everything. I don't even want to go into the office today," I groaned.

"Come on, Angelique. I told you, something is going to work out."

"What? We tried to figure it out last night."

"And we'll just keep trying."

I slid back under the covers. "I don't want to face the girls." I pulled the duvet over my head.

"Don't say anything to them yet. You still have a week and you don't know what God has planned for you. Plus," he paused, "I'm a real good problem solver. We'll keep working on this. Now, get up."

I didn't know why, but his demand made me smile. "And if I don't?"

"Don't let me come over there...."

He was kidding, but I wanted to tell him to come on. Instead, I pushed aside the duvet and said, "Okay."

"Call me when you get to the office."

And that's just what I did. I'd rolled out of bed, dressed and made it to work as if I wasn't giving up. I'd stepped into the office full of faux-cheer, and my demeanor even pumped Camille up.

"You're right," she said. "Let's do this. There has to be a way."

Yesterday was just like Tuesday. Blu called me in the morning with a rallying cry, sending me to the office with such hope. Camille and I brainstormed again, spoke to Walker, our consultant who worked with us to get sponsors, and tried to remember that one missing asset that we hadn't thought about yesterday. And then last night, I'd come home — with nothing.

In the two days that had passed, I hadn't even talked to Preston about it. He'd heard nothing about Black Girls Magic since Monday because this week, we hadn't even spent an hour together. He ran in late, he ran out early, and kissed me a couple of times in between.

The only highlight of my week was Blu. We'd left the app behind and now, we talked (mostly) by phone and every time I heard his voice, he was encouraging. Every time, he gave me hope.

But now, it was Thursday and though I had tried, I was just postponing the inevitable. I wasn't going to get this money, so I needed to get up, put on my CEO panties, and act like I was in charge. I needed to make some decisions, disappoint a few people, even possibly, cancel the event. Maybe I could just do the Friday night social and forego the gala and the scholarship presentations.

My heart was so heavy as I rolled out of bed, but what was the shocker was almost bumping into Preston when I stumbled into the bathroom.

"Whoa," I said, stepping back. "What are you doing here?"

He chuckled. "I live here, babe." He wrapped his tie around his neck.

"Could've fooled me." I grabbed my toothbrush from the holder, then spread toothpaste across the bristles.

"I know, I haven't been present much, have I?" He spoke to me through the mirror.

My answer to him: I glared at his reflection and pressed the on-button, sending my electric toothbrush spinning.

"I'm really sorry," Preston said above the humming sound. Looking at my reflection, he tightened the knot of his tie. "But I'll be home early tonight and then, we can brainstorm about what we can do with your foundation." He kissed my cheek and I kept my eyes on him — through the mirror. "Maybe we'll even go out to dinner or something."

All I did was move my toothbrush from the left side of my mouth to the right — and scrubbed harder.

Preston grinned before he stepped out of the bathroom, not having any kind of clue that if this toothbrush only had a jagged edge....

There was no reason to tell him that tonight would be too late. No reason to tell him that his absence did nothing to make my heart grow fonder. No reason because he wouldn't have heard me anyway. He never heard me.

When I was sure that Preston was at least out of our bedroom, if not already out of our house, I jumped into the shower. I longed to stay there all day, but I kept thinking, I was the CEO. There was a reason why Black Girls Magic was as successful as it was — whenever I was faced with adversity, I turned my fear into fight. I never went down, I always stood up. And today was going to be no different.

This morning, Blu didn't call until I was in my car.

"Good morning," he said, his voice filled with so much cheer, I thought I had missed a special holiday or something.

I wanted to ask him what was so good about it, but I refused to be negative. "Well, it's going to be good. I'm going to make the move today."

I braced myself for Blu's motivational assault. But he surprised me with, "I understand. You held on for as long as you could."

I breathed. "Thank you."

"For what?"

"For not trying to talk me out of it. Because I need to take care of this today."

"Well, I know that you put everything into the game. You can never be upset when you've tried your best."

"Thanks for saying that, but it's still going to be tough. I'm going to go through the schedule and the money that we have and see what we can salvage and see what has to go."

"Don't get down on yourself, Angelique. You still have so much to offer these young ladies."

I needed to get off this phone before I asked this dude to marry me. "Okay, well, let me go. I've got to get my head right, get my words straight to keep everyone motivated — starting with Camille."

"Call me when you get there."

"It'll probably be later. I have a lot to take care of today."

"Okay. Whenever. I just can't wait to hear your voice."

Yup, I was ready to buy this guy a wedding ring. We said goodbye and then, I did what I told Blu that I needed to do. I turned off the radio and settled in the quiet, trying to find the words that I needed to say to these girls. I could use this as a teaching moment — disappointment happens. We all have to live through it. What separates the successful from the unsuccessful is how we deal with it. Unsuccessful people sit down, successful folks use it to stand up.

I sighed as I swung the car into the parking lot. Now all I had to do was heed my own words and that was what I kept telling myself as I walked into the building and took the elevator to my office.

By the time I opened the door to my office, I was ready. And I was going to start with Camille. I'd practice on her, lift her spirits and then move onto the girls.

I took a breath before I pushed open the door, pasted a grin on my face, stepped inside, faced Camille…and her grin was bigger than mine.

"Hey!" Camille popped out of her chair. "We've been waiting for you."

Standing next to her desk was Walker, our consultant. And he didn't look like he sounded when I spoke with him yesterday. When I first told him our sponsor had pulled out, I thought I had just about made a grown man cry. But right now, there were no signs of tears. His face was shining as bright as Camille's.

Their grins weren't contagious because they made me frown. "What's going on?"

"I'm so glad you're here." Camille came around from the back of her desk.

"Ummm....I work here." My glance shifted between the two. "Did someone put an extra jolt of something in the coffee this morning?" Camille and Walker were beginning to look goofy to me.

Walker said, "We've been waiting on you."

"Yeah. Sorry I'm late," I said. "I was taking my time working it out in my head. Because today, we have to begin executing Plan B. I want to get the word out to the girls first and I was thinking that I would do that by...."

"But you're not going to have to do that," Camille spouted. "You're not going to have to do anything!"

"Yeah," Walker said, "you don't have to tell them anything because everything is going to happen."

"What are you talking about?" My eyes darted between the two.

"Let me tell her." Walker stepped toward me. "The conference is going to be move forward because...."

"We got the money," Camille jumped in.

Walker faced Camille, frowned, and almost pouted.

"What?" I said.

"We got the money," Camille repeated, ignoring Walker's glare.

I put my briefcase down. "Okay, the two of you...you better start explaining."

"We got another sponsor," Walker said. "So we have the money. The twenty-five thousand dollars, plus some."

"Shut the front door," I exclaimed. "How? When? Walker," I turned to him, "what did you do?"

He shrugged. "I wish I could take credit for this."

Camille said, "You have some powerful prayers. You could probably pray peace into the Middle East."

"What?" Now I wondered if these two were playing with me because they weren't making any kind of sense. "Please. Stop this. Just explain."

"Okay," Camille said. I was sure she felt my impatience because she got serious. "When I got here about an hour ago, before I even sat down, a courier came in and handed me this envelope. It had the foundation's name written on it, but no return address. So, I asked him who it was from. He said he didn't know, he was just told to deliver it and I had to sign for it. So I did, he left, I opened it because it said 'urgent', saw the check, and almost fainted. I called Walker right away."

He picked up the story. "I rushed over here, but when she showed me the letter and the check, I couldn't figure it out. We figured you knew what this was about." Walker handed me the oversized envelope.

I pressed back the flap and pulled out the letter. The check was wrapped in the folds of the paper and I studied that first. It was made out to Black Girls Magic. For thirty-thousand dollars. And with a signature that was unreadable, unless one could decipher the meaning of a couple of squiggly (and a couple of humps) lines.

My breaths came quickly as I read:

Please accept this donation for the good work that you're doing with Black Girls Magic. There is no need for any public acknowledgement nor any need to contact us. Our foundation supports good causes and we admire the work that you're doing.

That was it. No signature. No closing. Nothing to tie this money to anyone except the name that was on the check: The Taylor Foundation.

I felt a mixture of emotions. Like complete exhilaration, but then, some doubt. Because who would give this kind of money without some kind of acknowledgement? "They said we're doing good work."

"You are," Walker said. "So you don't know the Taylor Foundation?"

I shook my head. "I've never heard of them." Again, I looked at Walker.

But he gave me a blank stare. "It's not one of my connections," he said. "If it were, I would have called them up on Tuesday when you first called me. But there are a million foundations out there."

"Well, I was doing a little research just as you came in." Camille walked back around her desk and pointed to her computer monitor. I leaned over her shoulder. She said, "The Taylor Foundation was established in nineteen-sixty-three for the empowerment of African-American girls and women," Camille said. "There are a list of some of the programs they've supported, but it kinda stops like about five or six years ago. I don't know if they just stopped giving or if they became more private and haven't been sharing their information."

"The Taylor Foundation." I looked at the check again.

"It makes sense that they would support us. I'm just glad they heard about Black Girls Magic," Walker said.

"Yeah," Camille added, "just the right amount of money, just in the nick of time."

Just the right amount of money. "I want...I wish I could call and thank them."

Walker shrugged. "There are lots of philanthropists who remain anonymous because to them, it's about the good work not the recognition."

"I know...but, I just wish...."

"All I wish is that you would give me that check so that I can run to the bank and deposit it."

I scanned the letter again, stared at the check another moment, then grinned and gave them both to Camille. "What are you still doing here?"

We all laughed together and I was just ecstatic that the only email I had to send to my girls was, "Get ready to slay!"

I almost skipped into my office, thinking that God was so good and the Taylor Foundation was, too!

CHAPTER 12

Blu

Pulling into the driveway, I sat in my car for a moment. How many hours had passed since I spoke with Angelique? Seven? Eight? And she hadn't called yet. I felt such mixed emotions...exhilaration, but a bit of apprehension. Exhilaration, because I'd done the right thing. But on the other side, had I been right to support Black Girls Magic with funds from Monica's family's foundation?

That was where my apprehension came from. Usually, we didn't support a program unless it went through the board — even when it was something as little as thirty-thousand dollars. But Angelique needed this money quickly, and Monica and I could disperse anything that was less than fifty-thousand dollars without board approval.

We'd been very active with the foundation when we first married. I'd been impressed when Monica told me about her family's charity. It had started back in the sixties with a major endowment from her great grandfather. Timothy Taylor had bequeathed two million dollars to start the foundation, money he'd earned from oil wells his family owned in Oklahoma.

For the first fifty years, the Taylor Foundation had been everywhere, supporting school programs and civic events that lifted African-American boys and girls. But since Monica had taken over in 2010, her illness had gotten in the way of the foundation. I was the one who'd kept it afloat by contributing to one cause a year, which was what was needed to consider it active.

The timing had been perfect with Black Girls Magic — we hadn't made a donation this year, so I knew the board would have no problem since I was the CFO. I'd write up the proposal this weekend and submit it for the foundation's records.

Leaving my car in the driveway, I jumped out and strolled up to the door, just as my son opened it. "Hey," I said. "You came out to greet your old man?"

"Nah, I'm on my way to a basketball game at school."

I nodded. "Okay, come home right after. You have school tomorrow."

A car honked behind us and Tanner dashed out the door. "Okay, Dad."

"Did Ms. Ellis drop Raven off?" I shouted as Tanner ran across our lawn, even though I had told that boy to use the walkway.

"Yeah," he said, right before he jumped into the SUV.

"Drive safe, Ryan," I called out to Tanner's friend. But the Ford Explorer had taken off, going just a little faster than I would have liked.

I closed the door. I didn't know how parents did it. Every time my son went out, I wasn't sure what concerned me more — my teenage son being out, or my teenage son being out while black.

Sighing, I stepped all the way into the house and the moment, I closed the door, I heard the pitter-patter of Raven's small feet.

"Daddy."

Raven usually greeted me with a beam that came from the sun kinda smile and a hug around my knees. But today, she just shuffled toward me, her steps heavy as if she had a lot on her six-year-old mind.

"Hey, Munchkin. What's wrong?"

Her eyes watered and I did something that I hadn't done to Raven in a while; I lifted her into my arms and repeated my question.

"I just went and talked to Mommy."

The tremors in her voice let me know that she was one degree away from a full-out cry and it took everything in me to keep a straight face and not frown. What had Monica done to Raven?

I said, "And what did Mommy say?"

She wrapped her arms around my neck before she cried into my ear, "I asked her if she was going to take me to see *Despicable Me* because she promised that she would."

"Well, she can't take you today because you have school tomorrow."

"I know, but she promised and she said that we would go on Saturday."

"Okay. Well, today is only Thursday. So how do you know that she won't take you on Saturday?"

"Because when I talked to her, all she did was lay there. And then, she started crying. I hate it when I see Mommy cry."

I took a deep breath. One of the things that concerned me was the way Monica's illness was impacting our children. I'd been able to talk to Dr. Nichols about that and she had been as concerned as I was saying that children were always affected by a parent's emotions.

"*A parent's depression can often lead to a child's depression. So keep everything in your house as normal as you can. You're going to have to make up for the heaviness that your children feel with your wife.*"

I'd tried my best to heed the doctor's advice, but it was a hard task. What was I supposed to do? I couldn't keep the children completely away from Monica.

"Well," I leaned over, setting Raven on her feet, then led her into the living room. When we both sat down, I began again, "Do you remember I told you that Mommy is not feeling well?"

Raven nodded.

"And sometimes when people aren't feeling well, they cry."

"But Mommy cries all the time."

"I know, but sometimes crying helps her."

The way Raven cocked her head and gave me a what-you-talkin'-'bout look, I had to hold back my chuckle.

Fighting to keep my expression blank, I said, "It's hard to explain, but sometimes when you have a lot of sadness inside, you have to cry to get the sadness out."

She nodded as if my explanation made at least a little sense. But then, she asked, "Why does she have so much sad inside? Doesn't she love us?"

"Oh, Munchkin, she loves us and you especially. She loves you very, very much. That's why she's trying hard to get better. Because she wants to be better for herself, but she wants to really be better for you." I paused as Raven kept her wide brown eyes on me. "I know this is scary sometimes, sweetheart, but your mom is really trying. Just know that she loves you and I do, too. You know that, right?"

She nodded.

"And you know what?"

I wasn't sure it was possible, but her eyes got wider. "What?"

Leaning over, I got close to her ear, as if I were going to tell her a secret. I said, "If Mommy isn't feeling well on Saturday, and if your room is all cleaned up, I'm going to take you to see *Despicable Me*."

She gasped as if my words shocked her. "But you don't even like cartoons," she whispered back.

"Well, I love you, so I like anything that you like."

She was thoughtful for a moment. "I like bubblegum ice cream. Do you like that?"

"If you like it, I love it. Just like I love you."

She grinned for the first time and that made my heart swell with so much love. I said, "So whaddaya say? Just you and me, kid. You and me at the movies, okay?"

Raven jerked her head up and down. "Yes, Daddy." She wrapped her arms around my neck, but before I could her hug her, she jumped off the couch and dashed toward the hall.

"Wait! Where are you going?"

"To my room. I have to make sure it's all clean so we can go to the movies on Saturday."

She didn't give me a chance to respond, she was gone before I could say anything. I sighed, but again, I was filled with mixed emotions. I was thrilled that my daughter's smile was back, but on the other side, I was really saddened. I had to fight to remember that Monica couldn't help her illness. But it was hard because she was affecting her children and they meant everything to me.

"A parent's depression can often lead to a child's depression."

Leaning back on the sofa, I knew that I needed to go upstairs, check on Monica, at least let her know that I was home. But just saying hello could turn into an argument. So, I did the only thing that (besides my children) could make me smile. I slipped my phone from the side pocket of my briefcase and opened the *Word with Friends* app. What I wanted to do was talk to Angelique, but I needed to wait for her call.

So, I studied our game, moved around my tiles just a bit, then made a move that netted me fifty-seven points and put me twelve points ahead of her. I pumped my fist in the air and although, just a minute ago, I'd decided not to call Angelique, there was no harm in sending her a message:

Hey beautiful. Top that move.

I held the phone, hoping that I wouldn't be sitting for too long because I couldn't wait to hear from her. And Angelique didn't disappoint. She replied:

Can you talk?

My fingers couldn't move fast enough:

I sure can.

I jumped from the sofa and then paused. I needed to check on Monica, especially since she was home with Raven. But I wasn't going too far and I wasn't going to be long.

There was all kinds of pep in my steps as I first raced to Raven's room. I chuckled when I saw her in clean-up mode — pushing her dolls and toys under her bed. I'd deal with that later. Then, I dashed to the door, then trotted down the driveway to my Tahoe. The moment I slid inside and turned on the ignition, my cell phone vibrated.

Looking down at the screen, the name — *Angel* — with her photo from Facebook flashed up at me.

The moment I answered, she spoke, "Hey you."

"Hey gorgeous." I backed my car out of the driveway, feeling like I didn't want to talk to her this close to my home. "How was your day?"

"Absolutely splendid."

I smiled. I had the signature from the messenger service that the package had been delivered, but when I hadn't heard from Angelique, I wasn't sure if she'd even gone into the office.

But even though I smiled, I fought to keep the cheer out of my voice. "I love the sound of that. See? I told you this morning, it wouldn't be so bad. I knew you'd be able to handle whatever was in front of you."

"Well, that's true, but my attitude is because the event was saved."

"What?" I rounded the corner, then parked the car — one street over from my house.

"Yes! It was all saved," she said, her joy jumping through the phone, "because I received a check from an anonymous benefactor this morning."

"Wow, that must have been something." I hoped that I was at least in the running for some kind of acting award. Because I was trying hard.

"Yes, I'm just stunned because that check truly came out of nowhere." She paused. "I almost wondered if you had anything to do with it."

"Me?" I was incredulous — and shocked that she would think of me. "Of course not. I mean, how would I know how to get my hands on thirty-thousand dollars."

"I knew it!" Angelique exclaimed. "I can't believe you did this. I can't believe you did this for me."

I blinked. What had I said. "What are you talking about?" I said, trying, wanting to keep the charade up. Because I never wanted her to know. I never wanted her to think that this was anything more than one foundation reaching out to another. "Did what?"

"You're the one who donated this money to save my event."

She stated it as a fact, as if she already knew. "I have no idea why you would think that."

"Because you just said thirty-thousand dollars and I didn't tell you how much I'd been given."

Damn!

"Plus," she continued, "you're the only person I'd told that I'd be short five thousand."

Damn!

I hadn't counted on that. I would've thought that she'd told everyone.

All I could say was, "Busted."

"Blu...." She sang my name and right then, it became my favorite song. "I can't believe you did this...for me."

"Of course. You're doing good work."

"That's what you said in the letter."

"I mean that, and with you at the helm, Black Girls Magic will soar."

She paused for a moment before she said, "But...."

"Where did I get that kind of money?" I finished for her.

"Yes," she said. "Where? I wouldn't want you...."

"Donating that kind of money?"

"Yes."

This conversation made my heart smile. I was finishing her sentences. I felt *that* connected. But not connected enough to tell her the whole truth. So, I said, "Don't worry. It's not my personal money."

I heard her exhale.

"I work for...a local foundation and we're always looking for charitable causes and there was no one, no cause more deserving."

I felt her smile. We were *that* connected.

She said, "Oh, my God. Blu, you have no idea how much this means. How will I ever repay you?"

I stayed silent and thought about what I wanted to say versus what I needed to say. I needed to say, 'There's no need for repayment. You're welcome and have a good day.' But instead, what I wanted came out. "Have dinner with me." Then, I added quickly, "I mean, that's not a condition, the money is yours. It's just...Angelique, I enjoy spending time with you, but I don't want you to think at all that's why we donated the money to you."

Now, it was her turn to pause and the silence, as I waited, seemed to go on forever. It made me think that I'd gone too far, made me think that I'd pushed her away. Damn! Why did I have to ask her to dinner....

"I would love, too." Her words came softly through the phone.

I exhaled, feeling as if I was letting every bit of air inside of me, out. "Great. What about tomorrow night since it's Friday. And we can go somewhere on the other side of town like we did with the wine bar."

"Okay. I can't wait to see you."

"Me, too," I whispered and imagined what it would be like have dinner together. To just sit and talk to each other. Although if I were being honest, sitting and talking was not all that I wanted. Every time I spoke to Angelique or saw her, it was like I *needed* so much more.

But I would never disrespect Monica that way, never disrespect Angelique that way. So, I would settle for the beautiful thing that this was — friends with a connection.

"Okay, I need to get back home," I said, glancing at my watch. I'd been out for a little more than ten minutes and with

Tanner out of the house…."I need to check on my daughter," I told her.

"That's fine."

"We'll talk later…I mean, if that's okay with you."

"Anytime with you….I mean, no…I mean, any time I hear from you. That will be fine."

The way she stumbled made me smile. Made me want to say to her — I know what you mean. But all I said was, "You'll hear from me soon." Then, I clicked off our call.

If I hadn't been in my car, I could have just floated home. This was crazy. The time I wanted to spend with Angelique, the things I wanted to do with her.

I shook my head and tried to shake those thoughts away, too.

"Let this be, Blu," I whispered to myself as I turned over the ignition, then made a U-turn heading home. "Let's this be what it is — just a connection."

But then I prayed. Because I had no idea how long I could keep this connection without plugging all the way in. That thought would have been funny to me, if this situation weren't getting to be so serious.

CHAPTER 13

Angelique

Since I met Blu, there had been so many *justs* in my life.
It was *just* a game.
It was *just* messaging.
It was *just* phone calls.
It was *just* coffee.
It was *just* drinks.
And now, it was *just* dinner.

But I needed to take the word *just* out of my vocabulary, at least for this dinner. Of course, when Preston used to pay attention to me, he took me to the best of restaurants, though we had never been to Cafe Dubois. Reservations for this exclusive New Orleans eatery were six to seven weeks out.

So, I was already impressed when Blu told me that number one: we were eating at Cafe Dubois and two: we were eating at Cafe Dubois today when he'd only invited me yesterday. But from the moment I gave my name to the hostess and she asked me to follow her (to what I thought would be a table), I knew Blu had done something special.

The hostess passed all of the tables that were filled with patrons, and led me to the very back before she pushed open the door to what I realized was one of the private dining rooms. She stepped to the side so that I could walk inside...and I gasped.

There was so much for my eyes to see: the banner that greeted me that sloped against the far wall — *Congratulations Angelique! You're going to shake up the world!* Then, the second banner — *Black Girls ARE Magic.* Beneath the two banners were long tables filled with dozens of rose-filled vases.

But what captured me, where my eyes settled was on the small round table in the center of the room. And the man who stood beside it with a single rose in his hand. His smile was beyond his lips as he walked toward me, and my heart was beyond the moon.

"I'm so happy to see you," he said as he handed me the rose.

I would've told him the same if I could've figured out a way to speak. But since I couldn't, I stretched out my arms to hold him in a hug.

But why did I do that? A moment ago I couldn't get my lips to move, but now, I couldn't get my heart to slow.

Thank God he stepped back because with all of this, in another moment, all of my clothes would have fallen off. He took my hand and led me to the table.

I laid the rose on the table as he held out the chair for me to sit. "I thought we were just having dinner."

"You like?"

"You think?" I let my glance once again journey around the room and then I paused when my eyes met his. "I love. I just....wow. But how?"

He shrugged as he took his seat right next to me. "It helps to have friends in high places."

Leaning forward, I chuckled. "Okay, Mr. Blu. Let's talk. I know you're an almost-partner at PricewaterhouseCoopers, and now, I find out that you also work with the Taylor Foundation, but still." I paused and enjoyed all that was around me again. "This took a lot." I stopped for a moment again. "Cost a lot."

He said, "If you're wondering if I'm involved in any illicit activities, the answer is a resounding no. I'm too pretty," he stroked his chin, "to go to jail."

His words were meant to make me laugh, but all I could do was mumble, "That you are."

I guessed he didn't hear me because all he said was, "No, I just wanted to do something nice for a beautiful woman."

"And you do this?" Shaking my head, I added, "Whew, your wife is one lucky woman."

Maybe I should have measured what I was going to say because my words snatched his smile away and that made me want to bite off my tongue. Blu had told me a little about his wife in some of our message exchanges. But for the most part, we'd stayed away from the double elephant in the middle of our app — my husband, his wife.

But the way Blu's eyes saddened, I felt like he needed to talk. So, I listened.   He said, "If my wife were here, if I could get her out of bed long enough, if I could somehow convince her to leave the house, she would be complaining about the temperature of the water. It would be too warm or too cold, the room would be too dark or too light, my suit would be the wrong color, my shirt would be the wrong shade and that would all happen before the food was served."

When he paused, I didn't speak for a moment because I wanted to give him room. Then, after a few seconds, I said,

"I'm sorry." I said that for her, but I said that for me, too. For taking him to this space.

He nodded, his smile that I was so used to, still far away. "I'm sorry, too." Now, he was the one who paused and looked up at me for a moment. I knew what he was thinking — this was a territory we had not breached (at least not too deeply), respecting our spouses, respecting each other. To this point, except for a few mentions, our relationship was about us, about our connection. And like me, I was sure that Blu knew this was crossing a new line.

Still, I gave him a little nod, my agreement that I was going with him.

He breathed, then, he said, "You know, when you start out with marriage, you have all these dreams of what you think it's going to be."

"Tell me about it," I said, taking a short jaunt down my own jagged lane of memories.

"But what's sad is that it seems like they're just dreams that can never be achieved." He sighed. "I'm talking about regular everyday things. Just sitting together, talking together, laughing together." He paused and looked into my eyes so deeply that I gave him my own confession.

"That's all that I'd hoped for. I thought Preston was my perfect mate because there was a time when we were able to do all of those things together. But then, his business became his muse and his love and now, I can't tell you the last time my husband and I sat down for dinner, let alone, that he did anything romantic."

Blu shook his head. "I find that hard to believe. A woman like you, I would shower with so much affection and attention that you wouldn't be able to breathe."

Every organ inside of me flipped. He didn't say shower me with gifts. He was talking about those things that money could never buy, those things that were most important — to me.

His voice was so soft, I couldn't even call it a whisper when he said, "And you know what else I would do — to a woman like you?"

I shook my head because I didn't want to say anything that would break this trance I was in.

"After I made you feel good on the inside," he pointed to my heart, "I'd spend every day trying to make you feel good on the outside."

His words made me shift, made me swoon.

"I grew up dreaming about the kind of husband I would be. My father loved my mother until the day he died. And when I say love, I'm talking about the verb. Every action, he performed with my mother in mind. From working so that he could provide her with a life he believed she deserved, down to grocery shopping and always stocking the shelves with her favorite foods. Forget my brother and me, it was all about my mother." He chuckled and sat back in his seat as if he were remembering those good times. "He always told us 'Sons, this is how you treat a woman.' And then, when we got old enough, when we had that birds and bees talk...."

I nodded 'cause this, I wanted to hear.

"He told us to make it all about our woman and if we did that, it would always be more than good enough for us."

"Wow! He was some kind of dad."

"He was some kind of man." Blu nodded, his countenance covered with sadness, though different, this time. It was a sadness where he could still smile. "My dad taught me well, but unfortunately, I haven't had much need to use those how-to-please-a-woman kind of lessons...over the past few years."

"Years?" I whispered. I knew his wife was sick, suffering from depression, mostly. But had it been...years?

"My wife...her illness...yes. It's been a few years."

Before I could filter my thoughts or my words, I said, "So what do you do about that?" And then, I added — again, without a filter, "Do you have women on the side?" The moment those words came out of me, I wanted to take them back. I wasn't trying to insult Blu, it was just that I was so surprised. How does a man go years? But then...except for Preston's quickies, I'd done the same thing.

"Actually, I don't have any women," he said without a tinge of indignation. "I've honored my vows, I've honored my wife. I've worked hard to help her become better. I want to stand by her, it's just that...it's becomes harder. As time passes...it becomes harder."

"I understand."

"At some point, I have to think about me, right?"

I nodded.

"At some point, I have to chase my own happiness, I have to find my own life."

I didn't move because Blu had moved into a different space, as if he were no longer talking to me. It almost sounded as if these were his inner thoughts that had escaped into the atmosphere without his permission. These words were more for him than for me.

Leaning closer to him, I put my hands over his, my heart saddened by his sudden change in mood.

He moved closer to me and then suddenly, shook his head. "You know what?" His smile was all the way back. "I'm here to make *you* happy tonight, to celebrate Black Girls Magic. I want us to have a good time. To chat, to smile, to laugh."

"And I love doing all of that with you."

He shook his head at my words, his smile even wider now. "You know, if I'd met a woman like you back in college, there's no telling where I'd be, where we'd be today."

"Seems to me, you're in a pretty good space."

"Well," he began, "I am...at least when I'm with you."

I inhaled.

He said, "So, let's get this dinner started." He pressed something on his phone and less than a minute later, a waiter tapped on the door, then rolled in a tray filled with plates covered with silver domes.

"I hope you don't mind," Blu said. "I ordered dinner for us."

I smiled my approval. This was only our third time meeting in person, but I was sure that whatever Blu ordered would be perfect to my palate — and much more.

As the young man laid out one tray with cheese samplers and escargot, I marveled at all that Blu had told me. It felt like he'd gone deep, sharing some of his most intimate thoughts. And then, there were his other words, that I knew I would savor long after this dinner:

"A woman like you, I would shower with so much love and affection and attention that you wouldn't be able to breathe."

"After I made you feel good on the inside...I'd spend every day trying to make you feel good on the outside."

"If I'd met a woman like you back in college, there's no telling where I'd be, where we'd be today."

Just thinking about his words now made me weaken, made my heart want to beat to his rhythm.

When the waiter left us alone, Blu said, "Let me bless the food," as he reached for my hands.

We bowed our heads and while he thanked God for the food, I thanked God for him.

There was no way that I could prove it scientifically, but Blu's confession about his wife, his marriage and his aspirations for marriage drew us closer. I could see it in the way our conversation shifted once we began to eat. Now, it was more personal. When the waiter returned to serve us the filet mignon, grilled shrimp, grilled lobster and asparagus spears, we talked about our families. He told me how he'd been raised by loving parents and I told him how I'd been raised by parents who loved me, but not each other, even though they stayed together till the day my mother died.

"Wow, your parents," Blu said as his fork cut through a slice of the molten chocolate lava cake. "It seems like...we're both following in their footsteps."

Oh, my God! Were we doing that? Had I set myself up for a long-term marriage that would never fulfill me with love?

But before I could wallow in the sadness of that thought, Blu brought the joy back by talking about Black Girls Magic.

"Next weekend, is going to be epic," he said. "And I can't wait to join in with you."

I couldn't wait for that either. I wanted Blu to see me in my element. And though I couldn't explain it, I wanted him to see me with Preston. I was even hoping that he could bring his wife to the gala. Because him meeting my husband, me meeting his wife — that would ensure that we would stay what we should be. Just friends with a connection. Just friends trying to help each other navigate through this difficult period in our lives.

By the time we finished chatting and eating and talking and laughing, the restaurant was closing.

"I feel like someone should just roll me to my car," I told Blu as he pulled back my chair so that I could stand.

He laughed. "Why don't I just walk you out?" He took my hand and helped me to stand, but then, he didn't let go.

He held onto me as he led me out of the room, through the maze of now empty tables in the restaurant and through the front door. He held my hand as we stepped silently across the parking lot because there was nothing for me to say. I would never be able to speak with Blu this close to me.

Then, we paused at my car. Once I fished for my keys in my purse, he took the fob from me and pressed the remote.

I opened the door, tossed my purse inside, then said, "Thank you, for everything." By the time I turned to face Blu again, he was right there. I mean, literally — his face was so close to mine, there was nothing else for me to do.

Leaning in, I didn't pause at all. There was no need to hesitate when this was what I wanted. I pressed my lips to his...or maybe he pressed his to mine, I didn't know. All I knew was that it was the greatest feeling in the world. It was so gentle, so tender, and felt...so loving.

Loving, until our lips parted and we invited each other inside. Now, that loving feeling became passion. It was a slow grind, the dance that our tongues did together. The slowest of dances that went on forever, but not long enough.

When we stepped back, we were both breathless, though in shock. Even with that, I wanted so much more.

Through my heart that pounded like it was trying to get away from me and inside of him, I said, "Blu, will you...."

He pressed his fingers against my lips and shook his head. As if he knew what I was going to say. He said, "Let's just say good night."

This time when he leaned forward, he pressed his lips against my forehead, then opened the car door wider, guiding me inside.

I did as I was told, got inside, started the ignition, then waved as I rolled my Lexus away from him. But the whole time, my heart was still pounding. Not just from that kiss, but from what I almost asked him.

It was hard to believe those words were about to come out of me and thank God, Blu had stopped me. Still, I wondered what he would have said. What would his answer have been if he'd let me ask, "Blu, will you spend the night with me?"

CHAPTER 14

Blu

I deserved some kind of prize. Because if any of my boys from college or high school — heck, if anyone from elementary or middle school — saw what I just did, they'd swear I was on some special type of drug.

Trust, walking away like that right now had been one of the most difficult things I'd ever done. With all that we shared tonight, our connection was electric and could combust at any moment. But I respected Angelique. And even more — I respected my wife.

That was my thought as I rounded the corner, then edged my car into our driveway. As I slid out, I tried my best to shake away all thoughts of Angelique and tonight. I was with my family now and that was where my attention needed to be.

Inside our house, I first checked in on Tanner, knocking gently on his door. But I didn't wait for an invitation inside. I never did, even when he used to protest. Back then, I had to school him on who was the parent and who was the child, who paid the bills and who had no money at all. We had no need for further discussion after that.

"What's up, Dad?" Tanner said when I stuck my head in. He was laid back on his bed, with his Beats (as always) over his ears.

I walked over to him and bumped my fist with his. "What's good?"

He tapped his phone and I heard the music lower. "Everything's straight on the home front," Tanner said, and once again I felt that ache in my heart, for what my children had to see, for what they had to do because of Monica's illness.

One of the things I'd promised myself was that I wouldn't put the responsibility of taking care of his sister on Tanner. Growing up, I'd missed school activities and events because my parents believed that I was their live-in babysitter for my five-years younger brother. I was fifteen or sixteen when I made that vow about how I would treat my children, though, clearly, I was unaware, at that time, of the woman I would marry.

It was true, I hadn't pushed Raven onto Tanner, always hiring a babysitter when possible. But tonight, he'd volunteered.

I said, "Great. Raven's good?"

He nodded and slipped the headphones from his ears. "Yeah, she ate that nasty ravioli because she didn't want pizza and then, I made sure she got in bed. She's been asleep for a while now."

"Okay. Thanks, Tan. You always come through for me."

"No worries." He nodded, then slid the headphones back into place and I guessed that was my signal that he'd given me all that I needed to know. I guessed he knew what my next question would be and Tanner hated when I asked him about his mom. I always wanted to know whether or not there'd been any incidents.

And so knowing how much he disliked that, recently, I'd fought my urge to ask him, figuring that if there was ever anything he couldn't handle, he'd let me know.

Still, I hated that for him.

Right before I stepped out of his bedroom, he shouted out, "Raven's expecting you to take her to the movies tomorrow."

I paused, then remembered. "Yup," I said to him right before I closed his bedroom door.

Even though I knew Raven was cool because of her brother, I still peeked in, picked up her kicked-off blanket, and covered her once again. I had to chuckle as I looked around her room. To the ordinary eye, this six-years-old's room was pretty close to being considered for one of those designer magazines. But I knew the truth and feared for what I would find when I opened her closet and checked under her bed.

I kissed her forehead before I stepped from her room, then made my way over to our bedroom. I sighed before I stepped inside, hoping that Monica was asleep, and if she weren't, we wouldn't end up in a fight.

But when I opened the door, there were a myriad of matter that challenged my senses.

The first thing that hit me when I stepped over the threshold was that the television wasn't on. That was strange — the TV played just about twenty-four-seven because Monica watched it during the day and slept with it on by night.

Next, the assault was on my hearing:

"A chair is still a chair, even when there's no one sitting there..."

With Luther's voice in my ears, my eyes settled on the bed where Monica always lay. She *was* there, but she was a Monica that I hadn't seen in sometime. My wife was sprawled across our bed, in a red teddy and thong. It was quite a contrast, the red she wore against the white duvet. She looked like fire.

But it wasn't just the lingerie. My wife looked gorgeous with her usually-in-a-ponytail hair traded in for curls that cascaded over her shoulders. And she'd taken the time to put on makeup, though not too much. I always loved that Monica wore just enough to enhance her and not hide her.

My reaction was instant and it was real. I smiled. "Wow! What?"

She finished my question for me. "What is this?" She sat up just a little. "This is your wife waiting for you to come home." She paused. "You're a little late."

I stiffened as she glanced at the clock. My first thought was: this had been a set-up. She'd done all of this to lash out at me because it was Friday, it was after midnight, and I was just getting home. Stepping all the way into the bedroom, I braced myself for her rant, already thinking that I was too tired to sleep on the sofa, but I would do it.

But all Monica said was, "But I'm glad you're home now."

There was more than relief in me now, I was grateful to see that my wife was really trying. I walked over, leaned onto our bed, moving to kiss her. Then, right before our lips touched — a flash.

Angelique, turning to face me.

I shook my head, trying to knock that vision away.

"What's wrong?" Monica's eyes were filled with concern as she held the back of my neck.

"Oh, nothing. Nothing," I replied. But all my mind would let me manage as she pulled me to her was a peck on her lips.

When I leaned away, her frown deepened. "What was that?"

I stared at my wife laying there, ready and now, so willing. But before I could lean over again — a flash.

Angelique, her lips so close.

"Blu?" Monica called my name. "What's wrong? I'm lying here like this, waiting for you and that's all I can get? That's the way you kiss now?"

A flash — *Angelique, our kiss.*

"Blu?"

When I blinked away that memory, Monica, once again, came focused into my view.

Her frown of concern was morphing into anger and I rushed to stop that. "I'm sorry, babe. You look amazing." This time, when I leaned over Monica, I focused on *her* lips. And this time, I really kissed her. When I finally pulled away, I said, "It's just been a long day. I need a shower."

"Well, hurry up. Don't keep Mama waiting."

Inside our bathroom, I turned on the shower before I stripped my clothes. Not only was this not what I expected when I came home, but this wasn't what I wanted. Within an hour, I'd kissed two women — two women that I cared for.

That was my first dilemma — how would I stop those images of Angelique from galloping through my mind? And even if I were able to erase Angelique, I wasn't in the mood for this perfunctory sex. Every quarter or so, Monica felt like she had to perform her wifely duties — that was what she'd called it in the past. And once she'd said that, once she'd told me that sex with me was something she was supposed to do, that part of our relationship had lost its luster.

Under the shower's water, though, I decided that I would wait it out. If I took a long enough shower, surely, Monica would be asleep. But that was not the case. Even though at least twenty or so minutes had passed when I finally wrapped myself in my bathrobe and returned to our bedroom, my wife's eyes were wide open. And her eyes wasn't the only thing that was wide awake — she was naked, perched on all fours, and ready to ride.

A flash — *Angelique, smiling. Angelique, laughing.*

"I've been waiting for you." She crawled toward me and I wondered what kind of drugs had she taken? That was always my concern — was she taking her meds? Was she taking anything else?

She said, "I was hoping....thinking....maybe you know, it's been a long time."

She looked sexy, her voice was sultry, it was hard for me to see Monica this way. Hard for me to see her as sexy when all I saw in my mind's eye saw was the way this usually ended up in a flood of tears. Hard for me to hear her as sultry when all I heard in my mind's eye was the way I never knew what would send her spiraling downhill.

And then in my mind's eye, I remembered our last time. And how she'd just lay there, making me feel like we were in a remake of *The Color Purple*, she in the starring role of Celie, and me playing the villain of Mister.

No, I didn't want to do this. Not with the *other* visions that were still dancing in my head, the ones that could make me smile. I said, "Are you okay?"

Her eyes squinted a little. "That wasn't exactly the response I expected."

"I'm just saying, I hope this isn't your meds or something."

She raised up, flipped over and sat on the bed. Her arms were folded when she said, "If you're trying to kill the mood...."

"I'm not trying to do that," I lied. "It's just that I'm always worried about you."

Her glower was deeper now, as she stared at me first, and then glanced down at her nakedness before she returned her glance to me. "Really. This is the moment you choose to be concerned?"

"I'm always concerned. You know that."

"Well," she stood, wrapped her arms around me, and pressed her body hard against me, "the only thing you need to be concerned about now is how to take care of Mama."

When she tugged at my robe, I grabbed her hand, stopping her. "Come on, Angeli....Monica."

A flash — *Angelique, touching my hand, right before...our kiss.*

She paused, stepped back, folded her arms and with a little one of those neck rolls, she asked, "What did you just call me?"

I couldn't believe I'd made that mistake, and when I responded with, "Angel. I called you, Angel," I wondered if this was what cheating husbands had to go through. Being quick, making up lies. And then, as I moved toward her, I wondered what a cheating husband would do next.

I said, "Monica, I really appreciate you going through all of this for me, but...."

Her arms were back to being folded, even as she stood in front of me butt-naked.

I finished with, "I'm really tired. It's been a long day."

If she was fazed by my slip-up, she didn't let on. Her concern was elsewhere. "What? You're never too tired for sex. I've never heard of that from a man."

"I am today. I'll take a raincheck." I walked to the other side of the bed, needing to step away from her before I started sweating guilt.

But while I'd tried to put distance between us, she closed the space, coming to my side of the bed and stopping right in front of my face. "Really Blu? What's really going on?"

"I told you."

Her eyes narrowed as she studied me and I felt the heat of her stare. Before, I felt like a cheating husband and now, I felt like a criminal in one of those little interrogation rooms with the light shining in my face.

When Monica said nothing, I told her, "Let's just go to bed."

Now, she spoke, "You know my mama used to always say, if your man isn't getting it from you, he's getting it from somewhere else."

I shook my head, a move that was meant for Monica and me at the same time. I wasn't going to fight with her, so all I said was, "You know that's not what's going on here."

She sighed and stepped back. "I know and I don't want to fight. It's just that." She stopped there and pouted.

That was when I knew for sure that an argument and tears were not far away. For a second, I wondered if I could do this — just have sex with Monica because at this point, I knew that would make her feel better. But I couldn't — because of all the thoughts in my head of Angelique.

It was my guilt that made me say, "I'm going to check on the kids before I turn it." It was my guilt that made me rush away, moving past her and out the bedroom. Closing the door behind me, I leaned against it for a moment, thinking about what I'd just done to my wife. I prayed that she'd be well tomorrow because then…I could. Just not tonight.

Because I didn't want to be a total liar, I checked on the kids once again, then settled inside the family room. I clicked on ESPN, and although I really wanted to catch these highlights, my mind wouldn't stay on what was on the television.

Instead, I was back and forth — Monica and Angelique. Angelique and Monica.

I had no idea how I'd gotten to this place where Angelique occupied the same space as my wife. Yet, here I was about to sleep in my family room because when my wife wanted to make love to me, all I could think about was Angelique.

That was exactly what happened. I leaned back and closed my eyes, and fell asleep with Angelique all up in my dreams.

CHAPTER 15

Angelique

"I kissed him!" I declared, then pressed my hands to my face, covering my...what was it? Embarrassment? Excitement.

"You kissed who?" Sheryl and Cassidy said at the same exact time, then looked at each other and busted into laughter.

I was glad that my girls could laugh at what I'd just told them...well, at least, they laughed for now. But that was about to end because when I answered their question, I had a feeling all laughter would end.

The two of them were still in the middle of their fit of giggles, so I waited, grateful that I wasn't doing this over the phone. No, today, I needed a face-to-face girlfriend intervention and my transgression couldn't have come at a better time. Cassidy had gotten an international assignment, so she would be based in London for a while and had no idea when we'd be able to get together again. So she'd summoned us to her place, for our own happy hour. Only it was Saturday...it was one in the afternoon...and we had already finished off two bottles of Stella Rosa.

It had been a great afternoon of wine, appetizers and girl time, the three of us, just lounging on the floor, barefoot. Me, in sweatpants rolled up to my knees and Cassidy and Sheryl both in black leggings. But now, I knew I'd just taken our chatting to a different level.

Finally, Sheryl waved her hand as if that would stop her laughter, then she repeated her question.

"You kissed who?" She pressed her lips to her wine glass, taking another sip, though I wondered if we'd already had too many.

The way Sheryl and Cassidy looked at me, I couldn't figure out why they hadn't figured it out. I mean, how many people were in my life that I should have been kissing? It must have been the wine.

But since they still stared, still waited for my response, I said, "I kissed *him*. I kissed Blu."

And just like I predicted, the laughter stopped.

Again, they spoke together. "You kissed Blu." But this time, that didn't send them into a fit of giggles.

"Oh, my God!" Sheryl said and then, after a moment, a smile lit her face and she raised her hand to give me a high-five.

But before I could think about moving my hand to meet Sheryl's, Cassidy grabbed me. "Wait a minute," she said. "This doesn't seem like a moment to celebrate. I have some questions."

"Now that I think about it, I do, too," Sheryl said. "Like, all you did was kiss him? Why did you stop there?"

"He's married!" This time, Cassidy and I were the ones who spoke in harmony.

"And?" Sheryl said. "You're not trying to marry him, you just want to get your groove back."

"Ugh," Cassidy released her frustration. Then, she said, "Wait. Let's back up," Cassidy moved her arms in a reverse speed-bag-boxing motion. "What happened? When did you kiss him? And why?"

"Why?" Sheryl said. "You are the one among us who least needs to ask that question. You're getting more than me and Angelique combined and so I know you know why men and women kiss." She paused. "So, they can get it on." And then, she fell back, kicked up her heels, and giggled.

"Really?" Cassidy said. She swiped what would have been our third bottle of wine from the table, pushed herself up, then marched to the counter that separated the kitchen from the rest of her living room space. "Enough drinking for you." Turning back to me, she said, "Maybe we all need to drink some water so that we can talk about this," she glanced at Sheryl, "without getting hysterical at every little thing."

Cassidy traipsed back over, sat next to me, crossed her legs yoga-style and said, "Start at the beginning."

With my legs under the coffee table, I leaned back on the sofa. "He took me to dinner last night to celebrate me getting the funds for next weekend."

"Yeah, high-five on that, by the way," Cassidy said and Sheryl raised her hand, too.

I said, "Well, there's one thing I didn't tell either of you when we spoke this morning."

"Oh no," Cassidy frowned, "what else?"

"He was the one who gave me the money. I mean, not him. His foundation or rather a foundation that he works with."

"Wow, he gave you all of that money just like that?" Cassidy said.

I nodded.

Sheryl said, "Well then, you damn sure need to do more than just give him a kiss."

"Dang!" Cassidy said to Sheryl, but I stayed quiet.

My girls and I always shared the truth — at least that was what I wanted to believe. But there was one part of this story that I wasn't going to tell. I wasn't going to tell how I'd *wanted* to give Blu much more than a kiss. And the only reason it hadn't happened was because he stopped me, he stopped us.

"I wish you could take this more seriously," Cassidy said to Sheryl. "Because getting involved with a married man is a serious situation."

"Wait, hold up." I raised my hand. "I'm not involved with a married man. I just happened to kiss him."

My words made Sheryl buckle over in laughter and Cassidy glared at both of us. "Really?" That question was directed to Sheryl. But she had the same question for me and that was when I knew I needed to start explaining.

So I went back and told them about my phone call with Blu, his invitation and then, how he'd knocked me out with the private dinner last night. "We talked about everything and it's so easy with him. I mean, we talk about our connection all the time. I'm telling you, it's real."

"So that's why you kissed him?" Cassidy asked and folded her arms. "Because in case you've forgotten, you cannot be connected to him because of this thing called marriage." She leaned forward. "He's...married." She'd slowed down her cadence as if she were talking to children. Then, she lifted my arm and pointed to my hand. "And you are, too."

"I know," I moaned.

"He's married, she's married...and so?" Sheryl said again. When Cassidy glared at her, she added. "Look, I keep telling you I deal with this stuff every day. You keep telling her about how they're married and she keeps telling you about their connection. Come on, Cass, listen to her. She and Blu are connected."

"They can't be....they're...."

Sheryl held up her hands. "Please don't say it again because we've heard you. Angelique knows they're married, Blu knows they're married, we know they're married, the whole damn world knows that Angelique and that ninja are married, and not to each other." She took a breath, giving Cassidy a chance to say something, but she didn't speak.

"All right then," Sheryl continued. "Look, I know how the both of you feel about the sanctity of marriage and I get that. I get all of that forever and ever, sickness, health, richer, poorer thing. But with the kind of work that I do, this is what I know." The pause was so dramatic. "Angelique, you may be married, but did you marry your soulmate?" She held up her hand, stopping me or Cassidy from saying anything. "And if you have this connection with Blu, how do you know that he's not your soulmate?" Then, she slapped her hand against the table. "Boom!"

We were both quiet for a moment. I was silent because her words...wow! Soulmates?

But I guessed Cassidy was silent only because she was trying to think of a response. And she came back with, "Really, Sheryl?" She folded her arms. "So you want me to believe that Blu is Angelique's soulmate when she's known him for all of five minutes, and," she continued with her voice escalating, "she met him in an app!"

"And that's what I'm talking about," Sheryl said. "Who meets like that? Who has a connection like that?"

"People who want to hook up, meet like that. People who are looking for only one thing, meet like that. People who are looking for an easy find, meet like that."

Then, they both turned their eyes to me, but Sheryl shook her head.

"It's not lust," she said as if I'd told her that. "Not for Angelique, definitely, and I don't think it's lust for Blu."

"How would you know?"

"Hello?" I held up my hand. "I can see you, I can hear you and I can talk for myself."

"Well then, tell us," Sheryl said. "Is this lust or is Blu your soulmate?"

Really, I didn't know how to answer that, so I asked, "What's a soulmate?"

Sheryl grinned as if she'd won me over, even though all I wanted was clarification. I mean, I knew what I thought that meant — a person you were so connected to that you wanted to spend every moment, awake and asleep, with them. And that was how I felt about Blu. So...could he be...my soulmate?

Sheryl said, "I've been studying this for years and the best definition I ever found was from an American writer. He said, 'a soulmate is someone who has locks that fit our keys, and keys to fit our locks.' And I believe that only a soulmate can open up your locks and that's what allows you to be your authentic self. You can only do that with a soulmate. You can only feel totally complete inside when you've met that person."

"Wow," I exclaimed, but all Cassidy did was shake her head.

"So, are you saying that Angelique and Blu should be married?" Her tone let us know that she thought Sheryl's words were beyond ridiculous.

155

"No, I'm not saying that at all because being married to your soulmate, I think, is a very special thing. It doesn't happen very often. People tend to marry their life partners, but not their soulmates. They're with the dude who takes care of the bills, the female who takes care of the kids, but they're not with the person who knows them instinctively, who connects with them on the deepest level, and who allows them to grow in a relationship. That's a soulmate." She paused at looked at me. "Is that what you have with Blu?"

I nodded, but Cassidy answered for me, "It doesn't matter what she has with Blu. This," she pointed to the diamond on my finger, that even inside the apartment, shined, "is what she has with Preston."

"And no matter how many times you tell us this, we know it," Sheryl said. Then, turning back to me, she added, "So, answer my question. Is that...."

"Yes," I answered before she could finish. "That's exactly what I have with Blu. I mean, I connect with him...on that deepest level, like you said."

"Would you listen to yourself?" Cassidy put her arms up in the air. "How deep can it be? You've known him for five minutes."

I ignored her. "And though I haven't known him very long," I gave a sideward glance to Cassidy, "I know that I would grow with him. Because he respects who I am. I mean, he believes in it so much he was willing to give me money for my dream."

While Sheryl nodded, Cassidy said, "Or maybe he was just giving you money to get between your legs."

"What is it with you?" Sheryl asked Cassidy. "Why are you so down on this thing with Angelique and Blu?"

"Besides the obvious?" She shook her head as she turned to me. "I don't know how you can talk about someone you just met as a soulmate. You don't know him."

"But I do. I know him in my…." I paused.

Cassidy said, "Please don't say…your soul."

I nodded and Sheryl grinned.

"And I'm not even going to charge you for an office visit," Sheryl said. Then, her smile went away. "Look, I'm telling you what I know."

"And I'm telling you what I know," Cassidy said. "I don't think this is some divine intervention where God has introduced you to your soulmate because this meeting, the way you met Blu and who he is, is so out of order. What this meeting was all about for you is what's going on with you and Preston. And how he's been neglecting you. If Preston had been paying you any bit of attention, you wouldn't have even turned your head to look at Blu."

Her words gave me pause. Was that true? Was it all just about Preston? Then, I shook my head. "I'm not sure about that, Cassidy. Because Preston has been neglecting me for a long time, but this is the first time that I've ever connected with anyone. This is the first time I've even spoken to another man."

"Exactly," Sheryl said to me. Then, twisting to Cassidy, she asked, "And how do you know this isn't what God has for her?"

With the heel of her hand, Cassidy pressed against her forehead. "I can't believe you would ask me that when you go to church more than I do. I told you, this is out of order. How can this be of God when they're both married?"

"Here we go back to that marriage thing," Sheryl said as she stood, shuffled to the kitchen and brought back the bottle of wine that Cassidy had taken away. "For someone who's single, you sure talk about marriage a lot."

"Marriage thing? What God has put together let no man or woman take it apart." She turned to me. "So we know how you feel about your vows with Preston...."

"Hey, what're you trying to say?"

She ignored my question, but asked me one. "How do you feel about Blu's wife? If you go any further than that kiss...what about her? How would you feel if someone was doing this in your marriage?"

Sheryl rolled her eyes. "Talk about a buzzkill," she said, right before she took two gulps of wine.

"I'm asking that question with nothing but love in my heart for you," Cassidy said. "You can't fall for a guy who belongs to another woman because, Angelique you would die if someone did that to you. Don't do it."

I waited for a moment to see if Sheryl would come up with a good response, but all she did was sip, and sip, and sip.

So, I had to face Cassidy's words, straight-on and on my own. Her words were tough to hear, tougher to acknowledge. This wasn't who I was. What had I been thinking? I would never get together with a married man. Never!

I said, "Well, I guess you put a period where I'd been trying to put a question mark. Now, I feel so bad about this."

"You don't have anything to feel bad about." Cassidy shook her head. "You've been through so much. I just think if you're able to put the same amount of attention on Preston that you've been putting on Blu, you'll be good. I mean, if you really talk to Preston and open up and tell him about your keys and your locks, I think you'll find that he's your soulmate."

Sheryl released a chuckle that sounded like she was saying yeah-right. But that was the extent of her contribution.

Sheryl's sentiments were mine, too. At least about Preston. I had no hope for our marriage, especially since I'd been hanging out with Blu. Preston had chosen his mistress and I couldn't compete. And now, I had to question, what did I want? Was this how I wanted to live for the rest of my life?

But Cassidy was right about Blu's wife.

So now, the question was what was I going to do? And the challenge was how was I going to stay away from Blu?

CHAPTER 16

Angelique

"So, you understand, don't you?"

I sighed as I pressed my foot on the accelerator to catch the light as I made my way home. "I do," I told Blu. "Just know that this wasn't an invitation just for you; I invited all the sponsors."

"No, I get that, but we just want the Taylor Foundation to be an anonymous sponsor this time."

This time.

"Okay," I told him, hoping that I didn't sound as disappointed as I felt that he wouldn't be coming to any part of this weekend. Not even the gala. "But have I told you thank you?"

Even before he spoke, I felt his smile. "Every day. And have I told you that you're welcome?"

"Every day."

We laughed together and then, he said, "I hope this weekend is everything that you want it to be. You were born to soar, and I know you and these precious girls will do just that."

This was where I wanted to scream, 'Please come, at least to the gala.' But I knew that he would never do that.

"Call me on Monday and let me know how everything goes, okay?"

I noticed that he didn't ask me to call him over the weekend; I guessed he thought I'd be with Preston the whole time. So all I did was agree and then sighed so deeply that it felt like I was releasing years of pent-up frustration.

That was all I'd been doing all week. Sighing. Because I had made it through the entire week without seeing Blu.

Not that he had invited me anywhere and I tried not to think that maybe I'd run him off by the way I'd practically asked him to sleep with me. No, the words hadn't come out of my mouth, but he knew what I was about to say a week ago today.

Because...we were that connected.

But he never mentioned it and neither had I. Besides not making plans to see each other, everything else stayed the same. He still called every morning just to say: *Hey beautiful, make sure you make this a great day.* And we still messaged each other through the app, and we still played *Words With Friends* and I still beat him, most of the time.

But that physical space? It had been six full days. Yup, I deserved a medal because all I did was think of Blu. I thought about how he made me feel, I thought about how I wanted to spend all of my time with him. I thought about how...we were soulmates.

At least, that was what I thought, though now, I knew for sure that I'd never find out. Because even if I no longer honored my husband, I certainly honored another man's wife.

"Even if her husband is my soulmate," I whispered, right before I rounded my car around the corner and then into our driveway.

But then, my thoughts about my soulmate shifted to thoughts about my husband when I saw Preston's car.

What is Preston doing home? His car hadn't seen daylight in our driveway on a workday in…forever.

My heart began to beat in anticipation of what could be wrong. What would have Preston home and not at work? Someone died!

I jumped out of my Lexus, raced into the house, and bumped into Preston as I ran into the living room.

"Hey babe," he said, not sounding at all like someone had passed away.

"Hey," I said, confused. "What's wrong?"

He frowned. "What do you mean?"

"What are you doing home?"

"You know, you ask me that a lot. A man could get a complex." He chuckled. "What? You don't want me home? You trying to sneak some guy in here?" Then, he laughed, as if the thought of me being with another man was a joke. His laughter made me want to call Blu up and tell him to come right over.

"No," I said. "It's not that I don't want you home, it's that you're never home."

"Yeah, I know, babe. And I'm going to be working on that. As soon as we close some of these big deals. The clients have been rolling in, but once we get everything settled, I'll be all yours." He kissed my cheek, then moved toward the kitchen.

At first, I thought about just going up to our bedroom to pack my bag for this weekend, but I followed Preston deciding that I needed to take the time with him anyway and anywhere I could get it.

Inside the kitchen, I leaned back a little when I saw the four cartons of Chinese food lined up on the counter.

Wow! And, I'd just been thinking that Preston never thought about me. A bit of guilt swelled up inside. Preston had made this effort, at least so we could share a meal together, and even spend some time together afterward. After all, he was home at three in the afternoon on a Friday.

"You picked up something for us to eat," I said, unable to keep the surprise from my voice. "Thank you."

Preston laughed. "Actually the guy from Yee's who always delivers to us, was doing a delivery next door and no one was home. He was so pissed about it. So, I figured I'd help him out and buy it so that you'll have dinner."

I had to blink a few times to get his words to compute in my head. But even once I did that, I still wasn't able to come up with any words. He hadn't thought about me at all; his thoughts were about the Chinese delivery guy.

I wanted to kick myself for believing and then, slap him for making me believe. But all I did was stare at him in disbelief.

"Well...thank you...for *my* dinner." I'd noticed that he hadn't said that *we'd* have dinner. "So, where will you be eating?"

"That's why I came home. We have a big dinner tonight and I'd left the contract here." He shook his head. "I can't believe I did that. Gotta get them to sign it tonight." He paused. "But at least it gave me a chance to see you." He kissed my forehead. "So, you're gonna just hang out at home tonight?"

I kept my sigh inside because I didn't want to argue. I said, "No. I'm going over to the hotel for the social tonight. I'm going to stay there for the weekend, remember?"

His eyes fluttered like he was trying to figure something out. "What hotel?"

Now, I was the one who was confused by his words. "What do you mean? The Westin. Where I'm having the Black Girls Magic weekend." I paused. "It's this weekend."

"This weekend?" His frown was deep. "I thought the conference was cancelled."

Oh, this was hard. It was so difficult not to slap Preston, at least with my words. I had actually told him that I'd gotten the money, but this was my fault. I should've known when he'd said, "That's great, babe," he was really saying, "Can you get off this phone?" He hadn't heard anything that I'd told him.

But instead of letting the hysteria rise within me, all I said was, "No, I worked it all out. I told you and I even reminded you about the gala tomorrow night. Remember, I chose this weekend because you promised you'd be free."

He paused and I knew he was trying to remember. "Oh, okay."

"Preston…."

"What?"

"Please, you know how important this is to me."

"I know."

"And I want you there with me."

"Okay, I'll be there."

"And at six," I told him. "For the receiving line."

"I'll be there, babe. No worries. Tomorrow is Saturday, so it'll be cool. Nothing from work can come up."

"Okay," I said and then, I breathed a bit easier because Preston hugged me as if he were sealing his promise with this embrace.

When he stepped back, he said, "So, you're going to stay at the hotel."

I nodded. "Yeah, it'll just be easier for me to handle everything if I'm right there."

"Makes sense."

"That's for tonight, but for tomorrow…." I paused and looked straight at him. "I was hoping that it could be a special night…with you there."

When he smiled at those words, I felt like I had just swallowed the sun. I beamed. "That would be wonderful, babe." And then, when he pulled me back into his arms and said, "We don't get to spend enough time together and that's what I want," I swooned. He continued, "We'll do that tomorrow night and I'm thinking, maybe we won't even check out on Sunday."

Leaning back, I looked up at him. "Really?"

He nodded. "Wouldn't it be great to just stay in bed in the hotel all day Sunday? I mean, I'll have to go to work on Monday, but…."

"I'll take Sunday." I grinned.

He bent over and gave me the kind of kiss that had made me fall in love with him. And in that instant, just after this little exchange, I knew that Preston and I could make it.

I was breathless when I stepped back and not just because of the kiss. Preston had reminded me of how we used to be and how we could be once again.

His grin matched mine when he said, "I better get out of here or else I'll miss making this deal tonight and you'll miss your social."

Another kiss, and then when he turned from me, I gave him a slap on the butt.

"Do not play with me, woman," he exclaimed before he trotted out of the kitchen.

I laughed, feeling giddy. As I checked out the Chinese food, I marveled at how just a little attention from my husband was all that I needed, it was what I craved.

Well, I had that and I'd have more of that from Preston tomorrow night. Now, I couldn't wait for the gala and what would happen after.

CHAPTER 17

Angelique

This was why I did what I did.

There was only one word for the sight in front of me — amazing. The ballroom was filling up with the young girls and their parents. Seeing the girls, who were normally in jeans, dressed up in their gowns and after-five dresses made me swell with pride. With the five hundred or so people around me, I said a quick prayer to God, thanking Him for choosing me to do this before the next parent stepped up in the receiving line.

"Mrs. Mason, this was an amazing conference," Mrs. Johnson, Tonia's mother said to me. "I am just so happy that Tonia has been able to participate with you."

I shook Mrs. Johnson's hand and then hugged Tonia before I passed her to the next person on the line.

We were only a receiving line of six: Me, Sheryl (the only representative of the board), and our two sponsors and their wives.

"Mrs. Mason." The next parents stepped up with their daughter, Lara. Her father continued, "What we learned today about our girls going to college and the financial aid programs that are available to us...this was all priceless. Thank you for all that you do."

Again, I smiled and shook hands and hugged. Then, passed them along to say the same to Sheryl and the others.

Seeing all the smiles warmed me, let me know that what I was doing was right, made me feel like I was...soaring.

But though I smiled along with the girls and their parents, inside, I could feel the tears beginning to fill up the bucket inside of me.

I felt my phone vibrate inside my purse and I excused myself from the line. I was sure the incoming message was from Preston and before I clicked on the notification, I prayed that he was on his way.

I clicked my message icon:

Just want you to know that I'm thinking of you and wishing you well, always.

I wanted to smile because of who this was, and I wanted to cry because of who this wasn't. I responded:

Thank you.

He typed back right away:

Whoa. I didn't expect to hear from you. I thought you and your husband would be knee-deep in the celebration. Having fun?

It was because he'd been my sounding board that I replied:

Yes, to fun. No, to husband. He's not here. TTYL.

I tucked my phone back into my beaded purse and slipped back into the line. My smile was back, at least a little, because of Blu. At least he was my cheerleader.

It was an hour of meeting and greeting and hors d'oeuvres and the open bar. When the last family made their way through the reception line, I slipped to the bar in the far corner. As the girls and their families mingled and excited chatter filled the air, I brooded as I texted my husband:

Where are you?

I held my phone in my hand, staring at the screen for a moment, wondering if he would respond. But unlike Blu, my husband rarely responded to my texts within moments.

"What's up?" Sheryl said as she sauntered over to the bar. She ordered a glass of wine then turned to back to me.

I gave her a little shake of my head and Sheryl chuckled.

"You didn't really expect him to come, did you?"

"Yes, I did," I snapped at my best friend. "Because he's my husband. He's supposed to be here."

She raised an eyebrow. "Don't get mad at me."

"I'm not mad at you, Sheryl. It's just that you're always so negative about Preston."

Now, both of her eyebrows shot up. "I'm negative?"

"Yeah."

"Well, maybe it's just that your husband gives me enough material to be negative about."

I held up the palm of my hand because what I needed most right now was support since Preston wouldn't be here to give it to me. Didn't Sheryl understand that?

Rolling my eyes, I pivoted on my stilettos, then held my red gown up, so that I could trek to the ladies' room without tripping. I pushed open the door harder than I wanted to and was a bit surprised to find that there wasn't a line. I was grateful for that and stuffed myself into one of the stalls that certainly wasn't made for women in ballgowns, then, hiked up my dress and squatted down — even though I didn't have to go to the bathroom.

I just needed a moment. Because there would be nothing smiley about my face if I had to go back into that ballroom right now.

I shouldn't have blown up at Sheryl; I was deflecting, which is what she would say. She would tell me that I was taking out my frustrations with Preston on her because she was the most convenient person. If she said all of that, she would be right. But damnit (and I never cursed) why couldn't she be like Cassidy for a moment? Why couldn't Sheryl just root for me and Preston for once? Why did she always have to play the clinical psychologist who made me feel like I was on my way to divorce court?

Still, I owed Sheryl an apology. Because whatever she said, she was always right.

Standing, I smoothed out my dress, then, I went to face myself in the mirror before I had to face Sheryl. After I washed my hands, I pulled out my makeup case, though I knew that I was just trying to delay returning to the ballroom. I wasn't sure if I was trying to give Preston time to show up and surprise me. Or if I were just trying to prolong the inevitable.

I smoothed a bit of gloss onto my lips when the door opened and through the mirror's reflection, I watched Sheryl step in. She walked behind me, then, stood beside me, pulling out her own makeup case.

After a moment, she said, "Together, we look like Christmas."

I busted out laughing. She was right. My bright red gown next to her forest green one were not meant to be displayed side by side, I was sure. But I laughed because it did look like someone should plug us in and light us up....and that was my friend's way of apologizing.

I said, "I'm sorry, too."

Facing me, she whispered, "I just get so mad at Preston sometimes."

"I know. I know you're only looking out for me."

"I am. And I just think you deserve," she paused for a moment, "a soulmate."

I dumped my cosmetic bag back into my purse, then hugged Sheryl. "Thank you for always being in my corner."

"You got it." She stepped back and took my hand. "Now, let's go out there and you be as fabulous as you were born to be. Because no matter who's here, you are Angelique Mason, the founder of Black Girls Magic, a major foundation in Houston, Texas that has made a difference in hundreds of girls' lives and this is just the beginning."

Her words were a shot of fortitude that I rode back into the ballroom, and onto the dais. Even as I sat there, with Preston's empty chair next to me, I remembered Sheryl's words, and even Blu's. I didn't need Preston here. This was a success with or without his presence.

At the end of dinner of catfish, sweet potato soufflé, and collard greens, the mistress of ceremonies, Delinda Mauldin, stood up and began the program. In just a few moments, I would have to give my speech and I needed to focus on that.

I folded my hands and the light from the chandelier above, hit my ring, flashing a rainbow of colors across the tablecloth. That made me think of Preston once more. And that was the reason why, on the sly, I slid my phone from my purse and texted again:

Where are you?

And for the first time (at least in my memory) my husband's reply came right away:

Sweetheart, I meant to call. Not gonna make it. One of the partners didn't show up last night and we had to do it tonight. We have to close this deal. So sorry. But...

His text stopped there. I glanced at the clock. It was almost seven-thirty. This was something that not only he had known all day, but he could have taken care of today, too. Why did he have to do that dinner tonight? In the middle of my gala? On a date that I'd chosen to specifically fit him and his calendar?

I blinked and blinked and blinked back all the disappointment that I could. I needed to focus on the girls, not on my hurt. So, I turned off my phone because clearly Preston was going to send another text and I couldn't read another excuse that would bring me to tears.

I was still blinking when Delinda said, "And now, ladies and gentlemen, please join me in welcoming the woman behind this magical event, the woman who had the foresight to put together a program to build our young ladies, the woman whose commitment to these young women is never-wavering...let us all welcome, Mrs. Angelique Mason."

The room erupted in applause and I stood, pausing for a moment to allow the disappointment to drain from my head and flow to my feet so that I would be clear. With as much of a saunter as I could muster, I made my way to the podium.

When the hundreds before me quieted, I began, "Thank you all so much. I thank you all for coming, not only tonight, but for the whole conference. You know, I started Black Girls Magic because I wanted to make a real difference. In truth, I want every young black girl to know that she can soar."

My glance traveled from the left side of the room, to the right. Then, when I came back to center, I began again. Only this time, words did not come out of me.

I blinked because clearly I was so upset by Preston that I was having a reaction. I think they called this a mirage.

I blinked until I was sure that what I saw was real. I blinked until Blu came into full focus, leaning against the wall in the back, wearing a tuxedo, and watching me.

And then, I blinked, I smiled, and I continued.

"I...ummm...excuse me," I began again. "This is just so overwhelming."

"Take your time," someone shouted as if we were in church.

Laughter rang out through the room, just enough to help me relax my shoulders and move on. "There are few things that touch your soul, that you know you were put on this earth to see to fruition. Black Girls Magic is one of those things for me....."

Even from as far away as he was, I could see the way Blu beamed. And all of that pride he had, he had for me.

I completed my speech, then, we recognized the girls who were graduating out of the program and distributed the scholarships. After that, it was all about photo ops — with the graduating girls, with the girls and their families, with the sponsors...I stood in the middle of hundreds of photos.

And the whole time I kept my eyes on Blu. At first, he stayed in place, at the wall where I'd first noticed him, and later, as the photos began, he moseyed to the bar. As he sipped his drink, I watched him, watching me.

The room was almost empty by the time I was able to make my way over to him.

And before he said hello, he gave me a hug. "You're beautiful and you were so wonderful up there."

"Thank you," I said. "But what are you doing here? I thought," and I lowered my voice, "you didn't want to be recognized as a sponsor."

"I didn't. I didn't come here as a sponsor. I came here...as your friend."

"Because I told you that Preston wasn't here?"

"Is he?" The way he asked, he already knew the answer.

So, I didn't bother to acknowledge my husband. All I said was, "I'm glad you're here."

"Hey, Angelique," Sheryl's voice called out behind me. "What are you going to:...." She stopped as Blu came into her full view. Leaning back a little, she said, "Well." She held out her hand to him. "You must be Blu."

His eyes widened as if he were a little surprised and I guess he should have been. Sheryl had just committed a major girlfriend violation. She'd just told Blu that I'd been talking about him.

Oh, my God. How embarrassing was this? Because I was sure he hadn't mentioned my name to anyone.

"Uh, yeah," he said, looking from Sheryl to me and then back to her. He took her hand. "Yes, I'm Blu...Logan. And you have an advantage over me because I don't know your name."

"Really?" Sheryl said, feigning surprise. "So, she doesn't talk about me to you as much as she talks about you to me?"

My face filled with horror. No, not just my face, all of me. No, not horror. Horror was on my face, the rest of me warmed with complete humiliation. In fact, humiliation wasn't a strong enough word. I had to find a new one so that I could explain it to the judge when he asked me why did I kill my best friend.

Blu chuckled. "Ummm, I can't say that she's spoken a lot about you," he said. "But it's probably because when we're together, I only like to talk about Angelique."

Sheryl placed her hand across her chest and...sighed. I snatched her hand away from her heart and said, "Excuse me, Blu," and then, I dragged that six-figure earning dummy out of the room.

"Hey!" she exclaimed. "Where're we going? I wanted to talk to Blu."

Inside the hallway, I asked, "Have you lost your mind?"

"What?"

"Telling him that I talk about him?"

"Oh. That." She shrugged. "Sorry. But girl, you didn't do that man any justice. But I'm not sure that there are words that could describe him properly. That man is...."

"Married," I reminded her.

"Dammit. Cassidy done got to you."

"Sheryl, please. I just want to go back in there, talk to Blu for a little while, then, send him home and I'll go to bed, thinking about how my husband stood me up."

"Okay, bad decision, but your decision." She sighed. "Well, let's go say good night to Blu."

"No. No 'let's'. Just me."

"Awww man." And then, she grinned. "I knew you were gonna say that. Smart decision." She winked, gave me a hug, then whispered some crap about she wanted to hear all about tonight tomorrow.

I waved her away and then walked back into the ballroom. It was just about empty except for Blu who sat at one of the back tables now, two flutes of wine in front of him.

When I approached, he held up one of the glasses and handed it to me. "Thank you," I said, then sat next to him.

He clicked his glass against mine, then said, "Congratulations to a soaring success."

I grinned my thanks before I took a sip.

"So, tell me all about it."

"The conference?"

He nodded.

"Here?" I glanced around the room filled with hotel staff, clearing the tables, stripping them of the cloths, moving out the chairs. I had a feeling that any moment, we'd be carried out, too.

"You're right," he said. "Do you want to go out somewhere? I mean, since we're all dressed up and everything."

"But it's late. It's almost eleven."

"Well, it's early somewhere in the world. Come on." He stood up and took my hand. "Let's go celebrate a little. I won't keep you out long and I'll bring you back here to pick up your car."

"We don't have to worry about that. I'm staying here." And that was the moment when I decided. We needed to get out of this hotel. "Okay, let's do it."

I felt like a school girl sneaking out at night the way Blu and I tiptoed and exited through the hotel's back door. Not that I was concerned about anyone seeing me. Most of the girls and their parents had left — we'd only had the girls staying over last night. But even if someone saw me, I just didn't care. I wanted to go out and celebrate this big night. I wanted to be with Blu.

CHAPTER 18

Blu

From my peripheral vision, I saw Angelique's hair blowing in the wind. I'd traded in my Tahoe for my Mustang tonight, my 40th birthday gift to myself that I hardly had a chance to drive.

But tonight, my Mustang had been perfect, though I didn't know how perfect until this moment. Angelique seemed to love it, not having a single care about her hair.   Damn, she'd never looked more beautiful to me and that was saying so much because not only had she always been beautiful, but last Friday right before she kissed me, I'd had one of those angel visions again.

But tonight, there was something more than her physical beauty. It was everything about her as she'd stood behind that podium. She stood, so innocent, so vulnerable, looking like she was all alone. From that first moment when I saw her after I stepped into the ballroom, I was so glad that I'd made the rash decision to come.

It hadn't been hard to get out of the house. Monica was asleep — she would never notice. And though Tanner had plans, the fifty-dollars I'd paid him to change them put a smile on both of our faces.

So, I'd grabbed my tux from the back of my closet, dressed in the guest bathroom and rushed over to the Westin. As I dressed and as I drove, the whole time I imagined what I would do when I got there — and saw that her husband had finally shown up. But the way she looked when she walked up to the podium and began speaking — I knew he had failed her again.

How could her husband not see what he had with her? Damn, if she were my woman....

I sighed because she was not. And she could never be. Not even with what happened last Friday. Not even knowing that if I'd stood there a moment longer after we kissed, we would have found a place to do so much more.

If it makes any difference, I still love you, girl.
You're my weakness, you changed my world.

I bobbed my head to Kem, deciding to change up my music a bit. He may not have been of the eighties, but he was bringing it in this new millennium. 'Cause this song right here — I wanted to hit repeat, and play this part over and over.

You're my weakness, you changed my world.

I kept the music from my phone playing at I sped down I-45. Angelique hadn't even asked me once where we were going. She just sat back, let the wind mess up her curls and bobbed to the music like me. I guess it didn't matter to her where we were headed as long as we were together — and that pleased me.

Although when I finally turned off I-45 and onto Broadway, she sat up. "Wait a minute."

I gave her a quick glance and she gave me one of her smiles that seeped through to my soul. All kinds of desire rose up in me and I had to swallow it all back. It took a moment for me to get my words together. "Yup. I'm taking you to the beach."

"In the middle of the night?"

"Yup!" Then, I added, "Are you okay with this? I mean, dressed like that?"

She grinned. "I'm more than okay. This is perfect."

Just minutes later, I parked the car on the street, then, jumped out. Even in the dark, I could see her eyes on me as I rounded the front of my Mustang. Even in the dark, I felt her stare, warming every part of me.

When I opened the door and pulled her up, I had to hold in my gasp. We were so close, just like last Friday.

I slipped my jacket from my shoulders, then wrapped it around since her spaghetti straps would do little to fend off the night breeze, though I hated covering her up in any way.

"Thank you," she whispered.

"You know what?" he said. "We're gonna have to strip...."

Her eyes widened.

"Off our shoes."

She gave me a playful glare and I laughed. "I'm sorry. I shouldn't play like that."

"No, you shouldn't." Her tone frowned, but her face...she glowed.

"Come on." I kicked off my shoes and socks, and then stood back as she leaned on the car and unhooked each of the ankle straps on her shoes. God, I wanted to do that for her, but I didn't trust myself. I couldn't be that close.

She handed her shoes to me and I popped open the trunk before I dumped our shoes and her purse inside. Then, I pulled out the backpack that I'd packed in my trunk for such a time as this. I'd packed this bag awhile ago, not knowing when or even if, I would ever use it with Angelique. And now, the perfect time was upon us.

I slung the strap of the bag onto my shoulder, then reached for her hand. When she intertwined her fingers in mine, she squeezed my hand. I fought to keep my sigh inside. By the time we got to where the ocean met the sand, my heartbeat settled and we began a slow stroll, she in her red gown, with my jacket and me, hopefully looking some kind of dapper, though I'd unhooked my tie.

I didn't want to venture too far from the boardwalk. The half-moon was bright, but I preferred even more light.

"So," she said, "Galveston beach."

I chuckled. "I know this isn't Tahiti."

"What? This isn't Tahiti? I can't tell. Look at that crystal water," she pointed to the darkened ocean, "and this sand." She looked down and wiggled her toes and I did the same.

"Ouch!" I shouted.

"Oh, my God, what happened?"

"Something in the sand cut me."

"Oh, my God. We need to get you to the hospital." She grabbed my arm as if she needed to assist me walking.

I buckled over with laughter.

She frowned, stepped away from me, and folded her arms.

I said, "I'm sorry. I was kidding. I didn't know you would take it so seriously."

Her face softened as she moved back toward me, then, she punched my arm like she'd taken boxing lessons and this time I said, "Ouch," for real. "What are you doing?"

"Don't play like that." She pouted. "I would be so upset if something happened to you."

Her voice was so soft, her tone, so gentle. I couldn't help it. I pulled her into my arms. But even though I wanted to, I couldn't hold her for longer than a few seconds. If she'd continued to stand so close, she would have felt just how much I wanted her.

Taking her hand, we strolled again, moving only a few more feet.

I said, "Let's stop here." I dropped my backpack, unzipped it, pulled out the blanket, then flung it high into the air, before it drifted down to the sand. "Have a seat, madam."

She giggled as she hiked up her gown a bit, then flopped down on the blanket.

"And I have something special just for you." I pulled out a bottle of Stella Rosa. "Did you say this was your favorite?"

"I did." I smiled at the surprise and delight in her voice. She said, "I think we talked about it during one of the games. Where I was beating you and I asked if you were drunk, remember?"

I squinted at her. "Why you always have to bring up old stuff?"

"Old stuff? Didn't I beat you like...this morning?"

I waved my hand in the air, erasing her words and making her laugh, which is all I wanted to do. Well, it wasn't all I wanted to do, but it was enough to make me happy.

Inside my backpack, I had everything that we needed — a corkscrew, and two glasses. I filled both glasses and then handed one to Angelique.

I held up my glass. "To a successful conference, fantastic evening, and a beautiful woman."

She tilted her head. "Didn't we already do a toast back at the hotel?"

"You are always so technical. Don't you know that you can never have too many toasts nor too much wine."

"I didn't know that."

"And now you do." I clicked my glass against hers and we both sipped. Then, I sat down, close to her so that our shoulders touched. It took everything in me not to pull her back, not to have her lean against me or rest her head in my lap.

We sipped in the quiet for a few moments before I said, "So...tell me about the conference."

If this hadn't been a moonlit night, and if we hadn't been right by the boardwalk, the way Angelique beamed right now would have been enough to light up the whole beach. She talked and all I did was listen. It was easy to do because her voice...she sounded like she was singing to me.

She talked and talked and I felt like she wasn't leaving out a thing. She started with the social last night, which she said was a mix and mingle event, though some of the girls stood up and performed. She told me about the poets and the singers and the praise dancers and how the girls were all loaded with such talent.

"Then, today was filled with workshops."

Talking about the conference seemed like a shot of adrenaline for Angelique. It was like the more she spoke, the more excited she became. She told me about the workshops, the ones for the girls and then the others for their parents. She told me about all twelve that the girls had to choose from.

"It was just an amazing day."

As I refilled her glass, I said, "And then, the gala tonight."

"Yes, it was so special." But then, her smile dropped from her voice. "Until...."

I waited a moment and said, "Until I got there, and then it got better."

She turned toward me and again, her lips were right there. All I had to do was lean forward. All I had to do was kiss her and then this time…I shook my head.

"What?" Her voice was a whisper, but I heard her clearly because her lips were still right there. She said, "Why did you shake your head?"

"Nothing," I said. I let moments pass, then, "Can I ask you something?"

"What?" I looked at her for a moment, but then, turned my eyes out to the blackness that was before us. It was difficult to tell where the night ended and the ocean began. But that was a safe place for my glance. Because if I turned back and looked at her….

But right before I asked her the question, I did face her. Because I wanted to not only hear, but see her answer. I asked, "So, you told your friends about me?"

And then, I had to fight to hold back my laughter. Because the way she squinted, the way she pressed her lips together, I knew the thoughts in her head. She was going to kill her friend, Sheryl…a couple of times. But then, she smirked. "Yeah, I mentioned you a little. I had to tell them about the new guy in *Words With Friends* that I beat all the time."

I blinked. "Really? That's your answer?"

She nodded and we laughed. Together. The way we always did.

But I wanted her to know how much I appreciated her telling her friends about me. Because I knew how big that was. I knew because it had taken a lot for me to tell Lamar. "I'm glad you told your friends about me. Just means that I'm important to you."

She shifted her body so that she faced me completely. But she had moved back a little as if she didn't trust her lips either.

183

She said, "You are important to me, Blu. You've been such a fantastic friend. This weekend would have never happened without you."

I shook my head, though I kept my eyes locked with hers. "I doubt that. The way you are, you would have found a way. But," I continued because I felt her protest coming, "I am so glad that I was able to be there for you."

"It was a big risk for you to take. I mean, we'd just met."

"Not that big. I told you, I'd done my research. I knew that Black Girls Magic was something that our foundation would want to support."

"Tell me about the foundation."

She smiled, but it was her words that made me frown a little. It was a simple question, but I wasn't sure how to answer. I never wanted Angelique to feel anything but wonderful about what Monica's family's foundation had done. So, I just said, "We haven't been as active as we'd been in the past."

"Why not?"

"Well," it was hard to keep the hesitation out of my voice, "the CEO has kinda stepped aside. But with what we've done with you, I think we'll be moving back into finding good causes."

She nodded, though her stare revealed that her instinct told her that I wasn't sharing everything. But she left it there…or at least I thought she had until she said, "I'd really like to thank your board one day. Do you think that might be possible?"

No! But I told her, "Maybe."

And then, because I wanted to change the subject, I reached for her. She hesitated for just a moment, then moved closer before she twisted around and leaned against me.

I wrapped my arms around her, closed my eyes, and

didn't even try to hold my sigh inside. All I did was imagine what it would be like to hold her like this forever.

And then, I wondered…could one man be in love with two women at one time?

For the rest of the time that we sat out there, sipping wine, looking out onto the ocean, I pondered that question and searched in my heart for the answer.

CHAPTER 19

Angelique

I didn't realize it until Blu rolled his car into the driveway of the Westin. I didn't realize that I'd held my breath for the entire drive back. It was amazing that I hadn't fainted since we'd been driving for an hour.

But when he finally brought the car to a stop, I breathed. Then, I filled my lungs with more air before I turned and faced him. "I don't know what to say about tonight."

He grinned. "You've said it already. And I told you that you were welcome."

"You made this night so special for me."

"That's because that's what you are."

I nodded, then smiled, and I was so glad that we were in a convertible in front of the hotel that even at this late hour had too many people outside for me to lean over and kiss him. Because that was what I wanted to do so badly.

I slipped his jacket from my shoulders and handed it to him just as the valet came over to open the door for me. But then, Blu shouted out, "I got that, bruh," and the valet smiled and stepped back.

Blu jumped out, came around to my side, then taking my hand, he helped me to stand.

"Thank you, Blu. And goodnight."

"First, you really got to stop thanking me. And second, I'm walking you up."

"Oh no, that's not necessary at all."

He shook his head. "Now, I done already told you about my dad. If he ever found out that I'd let a woman walk to her room alone...." He made a slicing motion with his hand across his neck, making me laugh once again.

To the valet, he said, "The keys are in the ignition, but I'll be right back. Just park it right there," Blu pointed to the curb, "and give me five." Then, he turned toward the hotel and led me inside.

This night was really going to have to end because I was doing that non-breathing thing again. It was just impossible to do anything else except hold my breath when he was so close to me. And now, his hand was on the small of my back as we walked to the elevator. I was fully clothed, but I might as well have been naked the way his simple touch set me on fire.

We didn't say a word as we walked through the lobby and I was grateful that an elevator was waiting because as much as I love being with Blu, tonight needed to end. We stepped into the elevator and the silence stayed between us. All I had in me was enough to press the button for the 8th floor. When the doors closed, I glanced at Blu, but just as quickly, I lowered my eyes and bit my lip to stifle my giggle. Why did I feel like I was sixteen? It was nervous energy, of that, I was sure. But there was nothing to be nervous about.

The ride went on forever, but finally, the doors parted, I stepped out, but then stopped and turned so quickly, Blu bumped into me. We both laughed like he felt like he was sixteen, too, and it took us a moment to straighten up.

"I was just going to say that you can stop here. You don't have to walk me all the way down the hall."

"My father, remember?" And then, he made that slicing motion across his neck once again.

"Okay," I said. At least he had cut the tension from the air and I was able to walk and breathe at the same time. When we got to room 808, I paused and as I lifted my key from my purse, I had a thought — suppose Preston was inside? Suppose he'd finished with his meeting and decided to meet me here? He did say that he wanted to spend Sunday all day in the hotel. Maybe...maybe...maybe....

My heart was beating with hope when I opened the door, but right away that glimmer was gone. The lights were out, so unless my husband was sitting in the dark, he hadn't come. He probably wasn't even home yet. I wasn't even a minuscule thought to him.

The sadness of that fact rushed over me, washing away the best hours of this night. I was alone, that was the truth and that truth was so hard to bear.

When I turned to face Blu, I blinked to hold back my emotions. I wasn't going to cry. I didn't want his pity. But by the time I looked up at him, the first tear trickled from my eye.

"Oh," was all he said before he stepped into the room, closed the door and pulled me into his arms.

And then, I sobbed. I fell right into Blu's chest and cried.

I really didn't know why I cried. I'd been so used to Preston doing this to me. But this one hurt...or maybe, it wasn't this one. Maybe it was just that this one was on top of the Woman on the Move award, and that disappointment had been on top of something else, another time when he'd ripped out my heart.

Blu didn't say a word, he just held me and it took some minutes for me to back it up and get myself together. I leaned against the wall, looked down and tried to wipe my tears away. "I'm so sorry."

"There's nothing for you to be sorry about."

My eyes were still lowered because I didn't want to look at him. "No. After all you did for me tonight and I come back here and…." I shook my head because if I said anymore, I'd start all over again. "Please. Just go."

"I don't want to leave you."

"No, I'll be all right." I sniffed.

"No, Angelique." It was the way he said my name that made my eyes rise slowly. And when my eyes met his, they locked. But it was his lips that fascinated me. Because they were right there. Right there, when he repeated, "I don't want to leave you." It was his turn to shake his head. "Not tonight."

And then, with the most imperceptible of movements (I wasn't sure if he moved or if I was the one), his lips touched mine. It was easy enough, since just inches had separated us. I moaned as I pressed back again into the wall and Blu pressed into me.

His kiss was so gentle and there was a point, I was sure that we could have stepped back and away like we'd done before. But then, our mouths opened and our tongues met and we were one.

His desire for me was so apparent and I wanted to show him mine. My hands explored him as his hands traveled a journey over me and when his tongue broke away from mine and slipped to my neck, I groaned. Because it felt so good. But I groaned because I wanted his lips back.

And so, I found him and kissed him again as he pulled me from the wall, then without leaving my lips, lifted me into his arms. He carried me to the bed and with the gentility of a gentle man, he laid me down. I opened my eyes to find him hovering over me, staring. He spoke no words, at least not with his lips. But with his eyes, he asked. And I answered by moving my lips to his once more.

When he laid his body on top of mine, it was as if we were a perfect fit, like he was the missing piece to the puzzle that was my life. Like we were supposed to be.

I guess that was why I gave no more thought to anything beyond the two of us and this moment. All I had to give, I gave to Blu. And with my tongue, I gave him all the permission he needed to proceed.

He accepted my offer and kissed me with a fervor that he hadn't before. As our tongues danced, his hands made their way around to my back and I lifted up to give him access. He eased the zipper on my gown down, down, down, but then, he paused and pulled away from me.

He slipped the gown from my shoulders, but in the slowest of motions, gliding the straps across my skin. I stared back at him wondering if he were savoring this time or giving me a chance to change my mind.

I sat up, tugged the gown to my waist, then leaving him on the bed, I stood and wiggled until the dress slipped over my hips, then floated to my ankles. He gasped as I stepped free of the gown, his eyes bright with appreciation as he drank in my copper-colored bra and matching panties that were almost the same tone as my skin.

After a moment, he stood. "You. Are. Beautiful." His hands trembled a bit when with just his finger, he touched the lace on my bra. No, he didn't touch it, he caressed it, and through it, he caressed me. His finger was a feather as traced it along my skin, following the edges of my bra and sending a surge of sensations through every part of me.

I watched him, watching me and while his fingers moved, his eyes didn't. He stayed steady and so sensual. Sexier than any kiss. With his feather-touch, he teased me and made me want him in ways that I never remembered wanting a man.

His voice was husky when he said, "You are everything I ever imagined you would be."

I wanted to ask, had he been thinking about me? Enough to imagine this? But I never got the chance, because his lips were back to mine. And this time he devoured me as if I were his last meal. This time, he didn't play. He unhooked my bra and I wiggled it off until my breasts were set free. Then, he did the same to my panties and I shimmied until they were on top of my gown.

Only then, did he step back and stare.

Only then, did I notice that I was the only one naked.

I reached for his shirt, but he gently pushed my hand away. Instead, as I stood and he stared, he unbuttoned his shirt and slid it over his shoulders before he unfastened his pants — a striptease, just for me. I had no idea how his briefs and socks disappeared, but in a moment, he stood with me — naked heart to naked heart.

It was my turn to gasp as my eyes swallowed in all of him. Swallowed in how much he wanted me.

But then, he took my hand and led me away... from the bed.

No! That's what I cried inside, but no words came out because the vision that he was made me mute. All I wanted to do was see, not speak. All I wanted was to touch and never stop. But I followed him as he led me into the bathroom and to the shower stall. I tilted my head as he turned on the water. He stepped inside first, then beckoned me to come with him.

There was no hesitation inside of me. No thoughts of my hair, no thoughts of anything except for this black man named Blu who had given me the starring role in my fantasy.

Inside the shower stall, he pressed me against the wall and as the shower's rain soaked my skin, Blu kissed me, then licked the droplets away, every drop from everywhere. His tongue was fire against my skin and the water that dripped down onto me did nothing to extinguish the blaze.

I moaned, I groaned, I screamed in ecstasy, completely, spent in...what....two minutes?

But he was not done. Twisting me around, he pressed me against the wall and then lathered my body with soap from the dispenser. It was a body massage that sent me up the stairway, right to heaven's door. I swore I even heard angels' bells ringing.

By the time he took the shower head down and rinsed me, I should have been given a medal for the fact that I was still standing. His hands helped the water wash away the soap and when he replaced the shower head, I reached for the soap, my turn to give him a massage so that I could feel every part of him.

But he pulled my hand back and away. He shook his head. "Tonight is all about you."

He swooped me into his arms and I was so grateful. Because what he'd done to me had made me quiver, but the words he'd just spoken, had weakened my knees.

Outside of the stall, he wrapped me in a towel, then carried me, once again to the bed. He gave me a gentle kiss before he lifted up and moved away from me.

"No," I said because that was the only word I could think of.

He smiled. "I'm not going anywhere. But you know me." And then, as if he knew where everything was in the room, he plugged in his phone.

Before the first note played, he held himself up over me and pressed his lips to mine.

Let me hold you tight

If only for one night….

Luther sang our favorite song, and we swooned together. I pressed myself against him, realizing that no matter what I did, I would never get enough of this man. My hands traveled the terrain of his skin, my desire was to feel every part of Blu.

With each step of this dance, he took away my ability to breathe. I needed air, so I tried to inhale him.

I was ready to plead, to beg, to push him off of me and get down on my knees and pray for him to take me. "Please," I whispered in his ear.

He granted my plea. I screamed out as he filled me up. I moaned and stayed still for a moment because I wanted to keep this feeling with me forever.

And then.

With the part that made him a man, he gave praise to me as a woman.

"Open your eyes," he whispered.

And I was surprised when I was able to do so. And I was surprised at the way staring at him while he filled me so was amazingly sexy.

We danced and danced and danced, until we began to sing. Luther tried to sing with us….

Till the early dawn

Warms up to the sun

But we didn't dance to Luther's rhythm anymore. We had our own, our bodies, our movements, our all, in sync.

So I wasn't surprised when I called out to my creator at the same time that Blu did. And I wasn't surprised that we walked through that heavenly door — together.

It would be so nice...if only for one night.

For a moment, we just laid there as if we both were trying to figure out if the beauty of what just happened was real. And once we realized it was, Blu rolled away and held me — my back to his front, pressed together as if our bodies wanted to be one for real, one forever.

And Luther sang and sang and sang.

"I wish...." Blu began, but then he stopped.

I smiled. Because I wished, too.

And then, he fulfilled my dreams when he said, "I wish that you were mine."

We laid in the stillness, his words wrapping around me like the duvet Blu pulled up over us. And then held me as if his wish would come true. I closed my eyes and fell into a perfect sleep.

Because now, our connection was complete.

CHAPTER 20

Blu

It had been a beautiful night. A beautiful night that left so many questions and I didn't have a single answer.

Me and Angelique.

Where would we go from here?

I glanced at the clock on the dashboard — 6:27. I had kissed Angelique goodbye exactly thirty-seven minutes ago after I had finally found the fortitude to peel myself away. That was the way I felt. Like I was the skin that had been peeled away, but the fruit, the good part, had been left in that hotel room.

What had I done?

I slowed my car as I approached the street to my house, but at the last second, instead of making the right turn, I pressed the accelerator and continued straight. I needed a few more moments. I had time — this was Sunday morning, and Monica nor the kids would be up this early.

Swerving my car to the edge of the curb, I stopped, turned off the ignition, then leaned back and closed my eyes.

I rolled over it all in my mind. It was a set-up. Everything had been a set-up that led to the moment of last night.

Everything — from playing *Words With Friends*, to our chats, to sharing coffee, dinner, and then, the best time, sinking our feet together in the sand last night.

It had been a set-up that could only have one logical conclusion.

Only that had never been my plan. Yes, I was so attracted to Angelique, from the very beginning, loving her mind before I'd even seen her body. But it was the fact that we could never be that made me think we'd be safe. Made me think that we could go to the edge. We could flirt, hang out together and even share a kiss, though not too often. But it would never go further than that.

Only it did. Because when she walked into that hotel room and didn't see her husband, her heart cracked and all I wanted to do was put it back together. Not that she had told me that was what happened when she opened that door. But I knew...because we were that connected.

I sighed. Really, I wanted to remember all of last night, but it was difficult to shift my mind from that moment when she stood before me, the first time I ever saw her that way. Clearly, she had been sculpted by God, one of His master pieces of art.

There was that moment, and then all that followed. It had taken everything not to make love to her right in that shower. But I didn't want the night to be about me. I wanted to make love to her before I even entered her. But then, that moment, when our connection became complete....

I moaned all over again remembering the way she gave all of herself to me. And then...we slept together. But I'd had to open my eyes, eventually. Knowing that I couldn't stay till the morning's light. When Angelique stirred in my arms, I knew she was awake too:

My body wanted to fall...or should I say fall again. Because I'd already fallen for Angelique and now I wanted to fall into a deep sleep. But I knew I couldn't. So, I didn't allow myself to really sleep. I just drifted a bit, holding Angelique through the night.

But I must have felt like I was home in that hotel room because when I opened my eyes, I glanced at my watch. 4:13. I couldn't believe that my phone was still playing Luther, and I couldn't believe it was already time for me to leave.

I whispered in Angelique's ear, just in case she was asleep, though our connection told me that she'd awakened, probably at the moment, when I had. "I need to go."

"I know."

After that, there was nothing. I didn't move, Angelique didn't move. Luther just sang. It had taken me exactly ninety-two minutes to have enough fortitude to pare myself away from her. She lay in bed, watching me as I jumped into my clothes. There was no way I was going to make this a long goodbye. Because if I did, I would never leave.

So I moved quickly until all my clothes were in place. Then, I paused. And looked at this woman. Even though her hair was no longer in any kind of style and her make-up was gone, she had never looked more beautiful to me.

Leaning over, I kissed her forehead because her lips would have been a trap. I said, "I'll call you."

And she nodded.

I turned and marched through the door, never looking back because that would have been another trap that would have kept me with Angelique forever....

Opening my eyes, I shook away those memories because it was time to go home to my wife.

Turning on the ignition, I made a quick U-turn and within seconds, I pulled my Mustang to a stop in our driveway. I stared at the front of our house that was illuminated a bit by the beginning rise of the sun.

My house looked the same, but I wondered if now my home would be different.

I was somber as I slid out of my car, then made my way to the front door. The house was as quiet as it was dark, save for that rising sun seeping its light through the blinds.

Moving toward the staircase, my plan was to check on my children, then get a couple of hours of sleep on the sofa, but a voice stopped me cold.

"Glad you decided to come home."

I turned. I hadn't even seen her sitting in the living room. It took a moment for my feet to move, but I walked toward her, keeping my steps as natural as I could.

"Hey, babe." I leaned toward her, but she turned her lips away from me.

"It's almost seven in the morning and you think it's acceptable to come in at this time?"

"I'm so sorry," I said. I pecked her forehead anyway before I stood up straight. "I fell asleep over at Lamar's."

"And you couldn't call me?"

"Babe, if I was asleep, how could I call you?" I said.

Her eyes roamed over my tuxedo. "And so, you went to hang out at Lamar's dressed like that?"

"I went over to Lamar's after I left an awards dinner that my company asked me to attend — last minute. They'd bought a couple of seats, but it turned out that the partners couldn't go. And since I'm trying to make partner...."

She squinted as if she were trying to see if my words were true.

I continued my lie, "It was a boring, rubber-chicken night, so I called Lamar when I finished." I shrugged. "I would have come home, but you were sleep when I got the call and when I left. So...."

I stood there as if I were telling the truth. And I hated every moment of this.

"I'm trying to understand how you think this is acceptable. To come home like this."

I hated this interrogation, but I was so grateful that Monica wasn't screaming. It was like...this was a regular conversation.

"It's not acceptable, Monica and I apologize. I should have called you when I first got over there." I stepped to her, then, knelt in front of her knowing that I needed to put some kind of seal on this deal. I took both of her hands into mine before I kissed them. "Look, babe. I'm really sorry and you have every right to be mad. Because I would be pissed if you had done that. So, I get it. I can't apologize enough and I'll make sure it never happens again."

Concern was her only emotion when she spoke, "When I woke up, I thought you were on the sofa. So, I came downstairs to talk. But when you weren't here, I called Lamar."

I held my breath for a moment.

She said, "But it just rang and rang."

He never answered his house phone, the number that Monica had. And for a moment, I wondered now, if I'd given her that number, all those years ago, on purpose.

I said, "Because Lamar was sleep next to me."

"Next to you?"

"You know what I mean. He was on one sofa and I was on the other."

She shifted on the couch, then shifted her eyes as if looking at me from another angle would expose my lies.

"You know what?" I asked, trying to get her glare off of me. "Why don't you go get dressed and I'll take you out for breakfast." Everything inside of me hoped that she gave her usual, 'I'm tired' response because I was exhausted. And I was grateful when my wife did not disappoint.

"I don't feel like going to get anything to eat. I've been up all night worrying. Now, I   need to get some sleep."

"That's understandable," I said. "You go on back to bed, I'll be in the office. I want to send an email about the banquet last night and then, I'll take the kids to breakfast when they get up."

She was already climbing the stairs and she looked over her shoulder. "Well, bring me something back."

I watched her as she made her way to the top, then sulked down the hallway to our bedroom.

I staggered into the family room and collapsed onto the sofa. My wife was never awake this early. And I'd never come sneaking into our home at this time. Yet, she was awake, and I'd sneaked in.

What was up with that?

And then, I thought — maybe God was trying to tell me something.

CHAPTER 21

Angelique

When I pressed the garage opener, I paused for a moment before I edged my car inside next to Preston's. I was hoping that my husband would've been gone somewhere — playing golf, back to the office, a trip to the moon...I didn't care. It didn't matter as long as he wasn't home.

I chuckled, but it was filled with bitterness. All of this time I'd wanted my husband to be home and now that he was, I needed him to be gone. Because I needed some time. I needed to figure out me and Blu.

I should have stayed at the hotel longer, asked for a later checkout — anything not to come home. But the thing was, once Blu left, the room lost all of its air and all of its light. I didn't want to be there without him. I didn't want to be anywhere without him.

So I'd gotten up the moment Blu left. And I stepped into the shower, closed my eyes and remembered last night.

As the water ran over me, I relived the moments and wondered how I hadn't known — how did I not know that I'd been missing so much? Preston was a good lover, or so I thought, though it was hard to remember.

But what Blu had done, what we had done. Our bodies were meant to be together. Our souls were meant to mate.

And then, it dawned on me...we hadn't used protection. Who had unprotected sex in 2017? My desire for Blu had made me lose my good sense. Next time, I'd be prepared.

Next time.

I couldn't believe that I was thinking about a next time.

I sat in my car for a little while, trying to push aside all thoughts of this time and the next time. Preston had heard the garage door open — it wasn't silent. He knew I was home. Surely, he was inside planning what he would say to me. And that was why I was sitting in the garage because I needed to know what I would say to him.

When he said that he was sorry, would I tell him about Blu? When he asked me how did the event go, would I tell him about Blu? When he wanted to know what I did afterward, would I tell him about Blu?

Would I tell him about Blu?

Of course, I would not.

He's my soulmate.

Could it be? Could this be my chance for a lifetime of happiness?

He's married.

I sighed. No matter what happened from here, that would always be the thing that would bind me. Blu belonged to another woman. So could I ever be happy if I were the cause of that destruction, even with what I'd already done?

I wish you were mine.

Remembering his words made me want to shift my car into reverse and drive around the entire Northside until I found Blu's home. I wanted to go claim him, tell him that I wished that he were mine, too.

But I did the sensible thing, the realistic thing. I pushed open the SUV door, jumped out, ready to face my husband. Glancing at my suitcase in the backseat, I decided to just leave it there for now, not even having the energy to carry it inside.

I hesitated before I pushed open the door from the garage to our home and when I stepped inside and through the mud room, the first thing I noticed was the blue box. On the kitchen table. Another gift.

Stepping over to the table, I lifted the box and twisted it from side to side. Whatever was inside this box wasn't cheap and I found the greater Preston thought the violation, the better the gift. He knew he messed up, only this time, he had no idea how much. He had no idea that last night a man had taken more than what was between my legs.

I moved through the walkway, past the dining room and toward the living room. I wasn't looking for my husband; it would have pleased me if I didn't have to see him, at least not today.

But I found him in the living room, standing in front of the bay window. Two glasses, of what looked like mimosas, in his hand.

We stood there for a moment, staring at each other. I was a bit surprised that his expression matched mine. His face was stiff, absent of a smile. I'd expected him to personify joy right now. To try and make me believe that I didn't feel the hurt inside my heart.

I took the first step. I moved toward him and then noticed what he was wearing: black pants, though just his T-shirt. As if he'd started undressing and then, stopped. "Hello," he said and held out one of the glasses for me.

"Hi," was my only response. Well, it was my only verbal response. I took the glass from him and without taking a single sip, placed it on the table next to Preston.

His glance followed my movements and then, his eyes found mine again. He said, "So, I guess you're really upset with me."

I shrugged, turning away from him. What I wanted to do was just go up to our bedroom, crawl into the bed, close my eyes, and dream. But first, I needed to tell Preston what he'd done to me, to us. Maybe not about Blu, but I wanted my husband to know how he'd made me feel…and the only reason I wasn't still crying in bed was because of Blu. I was going to leave that part out, but everything else, he needed to know. But when I whipped around to face him, I was so weary that all I said was, "I'm not upset."

"Oh, yeah." He nodded. "You are." He stated that as if it were a fact, as if he were in my head. "You're mad about me not making it last night and Angelique, I had a really good reason."

"You always do."

"It was work, and you know it. It was unplanned and you know that, too. And if there was any way for me to be there, Angelique, you know I would have been."

I raised my hands, feeling so helpless because his words never changed. "Like I said, Preston, you always have a reason. You always have an excuse as to why I come in second, third, fourth place, why everything else in your life comes before me."

My plan had been to stand here, to give him more than just a piece of my mind; I wanted to give him my whole brain. But we'd had so many of these discussions. The same words, the same emotions. Nothing was ever going to change. And not only that, Blu had shown me....

He's my soulmate.

I shook my head. This wasn't about Blu. This was about Preston and me. But Preston and me...I was so done, at least talking about this right now. I needed time and space. Time to figure this out, space for my emotions to stop shooting around inside of me. I felt such love, I felt such hate. For two men. I needed to get away.

I spun around ready to stomp out of the room.

Until.

"Is that why you've put another man before me, Angelique? Is that why you had another man in your bed last night?"

There comes a time in every life when one must die.

I had no idea why that was my first thought. My second one was what would happen if I clicked my heels three times. And my third thought was about something that Sheryl always told me:

"Men-Admit-Nothing."

Clearly, I wasn't a man. So, I turned around and faced my husband.

It was amazing what had happened in the five, six, or seven seconds that had passed since Preston had flung those words into our atmosphere. It was amazing how one's eyes could go from normal to bloodshot. That was what happened to Preston. Or maybe his eyes had been that way when I walked into the room and I hadn't noticed because there was such anger in mine.

But now his red eyes glared at me filled with more hurt than fire. Slowly, he placed his glass on the table and I followed his movements. I followed every gesture, every blink because

I had no idea how to react in a situation such as this. I had no idea what he would do, what I should do.

He stood straight, said, "I was so sorry when I couldn't get there for you, Angelique. I could hardly sit through my meeting. But I did because it was about business. And this was an important contract. Then, right after it was over, I rushed to the hotel. You know why I was able to do that, Angelique? Because I was already wearing my tuxedo." He glanced down at his pants.

That was when I noticed — his pants to one of his tuxedos.

"I went to a business meeting wearing a tuxedo so that I could get straight to you." Now, he shook his head. "I prayed that I would get there in time for at least the end of the program. But even if I missed that, I wanted to spend the night with you." He paused. "Because I wanted to be there, as soon as we ended, I called you. I called and called your cell."

My cell. Turned off. Because I didn't want to hear another excuse from him.

"I wanted you to know that I was going to be there."

The lump in my throat expanded with shock and fear…and guilt. Because his hurt was so apparent.

"Why, Angelique?"

There were so many tears in his voice that my knees buckled, but I broke my fall; I grasped the back of the chair, thankful that our Feng shui designer had placed it right by the door for a time such as this. Holding onto the back of the chair, I edged around until I lowered, first my butt, then my head, my eyes.

"Why, Angelique?"

The fact that he repeated let me know his question wasn't rhetorical and I wanted to respond, truly, I did. But when nothing came out of me, Preston filled in the why for me. He said, "Were you just that unhappy with me?"

He spoke like he was incredulous. Like the idea that I was unhappy couldn't possibly make any sense.

Now I raised my eyes. "First, it didn't happen because you didn't come to the gala."

Now, he was the one who stumbled. His steps were short, almost drunken as he moved toward me, then he flopped onto the sofa. Sitting across from me, he rested his arms on his legs and leaned forward, though he kept his eyes away from me. His head bobbed, though I couldn't tell if he were nodding. But then….he looked up and his red-rimmed eyes were filled with a mist that made me gasp inside.

"I didn't know," he whispered. "I didn't know for sure."

He didn't know? What was he talking about?

"I saw you walk into the hotel last night. I watched you from the bar, walk in and then away from me with him. And it left me — kinda frozen because I couldn't believe what I was seeing."

Oh. My. God.

"But I told myself that he was coming right back down because I watched him, from the window in the bar…I watched him signal to the valet that he would be right back. But I was frozen because of the way he looked at you." He paused and I watched his Adam's apple rise. "The way you looked at him."

Preston. Saw. Me.

"I should have called out. I should have run after you. And if I had to do it again, I would…I think. But I was just frozen from such shock." He paused. "But if I had stood up, then none of this would have happened." Now, he looked up. "Would it?"

I swallowed and then, tried to breathe because I needed the air to speak. But I could only release two syllables, "Preston."

"Or has this been going on...."

"No," I stopped him with my words and with the way I shook my head. "No, it..." I squeezed my eyes shut. "No. Never before. Ever."

He nodded just a little and he blew out a long breath. "Still, I should have called out because if I had...."

"Preston."

"I called your room, you know."

I closed my eyes. He called? I never heard the phone. And then, I remembered...the shower. And the angels' bells ringing....

"I called your room, then waited. Called your room, then demanded that the front desk give me a key. But you didn't have my name on the room and apparently, they give keys to no one — not even husbands." Red-rimmed, mist-filled eyes stared at me. "I guess they do that for protection." He took a breath. "Are you going to answer me? Are you going to tell me why?"

How was I supposed to answer a question like that? But I told him what was inside my heart. "I have felt so," I paused and thought about Blu, "disconnected from you."

"And so you sleep with another man?" He shook his head like he couldn't believe it. "I don't know why you feel that way, Angelique. From the moment we met, we've been connected. I've wanted to live my life doing everything for you. I have never cheated, I've never looked at another woman. It's been all about work for me so that I can take care of you."

"But the way you take care of me...."

"I do it by giving you everything!" His voice rose and so did he. "I work hard so that I can give you the world —

diamonds, furs, a new car every two years." His arm swept through the air. "This is a five-thousand square-foot home," he said as if he wasn't sure that I knew. "And it's just for you and me."

"But listen to what you're saying, Preston," my imploring was all in my voice. "You've given me a list of material things. Yes, I have every *thing*, but what I haven't had in a long time is what I wanted most — and that is you."

"I asked you to be patient."

"And I have been. But this has been never-ending and it hasn't been worth it to me. God, I would rather you work for UPS than what you're doing at Wake Forest."

He shook his head. "I don't believe that. I thought you loved Wake Forest."

"No, I love you. And I supported you in your business because of that love. But for me, Preston, the happiest time in our marriage was in the beginning. When you struggled to make thirty-thousand dollars a year and when I made even less. And we would go to Waffle House for breakfast so that we could have a feast for five dollars, or we'd go to the all-you-can-eat buffet and stuff as much as we could inside my purse."

The glare on his face, the shaking of his head — my words were nonsensical to him.

I said, "That's when I was happy, Preston. Because it was just you and me, together all the time. I understand striving and I have supported you. But this has been crazy. We're not man and wife, we're business partners . We're not soulmates, we're roommates."

"You're not being fair."

"I have been fair for years. I've been patient and then when that ran out, I tried to do everything that I could to get your attention. Hell, I even ordered a stripper pole but never accepted the delivery because I didn't think it would matter."

"What do you want from me?"

I paused to give him a moment to think about his words. Because I'd been telling him for years and we'd just spent these minutes...but still, he couldn't hear me. "What I want Preston, is your time, your attention. But it seemed like you just didn't have that to give...at least not to me."

He nodded. "And...he...did."

I didn't want to talk about my soulmate with my husband. "It wasn't like that, Preston. It was..."

"Oh, no." He held up his hand. "I don't need to know the details."

I lowered my eyes once again and nodded. And massaged my fingers. When I looked up, he was staring at me.

He said, "I can't believe you did this to us."

I wanted to say I was sorry, but to this point, I hadn't told Preston any kind of lie. So, I pressed my lips together and kept the truth inside.

In the silence, he stared, and as the quiet became louder, I watched the metamorphosis of his emotions. It played right in front of me. His face had been stiff, but his hurt had been evident. Now, though, fire burned behind his eyes, in the flare of his nostrils, in the curling of his lips. His hurt had been displaced.

"I have to get out of here." He moved past me, grabbed his keys from the console in the foyer.

I popped up from the chair. "Where are you going?"

He didn't look back. "I don't know."

"What...what...do you want me to do?"

Now, he turned, now he looked at me. The one thing I could say about Preston was that while I'd hadn't felt his love in a long time, I could always see it in his eyes. That was what kept me. But it wasn't there now. "I don't give a damn what you do." And then, he stomped out of the front door. As if going through the kitchen to the garage would make him have to spend too much time in this place with me.

For the longest moment, I just stood there, staring at the door that he'd just slammed. And then, I stumbled to the staircase. But I didn't have the energy to move up the stairs. So, I just sat down at the landing, held my face in my hands.

And I didn't shed a single tear.

CHAPTER 22

Blu

The memory of Saturday night with Angelique consumed me. I fell asleep with it on Sunday, woke up with it yesterday. And now, it had followed me onto the basketball court today with my boys.

"Negro, get your head in the game!" Lamar shouted at me. "You're the one who called us out here." He dribbled the ball coming at me. "Who does that in the middle of the week anyway?"

"Tuesday isn't the middle of the week," I said, posting up in front of him, determined that he wasn't going to score on me again.

"Whatever." Lamar dribbled the ball between his legs, then crossed the court like I wasn't even there, hit a bank shot, then bumped fists with Terrence.

"Ah, man!" Reggie, who was on my team, threw his hands up in the air. "You really half-ass playing tonight."

Lamar and Reggie were right. We were at our favorite place to have a pickup game, the neighborhood court by Lamar's house. Usually, I loved these get togethers, called by any one of us. It was a chance to hang with my boys and get a good workout in, but today, my mind wasn't in the game. It was hard to focus on dribbling when I was in such an internal battle between right and wrong.

"I'm out, bruh," I said, walking past Lamar and leaving my three friends on the court. "Got some stuff I need to work out in my head."

Lamar looked like he wanted to protest, like he was about to say something smart. But the expression on my face must've made him have a different thought because he turned to Reggie and Terrance and said, "Yo, it's a wrap. We gotta bounce."

"How you bouncin' in the middle of a game?" Terrance asked.

"Look at it this way, we won, Terrance. Reggie and Blu forfeited." He laughed.

There had been many times in my life when I was grateful to have Lamar as a friend, and I would have to add this time to my list. He knew me. He knew that I needed some time, probably needed to talk.

Terrance grabbed his ball and his bag, bumped fists with all of us and then strolled out of the park. But Lamar and Reggie followed me to the bleachers. I sat back on one, Reggie took the one above me and Lamar straddled the one I was sitting on and faced me.

Without me saying a word, Lamar went in, "I swear you should be the poster child for the 'It's Complicated' status on Facebook."

Since our first talk, I'd been filling Lamar in on every part of the progression of my relationship with Angelique, though I hadn't told him about Saturday....

He said, "So which woman is it?"

While I'd shared this with Lamar, Reggie didn't know a thing and his confusion showed in the way he squinted his eyes and tilted his head. "Which woman?" He chuckled. "Not Faithful Freddy," Reggie quipped. "I know the last good man standing ain't stepping out."

"Ahem," Lamar coughed and pounded his chest. "Blu ain't the last good man. I'm here. Just because you're the head of the canine club, don't lump us in that cage with you."

Reggie waved him off and Lamar turned back to me. "So is it Monica or Angelique?"

I shook my head, then nodded. That was how confused I was. "Both."

"Ah, man." Lamar threw his hands up in the air. "I get Monica being all in your head, but Angelique? I don't know how a woman you ain't sleepin' with is giving you so much mental grief."

And there was silence.

Lamar cocked his head, Reggie cocked his head, and the silence got so loud that it gave my secret away.

"You have?" Lamar whispered, though he didn't give me a chance to lie. He said, "You have!" and shook his head.

While Lamar's head was lowered, Reggie raised up. "Welcome to the wild side, my brother," he said, reaching out to give me some dap.

I let out a long sigh and left Reggie hanging. "I know this may sound sappy but this isn't about sex with Angelique. I have never stepped out on Monica before, never planned to, never wanted to, not even with all that we've been through." I shook my head. "But Angelique, she's different. It's like we have this," I didn't want to say it again, but I had no other word, "connection. We have this deep connection."

"Bruh," Lamar began, "don't start talking like you're in love. That ain't love. You've been standing by Monica and battling her illness. Your wife left you out there high and dry.

So this is nothing more than the first piece of outside ass that you've ever had. You're sprung, but just for the moment. It'll pass."

"I feel like I'm missing pieces of this story." Reggie frowned.

I ignored Reggie, but shifted a bit so that I was looking at Lamar face-to-face. "First of all, you're gonna have to slow your roll on being disrespectful to Angelique." Lamar's eyes widened a bit. "She's not a piece of outside ass. Secondly, I've been having problems with Monica for a while now, and there has never been a woman who I even wanted to talk to. Check my phone...I don't collect numbers. I ain't into all of that. I was into my wife, my family. No one ever made me want to risk everything."

Lamar held up his hands as if my words had made him surrender.

I nodded. "But then, I met Angelique and she makes my heart smile. She makes every part of me smile."

"I bet." Reggie laughed.

"I'm not talking about all of that. Seriously, this is like a mind thing with Angelique, but I'm so...I don't even know the word. Confused, maybe. Because there is no doubt in my mind that I love Monica." I paused and then, repeated that truth. "I love my wife."

"I tried that line with my last girl," Reggie shook his head, "and it didn't work. She told me that I must not have loved her too much if I could step out on her so easily."

"It wasn't easy. It wasn't planned." I paused as another truth settled in my heart and then, I spoke that one aloud. "And I would do it all over again."

"Wow!" Lamar and Reggie said together.

Reggie leaned back. "Just make sure you're playing it safe. The last thing you need is an outside kid."

"Now on that, you're an expert." Lamar laughed since Reggie had four kids by three different women.

I groaned. I hadn't even thought about that. Angelique and I felt so connected - so natural, that I don't think either of us thought of that. I wanted to slap myself. That was a bit of information I definitely wouldn't be sharing with my boys or I'd spend the rest of the conversation getting roasted.

Lamar turned back to me and added, "Look, I get it. It's like you've been dehydrated and someone comes along and offers you a tall glass of water," he said. "Or was she more like a shot of tequila?"

Lamar was my boy, but I wanted to punch him in his face when he bumped fists with Reggie and they both laughed at my pain.

But then, Reggie said, "Or maybe she wasn't a glass of water or a shot of tequila. Maybe she's just your soulmate and you're just now meeting her."

His words stopped everything. I mean, everything: I didn't move, Lamar didn't move, the air didn't move. It was right at dusk and the streetlights hadn't yet come on, but it seemed like a spotlight focused in on Reggie.

Finally, Lamar broke the silence. "Ah, bruh, don't tell me you believe in soulmates?"

Reggie shrugged. "Personally, I only deal in *sole* mates, chicks who fit my needs at the moment, like a good pair of Jordans." He was the only one who laughed.

"Bruh, for real?" I asked.

"But," Reggie continued, seriously this time, "I believe the universe is responsible for specific people coming together at a specified time. So the term, soulmate, is not just some

216

rationale for understanding or justifying the depth of intimacy in a highly compatible relationship, the term signifies the reality of such a situation."

We stared at Reggie for more than a couple of seconds, then both of us busted out laughing.

"Negro, is you high?" Lamar asked.

Reggie patted his pocket. "Not yet, but I will be. But I don't need to be high to spit this knowledge." He leaned forward like he was serious about schooling us. "Women fall into five specific categories." He counted off on his fingers: "Hit it and quit it, friends, friends with benefits, life partners, and then the ultimate, soulmates."

I stared at Reggie because he didn't sound high at all. But, the thing about him was that he never got philosophical without being stoned out of his mind.

Our expressions of bewilderment made him shrug, but he still flashed a smile. "Y'all can discredit me all you want, but your boy knows what he's talking about. I'm the only one among us who's had a woman in every one of those categories — well four of them. I'm still looking for my soulmate. The one who will make me put all the other women aside."

Lamar shook his head. "Man, soulmate ain't a category. It's an adjective. It describes compatibility. So you can have a soulmate who's a friend, one who's a friend with benefits, and definitely one who's a life partner," he said. "You can have multiple soulmates, but I don't believe that God's out there designing that one," he used air quotes, "who's for you and only you. It's like a buffet. You choose what you want and when you're ready, you make her the one."

Reggie wagged his finger back and forth. "Ah grasshopper, that's where you're wrong and I can prove it." Reggie turned to me like he was about to use me in a science project. "So, you love your wife, right?"

My plan had been not to fall into his trap. I didn't really want to be a part of this conversation, but when he asked that question, I had to tell the truth. "Of course I do. I really do. I love Monica with all my heart."

"Do you love this Angelique, chick?"

I paused. "I wouldn't call it love, I don't think. I mean, I don't know her well enough to say I love her. We've only been in each other's presence," I had to pause and count, "three times, no four times. But I have some intense feelings for her. We're compatible in everything — from sports to books, to TV shows and movies. And then, there's the music. She loves what I love. We laugh like we've known each other forever and we can even finish each other's sentences. If I could read her mind, I'd bet we had the same thoughts. And then, there's this...I can't stop thinking about her and wanting to be with her." I stopped again, long enough to let another thought settle on my heart. "No, I don't think I love her, but I could. And if I spent any more time with her, I would."

Reggie held his hands up in the air like a referee signaling a touchdown. "Yeah, bruh. She's definitely on the line of being your soulmate. You know how I know?" He didn't give me any room to ask him how. "'Cause you listed all these things and didn't even mention what was going on between her legs."

I cringed at his crassness, even though that was the truth. I loved making love to Angelique. There was a passion with her that I hadn't felt with Monica, at least not a passion that I could remember. We just...fit together. And Saturday night, we connected. But while the sex made me want to go back for more, that wasn't what was most important with her.

Reggie continued, "Now, all we have to do is figure out which category she falls into."

"Are you kidding me?" Lamar said. "So you have soulmate categories, too?"

He nodded. "Take notes and learn something today, my brother."

He laughed, Lamar shook his head, and I stayed with my eyes on Reggie. Because even though he was my good-time friend, it seemed that there was more to him than just getting high, chasing women, and playing ball. I'd known him for what, fifteen years? I'd never seen this side of him.

Reggie continued, "There are actually three different kinds of soulmates. First, there's the life lesson soulmate, the woman we think we want, but she's just there to teach us a lesson. With these women, love isn't always enough, love can't keep you together because you're not meant for anything more than the lesson. You feel connected, compatible, but it's not for life."

I wondered — was that what Angelique was to me? Was she only here for a lesson?

Reggie said, "Next, there's the forever soulmate. She's your platonic friend that you will always be connected to, but there will never be any romance. But the friendship is strong. You may not see or speak to her for weeks, months, sometimes even years, but when you connect again, it's like yesterday. Not a beat was missed."

I couldn't imagine that with Angelique. I wouldn't want to be apart from her for weeks, or months, or years. I couldn't stand the fact that we hadn't communicated much at all since Saturday. I'd sent her a text on Sunday because I didn't want her to think she was part of Reggie's first group — the hit it and quit it clan. I didn't know what this was that she and I had, but I wanted Angelique to know that whatever, I was in this with her.

But when I'd texted asking her if she was okay, she'd texted back that she needed a couple of days. I got that. I needed those days, too.

"And finally," Reggie said, cracking through my thoughts, "there's the 'right time' soulmate. This woman brings out the very best in you and you meet each other precisely when you're both ready, not a moment before or a moment after. She's everything that the other two have, but she has the right time. Because we all know that timing is everything." Then, he leaned back on the bleachers like he'd just given his dissertation.

Lamar chuckled, but I didn't. I was too deep into my thoughts and that must've bothered Lamar because he said, "Man, don't listen to Reggie. This dude watched three episodes of Doctor Phil and now he's your relationship guru. You know all that weed has punished this dude's brain. Real talk, how do you know it's not infatuation you're feeling, like when Raven gets a new toy. You're always joking about how she plays with her new doll all the time, taking it to bed with her and everything, but by week three, she can't even find it anywhere in the house. Maybe Angelique is your new toy and you're just a kid who's never had a toy before."

I shook my head. "She's not a toy." That I knew for sure. "Listening to Reggie...."

"Ah, man, don't say it...."

"She's my soulmate."

"Boom!" Reggie shouted.

Lamar slapped his hands on his legs. "Didn't I just tell you not to say it?"

"But I had to." I thought for a moment. "Because I think it's true."

While Reggie grinned, Lamar asked, "Okay, so what about Monica?"

"She's my wife," I answered right away. "The woman I love and the one I'm supposed to be with. And I would never want to hurt her."

"Too late for that, bruh," Lamar said.

I tried to ignore that truth. "I just feel," I began, "that Angelique was created for me."

"Man," Lamar waved his hand in the air, "that's some let-me-try-to-justify-my-cheating bull if I ever heard it," he said. "You just trying to eat two cakes. I'm sure her husband thinks she was created just for him."

"Wait. Hold up. Stop everything." Reggie moved to the edge of the bleacher. "She's married?"

I nodded.

"What the hell?"

"See," Lamar jabbed his finger at Reggie, "this is why you didn't need to be talking all that soulmate bull to this dude. She can't be his soulmate when she belongs to someone else."

"Wow." Reggie looked at me as if my complicated life had given him new respect for me. "This is deep. Well, all I can tell you is that what it sounds like to me...."

"Shut up, Reggie," Lamar interjected. "You've already messed up his head."

"Is that you," Reggie continued anyway, "are one of the few who have found two soulmates. Now all you have to decide is which soulmate you want to live the rest of your live with."

And right there, the one in my crew who never felt there was anything more important in life than finding new ways to get high, had just broken down the truth. He'd just thrown my dilemma right in my face.

We all sat there, quiet again, no kids around us since it was Tuesday night. Just a few passing cars, heading to their homes in the neighborhood.

But in that quiet, I had to face the facts. I didn't want to leave my wife. I loved her and she needed me. But the thing was, I didn't want to give up Angelique either. We were on this path of something that I'd never felt before, something that I really believed could be life-changing for me and hopefully for her, too.

But since I wasn't Reggie and since I wasn't in the business of hurting women, I had a decision to make. Seriously. A hard decision that had to be made now...that could not be put off for later.

CHAPTER 23

Angelique

I strolled from Sheryl's kitchen, cupping the mug of tea in my hands, feeling the warmth and loving it since every other part of me had felt so cold. It was like I couldn't stop trembling. Hadn't stopped since Preston had walked out on me two days ago.

Stepping out onto the covered patio, I sat on the love seat that was part of a four-piece ensemble that made Sheryl's outside look a lot like her living room. Tucking my feet beneath me, I sipped. And thought. The green tea was soothing, my thoughts were not.

Sipping and thinking was all that I'd been doing since Sunday when I called Sheryl and told her I needed a place to stay.

There was not even a moment of hesitation from my friend. All Sheryl said was, "Are you all right? "and "Do you need help packing?"

I'd told her yes and no, then grabbed a few pair of jeans, a couple of tops and stuffed my clothes into my weekender, right next to the toiletries that I didn't have to unpack from the weekend. Then, I made my way to Sheryl's, but not before I left Preston a note. It had taken me a minute to decide where to leave it and I'd finally settled on his pillow:

I'm going to Sheryl's for a few days to give you space, to give us space. Call me when you want to talk.

I sighed and placed the mug on the side table thinking about what I'd done after that. I'd taken my suitcase back into the car, slid inside and buckled up, put the car in reverse, when I had a thought. Really, it was more than a thought. It was a gnawing in my spirit. I'd set the car in park, jumped out, ran back inside and added: *I love you* to my note.

That was the truth. No matter what was going on now, no matter what would happen next, I loved Preston.

But then, there was Blu.

And all the things that he'd said to me:

A woman like you, I would shower with so much affection and attention that you wouldn't be able to breathe.

If I had a woman like you waiting for me at home every night....

I wish that you were mine.

The front door slammed, but I stayed in place, knowing that Sheryl would search for me. She didn't have to look very hard; this was where I'd spent most of my hours once I got here on Sunday and then yesterday when I wasn't finding solace from sleeping in her guest room.

"Hey," she said when she came to the edge of the patio door.

I glanced up. "Hey."

She looked me up and down as if she were my psychologist and she was studying me. She said, "You took a shower, you got dressed."

It wasn't a question, so I didn't answer. It was just her observation that I was already improving since I hadn't been able to do this much yesterday.

She sat down in the chair across from me. "You look good."

"I guess that's better than looking bad."

"It is." She sighed. "You know, I still can't believe it. I can't believe we're in this space."

I loved how she said 'we'. She'd been using 'we' and 'us' since I'd arrived. I wasn't even sure if Sheryl even noticed the way she spoke, but she was my girl and that was her heart telling me that I wasn't in this alone.

She continued, "All this time, I've been telling you that you needed to do something. That since Preston didn't appreciate you, you should leave…or do something. But not this." She shook her head. "Any decisions yet?" Before I could answer, she held up her hand. "I'm not rushing you, just want you to know that I'm here if you want to talk. Because talking is good."

"I know. It's just that it's hard to talk because then, I'll have to think. And it's hard for me to think when my heart hurts so much."

Sheryl nodded.

"I just can't get past how much I hurt Preston." I closed my eyes and shook my head, though that hadn't been enough in the last forty-eight hours. Shaking my head didn't erase the pain on Preston's face when I'd confirmed that I'd made love to another man."

"I know," Sheryl said.

"But what's worse, what makes guilt burn inside of me, is that even knowing how much I've hurt Preston and even though I really do love him, I still long for Blu."

She nodded. "Have you spoken to him?"

At first, I wasn't sure which 'him' she was referring to — but then, I decided that it was the 'him' she knew I wanted to talk about. "No. Except for answering Blu's text on Sunday…nothing. I took your advice, no contact while I'm trying to figure this out. No need to muddy water that's already so dirty." I shook my head. "This is so hard."

"It is hard. Because life is hard and relationships make life even tougher." Sheryl leaned forward. "But I want to ask you something."

I nodded, then braced myself for one of Sheryl's psychological questions that always went so deep. And she didn't disappoint. "What is it that you want, Angelique? If you could have everything that you want in this situation, not thinking about who would be hurt or how you could make it happen — what is it that you want?"

All I could give her was silence.

She said, "Don't overthink it. Don't say to yourself, 'Oh, that will never work.' What would be your perfect world?"

This time, I didn't hesitate. " In my perfect world, I'd have them both."

For the first time since Sunday, I laughed. Not because of what I said, but because of Sheryl's reaction. She almost fell out of her chair. Really. If she hadn't grasped the arm, I was sure that she would have slipped right down onto the deck.

"Well damn, girl," she said, her psychologist facade gone. "I never took you for a bigamist. You're just like a dude."

"No, I'm not. That's not what I meant. I would roll them together, create one man."

She gave me a side-eye.

"Look, you're the one who asked the question. You said my perfect world." I shrugged. "That's what I would do."

"Well, I guess I should have been more specific. I meant what would you do that's realistic?"

I waited a moment, swung my legs off the love seat, then leaned forward, almost mimicking Sheryl. "Remember the other day when you were talking about soulmates?"

She nodded.

"Not only did I listen to you, but from the bottom of my heart, I think Blu is my soulmate. At least it feels that way. When you described a soulmate, you described us. You described everything that I have with Blu. And even with all the love I've felt for Preston, I've never felt this way about him." I paused. "And just know that I'm not factoring in all the years of neglect from Preston. I'm talking about even in the beginning when Preston and I were really happy. Yes, I laughed with Preston, but when I laugh with Blu, I laugh from my soul. Yes, I talk to Preston, but when I talk to Blu, I talk to him from my soul."

"Wow, girl, this is deep," she said.

I guessed she'd never had a case like this before. "It is. That's why I can't understand it. I don't get why God would introduce me to this man."

"I know, the timing."

"It's more than the timing. It's Blu's wife. As much as I didn't want to hurt Preston, Sheryl, I'm not like this. I'm not the woman who doesn't care about other women. I'm not the woman who would go after someone else's husband. I'm not the woman who would want to be responsible for another woman's pain."

She leaned over and covered one of my hands. "It's not like you went after him."

"No matter how you describe it, or define it, he's married."

"But he's unhappily married."

"The adverb doesn't matter."

"Well…you're married, too."

"That does matter. And that's what makes this so bad. I saw Preston's pain, so I know what Blu's wife...." I stopped.

She sighed. "You know, I help couples through this all day long. But when it's right in front of your face with your friend." She shook her head. "I don't know, Angelique. I don't know how to advise you."

"You've been great — letting me stay here, helping me to talk this out, encouraging me to take my time and respect the space that we all need."

She nodded. "But you can't take too much time, or too much space. Decisions have to be made because of people's emotions. Four of you are in this."

"Well, let's hope it's just three. Let's hope that Blu's wife didn't find out the way Preston did."

She nodded. "I have another question."

"Oh, lawd. Haven't we gone deep enough today?"

"No." Then, she continued like the head doctor that she was. "You talk about Blu as your soulmate, but...do you love him?"

That made me pause.

I wish that you were mine....

"I don't know if I can say that I love him because I haven't known him long enough, but I believe that it wouldn't take much to love him."

She shook her head as if I fascinated her and I understood. My life — I'd always felt so ordinary. I was a wife, a mother-figure to many of the girls in my foundation. I was a friend, a businesswoman, a churchgoer. What I wasn't was an adulterer.

Until now.

It was sadly fascinating.

"So, are you going to tell Blu that Preston knows?"

I shrugged. "I don't know. I guess it depends on what it is that I decide that want. If I want to stay with Preston...."

She held up a finger. "But he might have something to say about that."

"I know. To be honest, I can't imagine Preston wanting to stay with me after this. I mean, if he had cheated on me...." Covering my face with my hands, I shook my head.

"So, does that mean you want to be with Blu?" When I peeked at her with one eye, she added, "Never mind." Then, she said, "But suppose Blu decides that he wants to be with you?"

I shrugged, not really sure of that answer.

"One of your challenges, Angelique, is that you're waiting for these men."

"No, I'm not."

"Well, you are kinda sitting around wondering if Preston is going to want you back or if Blu is going to stay with his wife." She shook her head. "I think you need to decide what you want and then make that happen. Decide what you want so that you're the one making the decision about your life." She held up her hand to stop my protest. "And I know what you're going to say — you could decide that you want one and he's the one who doesn't want you. But at least you'll be walking into each conversation knowing what it is that you want."

That made sense.

Suddenly, Sheryl popped up from the chair.

"What happened?" I asked.

She waved her hand and dashed into the house.

I shrugged, thinking that she probably had to go to the bathroom or she'd just remembered a call she had to make. I lifted my feet, tucked them back in place, and picked up my cup of tea that was lukewarm now. But I was too comfortable to get up and heat it in the microwave or make a new cup. So, I sipped the tepid tea and waited for my friend to come back and finish helping me to solve my life's problem.

A couple of minutes later, she did return. With a bottle of Stella Rosa and two glasses. And right away, I thought of Blu. But, I didn't say that to Sheryl.

"Here, this will definitely help the decision process."

She filled up the two glasses and then, we sipped, said nothing. Just thought.

And, of course, all of my thoughts were ones of Blu Logan.

CHAPTER 24

Blu

"I need to open a business. Lamar's Get Right Shop."

My friend's hearty laugh filled the speakers in my Mustang as I turned into my driveway. I'd been driving this car since Saturday, as if I were trying to live inside the memory of that night.

"I can't believe this is all that we talk about, bruh," Lamar said. "I wanna get back to our normal important conversations. Like when are the Rockets gonna finally get a team? And wouldn't it be great if the Texans went to the Super Bowl?"

As I turned off my car, I agreed with my friend. I longed for the days when we talked about nothing more than sports, music, and what was going on in the news. But since our pick-up game yesterday, I'd called Lamar about a dozen times, more in twenty-four hours than I'd spoken to him in a month. All because I needed to talk to someone as I was trying to figure out this maze that I called my life.

"I'm sorry to keep calling, but I'm just trying to talk this out, make it clear in my head."

"Hard to be clear when you love two women."

"I told you, I'm not saying that, but...."

231

"Yeah, one's your wife and the other's your soulmate."

"Look, you're the one who told me that I needed to get out. That I shouldn't be going through all of this."

He raised his eyebrows. "Man, is that why you're in this situation? Because of what I said? Bruh, you need better friends 'cause that was some bad advice."

This time, I laughed with him, even though my heart still ached with indecision.

"Why's life so complicated?" I said, finally easing out of the car.

"Because God ain't playing with us. He's like, 'if you want to get up here to heaven, you better get all your mess worked out down there, 'cause I ain't tolerating no drama.'"

I chuckled because, for a moment, I could actually imagine God saying something like that, telling me to handle my business 'cause that was what I sure needed to do.

Stepping into the house, I listened for sounds of my family. I knew Tanner was still at school with band practice, though Raven should've been home. She was probably hanging out in her favorite place — her room.

Dropping my briefcase into the kitchen, I headed to the patio; I'd check on Raven once I ended my call.

"One thing I didn't ask you yesterday," Lamar began, "are you staying with Monica because of the kids?"

I paused to really think about that. Then, "You know, that's a good question because a few times, I thought that was a reason to stay. But sometimes, I think that's a good reason to leave, too, and take the kids with me to get them away from her illness, like you suggested a while ago.

"But honestly, I love my wife. I don't love who she is now, but I know that the woman I fell in love with is still there inside of her. Beneath the depression and the medication. I just have to figure out if I can wait it out."

"And then, there's Angelique," Lamar said, bringing my complication back to me.

"Who makes me feel — don't laugh — warm inside."

"So does gas."

Even I had to chuckle at that.

"Well, all I can tell you is that you can't have a wife *and* a soulmate."

"That's what you say."

"Nah, bruh. I know there are guys out there who can carry that off, but that's not you."

I shook my head. Lamar had misunderstood my response, but I didn't correct him. I wanted to know — why couldn't your wife be your soulmate? Isn't that the way life was supposed to be? "Yeah, I'm not that dude," I responded to Lamar.

"Look man, I'd love to keep playing your psychologist, but since you ain't payin' me, I got my own life and my own wife and she's beginning to give me the stinky-eye because of all the time I'm spending on the phone with you."

I laughed. "Go take care of your wife. Catch you later." I clicked off the phone. At least I was smiling, though I was no closer to knowing what to do.

Just as I was about to put my cell down, my phone vibrated from an incoming text:

Can you talk?

I breathed in deeply. Angelique. Ready. To talk.

It took me a moment to reply:

Not right now. In a little while?

She replied: *I'm at my girlfriend's. U think u can drop by tonight?*

At her girlfriend's? What the hell? Was she staying there or was she just hanging out? Had something happened with her husband?

My stomach tightened when I glanced at my watch. It was almost six. I replied:

Can we do it around 6:30/7?

Cool. Here's Sheryl's address.

Sheryl. Her friend from the gala. What was going on?

I wanted to ask her so badly, but this couldn't be a text conversation. That fact didn't stop the questions in my mind — was she staying at Sheryl's? Had something happened with her husband? What were the implications of that?

Opening the *Words With Friends* app, I pulled up Angelique's profile and the moment I looked at her picture, my heart contracted. Like she was squeezing it, a reminder that she touched me in the very center of my being.

"Everything okay?"

I jumped and my phone crashed to the floor. I hadn't heard the patio door open and when I glanced up, Monica was standing right there. Looking over my shoulder. How long had she been there? Had she been reading my texts? Seen Angelique's picture?

Nah, she couldn't have been there that long.

As I picked up the phone, she said, "You seem nervous."

"I'm not; you just startled me." I stood and smiled. "I didn't hear you come downstairs." I glanced at Monica dressed in jeans and a white tailored shirt. She'd been dressed when I came home after the basketball game last night, too. "You look nice," I said.

She nodded. "I was thinking...I would come downstairs."

Such a simple statement that I knew had taken so much effort.

She said, "I ordered pizza…for dinner."

"That's good," I told her. It wasn't cooking, but it was a start since the kid's dinner had become my responsibility.

"I know it's only pizza. Maybe tomorrow…I can cook."

I smiled. "That would be great, sweetheart. You up to that?"

She nodded, though her tone sounded unsure. "Maybe if you can help me."

"I'd love to do that. We can cook together, just like we used, too."

Now she smiled, though hers looked a bit forced. Still I accepted it. "How was your day?"

I could not remember the last time she'd asked me that, and though the question sounded like it had come from a robot, I still responded, "Oh, it was good. What about you?"

"It was good…better."

"Are the kids upstairs?"

She nodded. "Raven is, Tanner is still at school."

My eyebrows raised. I knew that, but she knew that Tanner was still at school? She hadn't paid attention to the children's schedules in so long.

She glanced back at the house, looking as if she wanted to run back inside. "Can you pick up the pizza?"

"I sure can," I told her. "I'll pick it up, then drop it off. I need to…run by the office…for something."

She gave me a long look as if, she didn't believe me. But then, a moment later, she nodded and smiled again. "Okay. Well, I'm going…back inside…upstairs." She turned toward the door, then paused, took the few steps back to me, stood on her toes and kissed my cheek.

It was a quick peck before she scurried away, as if she weren't sure about what she'd just done.

I stood there for a moment. And finally smiled. Monica was unsure, but that was all right. Because I was sure enough. For both of us.

***

I edged my car to the curb in front of the address that Angelique had given to me, then sent her a text:

I'm outside.

Anticipation had me shaking. It was because of all of the thoughts in my head. On the drive over, I relived every moment of Saturday with Angelique, and then, the moment I just shared with Monica.

Let me hold you tight, if only for one night....

When Angelique stepped out of the townhouse, my heart did that squeezing, quickening thing again. But this time, it didn't make me smile. As she walked toward me in jeans and a white shirt (just like how Monica had been dressed) in my mind, I saw her — naked, giving herself to me.

And I sighed.

She opened the door to the Mustang and the moment she slid inside, I wondered if I should have driven my Tahoe.

"Hi," we said together.

I won't tell a soul....

I clicked off the music.

After a moment of silence, Angelique leaned over and kissed my cheek. That surprised me a bit, it was so open, such a public display...and it felt, so awkward.

Then, "How are you?" we spoke together.

I guessed she felt as awkward as I did.

We studied each other inside more silence. She was the first to ask, "Is everything okay?"

That was supposed to be my question. I nodded. "What about with you?"

She sighed. "I'm staying here with Sheryl."

I sucked in a lot of air. "Did you and Preston...break up?"

She was silent and very still for a moment. "No...not yet...I mean, I'm not sure."

I didn't have enough nerve to ask the next question, but from somewhere deep, the words came out. "What happened?"

"He found out...about us."

I wished I'd never asked. "You told him?"

It must have been the incredulity in my voice that made her eyebrows raise. Patience was peppered all through her tone when she said, "I'm not going to go into the whole thing, but I told him because I had to. He saw us."

My eyes widened and I wondered if I had the right to ask anything else. I wanted to know more.

She said, "He saw us enter the hotel and he never saw you leave."

Now, I nodded. A clearer picture in my head. "I'm really sorry, Angelique."

She tilted her head. "About what? About what happened or about Preston finding out?"

My answer came quick because I wanted her to know the truth about my feelings. "I never wanted to hurt anyone. Never wanted to hurt you or your husband or my wife. But...."

"But Saturday was special for us," she finished for me.

I nodded.

"To be honest, I don't regret it either. I regret hurting Preston, but...not you and me."

I breathed, grateful for her words. "So, what do you think is going to happen? I mean, you're going to try to get back with him, right? You're not going to walk away from him?"

I thought my words were simple, but the way she stiffened, I could tell that I'd offended her, somehow.

She squinted, though it was more of a frown. "Our connection, on Saturday and even before then has been special to me. It's been real, something I never felt before, but I would never just up and leave my husband…you're married," she said as if she thought I needed a reminder.

I exhaled relief. "I know." I took her hand and looked down at the way we fit. "We're married to other people, yet so connected to each other."

"We're married, yet we've both said things…."

She left it there and I had no idea where she was going. She paused as if she were thinking. And then, she said, "I wish…."

And, I remembered. What I said Saturday: *I wish that you were mine.*

It took a moment, but then I responded with what she'd told me on Saturday. "I wish, too."

She looked down and away from me, but she nodded as if she understood. She nodded as if she'd asked the question and I'd answered. Without a spoken word, she nodded. Because we were that connected. Soulmates. But I would never tell her that. Didn't want to complicate our hearts even more.

With my fingertips, I outlined the line of her jaw and we sighed together. Then, I guided her chin until she looked at me. A mist covered her eyes and I was surprised that I was able to see it through the mist that covered mine.

"I just want you to know that I've never felt this way about another woman."

"I know."

My hand cupped her cheek and my palm heated. "And, I'm so grateful that I met you."

"I know."

This time, I was the one to say, "I wish…."

"I know." She blinked and a tear trickled down her cheek. Still she smiled, receiving my message.

And then, she gave me her message. She leaned across the console and kissed me. She kissed me the way we kissed Saturday. That night, our bodies said hello, but there was no doubt that this was our goodbye.

When she leaned back, the tear that fell came from my eye and I swiped it away.

Now, she cupped my cheek. "Thank you, Blu Logan."

I nodded because I was afraid if I spoke, another tear would fall and what kind of man would I be? Damn — this woman had me out here in the middle of the street with the top down on my car, crying. I needed to buck up quick.

But I was gonna have to wait until she was gone. Because my eyes were still misty as she opened the door, slipped out, then did that little saunter up to her friend's front door that made me sigh and made me wish some more.

I wanted to shout out to her. Tell her to call me if she needed me. Because I didn't want her to feel like she was alone. I wanted to help her through this, whether she got back with Preston or not.

But telling her that, keeping our connection would only delay the inevitable. Would only hurt our hearts. Because I loved Monica, I loved my wife. And I was going to do whatever I could to put us back together and help her get well.

So, I had to say goodbye to Angelique. And just be grateful for this moment in time. Just be grateful for that one night.

Even after Angelique stepped inside her friend's home, I sat there for a moment watching the door. Thinking how simple this finale had been and if it were so simple, why was my heart so heavy?

I sighed, grateful this was over, then turned over the ignition. The Mustang roared and I wondered if I would ever want to drive this car again?

Glancing to my left, my eyes first hit my rear view mirror. And then, I looked up.

And saw the silver Infiniti across the street and the woman behind the wheel, staring at me.

The woman. My wife.

"Monica," I whispered her name.

Even from where I sat, I could see the water in her eyes. "Damn."

I slammed the car into 'park' and jumped out, leaving the Mustang running. "Monica!"

I watched her shift her gears, and then with tears streaming down her cheeks, she screeched away.

CHAPTER 25

Blu

Yesterday — six o' clock. Today — it was almost three. I counted the hours the way I'd been doing. Twenty-one hours. It had been twenty-one hours since I'd seen my wife.

And all I'd been doing in those hours was looking for her. I hadn't gone into work, I hadn't eaten, definitely hadn't slept. All I'd done was put on a facade for our children who didn't notice that Monica was gone at all.

But while I'd kept their life as normal as I could, I'd searched for my wife, calling every friend, driving by any place where I thought she might be.

And I called her phone...one hundred times. No, a thousand. More than that, thousands of times. I called her until I filled up her voicemail, apologizing, begging, telling her on every message, "I love you!"

But, she never answered.

The only thing that saved me — the text that she'd sent about an hour after she'd sped away from me:

I need time.

Her text was the only reason why I hadn't called the cops, though I wondered if I should have because of Monica's illness. Wouldn't that make her a priority with the police? I decided not to make that emergency call. That had been my decision last night. But if we got to twenty-four hours.....

My phone rang and I grabbed it from the passenger seat. But the picture that popped up on my screen, let me know it wasn't Monica.

Still, I answered, "What's up, Lamar?"

"Just checking on you. Any word from Monica?"

My best friend had been the first one I called and last night, he'd hit the streets with me. "Nah, just that one text. I'm going out of my mind with worry."

"I know you are, bruh, but she'll be home. I know it. She's just hurt."

Shaking my head, I said, "I can't believe this."

"I know, but in your defense, you were breaking it off with Angelique when she caught you."

If he were trying to be my attorney, he would've lost the case. He hadn't convinced me because I was guilty. What hurt the most was I had no idea of my offense. I had no idea how long Monica had been there, watching us. Had she seen the way I'd touched Angelique? Had she seen the way Angelique had kissed me?

Those memories made me groan. No matter how long she'd been there, she'd seen enough, seen too much. Enough, too much to make her speed away and stay away from me.

"So what you doing now?" Lamar asked.

"Still driving around. I've been checking every single hotel for Monica's car."

"How long you been out?"

"Just about all day. I gotta get back soon, though. The kids will be home and I don't...."

My phone beeped.

Monica!

I didn't even say goodbye to Lamar, I just clicked over.

"Oh, my God, Monica," I hyperventilated into my phone. "Oh, my God. I'm so sorry."

"Why?" was all she asked.

I wasn't sure what she was asking. Was she asking why I was sorry? Or why had I been with Angelique? Either way, I wasn't sure how to answer. What was the best approach? What would keep her safe, make her feel better, let her know how much I truly loved her?

I had no answers, so all I said was, "Baby, come home. Let's just talk."

"Do you love her?"

Even though I was driving, I closed my eyes for a second. "No, I don't."

"I don't believe you."

I frowned. For the first time, I noticed. Monica sounded groggy, like she was just waking up. Had she gone somewhere and just slept all day? "No, really, Monica. I love you."

Her voice was soft. "I saw you with her. I saw how you were together. You love her."

I shook my head, wishing to God that she could see me. Wishing to God that she were here so she could see the truth. "No, I don't."

"I wondered. I kept wondering. You didn't want to make love to me. Then, you called me by her name…."

"No…."

"Then, it was your phone. You were always on your phone. And you came home later…or not at all. I knew. That's why I followed you."

Oh my God! I thought Monica spent her days in bed, not thinking, not caring, not paying any kind of attention. But she saw, she knew.

"I knew, I just wanted to make sure. I had to see it for myself in order to get my heart to believe it."

Her voice was so soft, but still I could hear it — her hurt. And her hurt made me ache. "Please come home. I was out trying to find you, but I'll go home and wait for you and we can talk about this."

"I'm already at home," she said. "I wanted to come home for this. Goodbye, Blu."

She clicked off the phone, but still, I called her name. Tossing my phone onto the passenger's seat once again, I made a sharp U-turn, made the wheels of my Tahoe scream.

Monica was home and I needed to get there.

But, oh, my God. The way she sounded. Had I sent her into a deep depression forever?

"God, I hope not," I whispered.

And then, I prayed. I prayed and I called. Over and over. She never answered, but I kept calling.

I drove as if there were no traffic lights, no traffic signs, no speed limit. I drove until I was home, making that twenty minute drive in a little over ten. I breathed when I saw Monica's car in the driveway.

I jumped out of the car, and it wasn't until I hit the front door that I wondered if I'd turned off the ignition. But I didn't return to check. I just slammed through the door.

"Monica," I screamed as soon as I made it inside the house. When she didn't answer, I called her again and again, even as I took the stairs two at a time, even as I raced through the hall, to our bedroom.

The first thing I saw was Monica rolled up in the bed. I exhaled, until I rushed to her and saw her eyes. Open, but rolled back.

"Monica!" I shook her shoulders. "Baby, please." I lifted her into my arms, and then I stopped. Six bottles of pills lined up on her nightstand. "Oh, baby," I moaned.

"Dad?"

I glanced up at the sound of my son's voice and took in the sight of my children, just coming home from school. It was a curse that they were coming in now. It was a blessing that they'd come home together, something that only happened on Thursdays.

Still, the sight of them made me moan as I laid my wife on the floor.

To Tanner, I cried, "Son, get your sister out of here and call nine-one-one."

They didn't follow my orders. Both stood, stiff with shock, their backpacks still on their shoulders.

Tanner said, "Dad, what's wrong with mom?"

"Please son," I yelled, "just do what I said."

"What's wrong with mommy?" Raven was the first to move. She knelt over her mother. "Mommy? Mommy, wake up," our daughter cried.

"Dad, is mom dead?"

"Mommy's dead?" Raven screamed.

"Tanner, please call nine-on-one," I said.

I positioned Monica, prepared to give her CPR. First, I checked her wrist for her pulse and felt a slight beat.

Behind me, I heard my son, "My emergency is my mom. Something's wrong with her." He paused before he said, "I don't know." Then, "Dad, is she breathing?"

"She is." I had to shout above Raven's cries. "She's breathing barely."

Then, Tanner's voice. "I don't know, " he said into the phone. Then to me, "Do you know CPR, Dad?"

"Yes," I told him. "But please, tell them to hurry."

As my son stayed on the phone with 9-1-1 and my daughter cried until she was heaving with hiccups, I focused on breathing life into my wife.

Thirty pumps, two breaths.

I remembered the lessons from the CPR class that Monica and I had taken together, and I began the compressions: one, two, three, four, five....

I pumped until I got to thirty, then I breathed my life into her — twice. Then, I started all over again: one, two, three, four, five....

I pumped, I breathed, I prayed.

*****

Four hours, thirty-three minutes, and twenty-seven seconds.

I'd been counting how long it had been since my heart had stopped. That was how much time that passed before I glanced up, and saw the Emergency Room doctor coming to me.

As he approached, my heart felt like it stopped for real now. But then, he nodded slightly, making me able to stand.

He said, "Your wife is going to be fine."

Those words had brought tears of relief to all of us — me, Lamar and his wife, Tanner and Raven. I had wanted my children to go home with Lamar. But my six and sixteen year old had told me, in not so polite terms, that they weren't going anywhere except for with me and their mother.

So, I'd acquiesced because I wasn't sure what to do in a situation like this. They'd already seen their mother, sprawled out, looking dead. Whatever happened here at Houston

Memorial Herman Hospital couldn't be worse than that. Well, maybe one thing — but it seemed that I wouldn't have to worry about that.

"Your wife gave us quite a scare, Mr. Logan. But we managed to pump her stomach." He glanced at my children.

That made Lamar say, "Okay, now that your mom is doing okay, y'all are going home with me."

It was exhaustion that made my daughter agree right away, but I had to give Tanner a pat on his back to let him know that it was fine to leave now.

I said, "I really want to concentrate on your mom and it'll be better if you're with Lamar."

"She's gonna be all right?" My son looked at me and the doctor.

We both nodded back. I hugged my children and Lamar's wife, gave my man, dap, before he hugged me and then, I watched them walk through the doors.

Turning back to the doctor, he continued his explanation. "Her heart never stopped, which is a good thing. And she's stable right now. I do have to speak to you about her recovery." He glanced down at his tablet. "Her admitting paperwork. Your wife, she suffers from depression?"

I nodded. "But she's never done anything like this before."

"Unfortunately, this is not uncommon. She's being treated, though." Again, he glanced down at his table. "Doctor Nichols, I know her."

"She's really good, but it's my wife. Her visits have been sporadic and she takes medication, but not regularly."

He paused. "Well, you do understand that she will have to be admitted under a seventy-two hour hold for observation."

Even though I nodded, I didn't know that.

The doctor explained, "This is standard procedure when we believe someone is a substantial risk of serious harm to himself or others, so this is something that we have to do. Your wife will be admitted to West Oaks Hospital. "

I had lots of questions about this, but that wasn't my priority right now. "Okay, but can I see her?"

"Of course. She's still groggy. She's going to be for a while. But she'll be under observation so we'll get her whatever she needs."

He led me through the door, then past several draped-off areas before he stopped. He pulled back the curtain, and I caught my breath. I heard the curtain close behind me, but I didn't look back. My eyes stayed on Monica and I moved toward her. My wife, she looked as fragile and as innocent as our daughter.

"Hey," I whispered.

She turned her head toward me, and smiled at first. But then, it was as if she remembered, I watched tears come to her eyes. "I'm sorry."

I pulled the chair next to the bed up close, sat down and took her hand. "You don't have anything to be sorry about."

She licked her lips, nodded a little, and closed her eyes. For a moment, I wondered if she'd fallen back asleep — she'd taken so many pills. But then, she opened her eyes.

"Don't leave."

"Oh, no, baby. I'm going to stay right here. I'm not going anywhere."

She shook her head a bit. "No, don't...leave...me."

Then, I knew what she meant. "Oh, no, baby. I'm not leaving you. I was never going to leave you. It's just...." I swallowed back tears. "I love you. Do you know that?"

She didn't move.

I said, "I love you," again and again, until my wife nodded.

She nodded and said, "I love you, too." Then, she closed her eyes, but my heart sang. Because she closed her eyes and there was a smile on her face.

I stayed in my seat, holding her hand, and I was going to stay there until she woke up. I was going to stay there until she was admitted under the seventy-two-hour hold. I was going to stay there even if she needed to be admitted to a longer term facility.

I was going to stay and stand until my wife got well.

I was going to stay and stand because I loved Monica. From my heart, to my soul. And even with my transgression, all my imperfections and Monica's illness that was the kind of love that lasted forever.

CHAPTER 26

Angelique

"Okay, Preston. Five o'clock. I'll meet you there."
I clicked off my cell, right before I had the urge to say, 'I love you,' then turned and looked straight into the face of my friend.

We stared at each other for a moment before Sheryl said, "Before you tell me what he said...here."

I took the glass from her. "You know this isn't healthy, right?"

"What?"

"Filling me with all of this wine all of the time. And never, ever any food."

"You need food?" She shrugged. "I drink my dinner."

"And your breakfast and lunch, too." I took a sip.

"Girl, today is Saturday. This is an all wine, all day, kinda day. Plus, didn't I feed you a hella dinner last night?"

I chuckled. Yes, she had. She'd served me the one dish that she knew how to make — macaroni and cheese. That was it. Just mac and cheese and wine. But like she said, it was hella good, and I hadn't had to cook. So, who was I to complain?

While Sheryl sat at one of the bar stools at the counter, I set my glass down, then searched her pantry that was loaded with food that would never be prepared unless Cassidy or I came over. But for the week that I'd been here, I hadn't had the energy to do more than sleep, think, and drink with my best friend.

I grabbed a half bag of potato chips and a box of crackers. Inside her refrigerator, I found a block of cheese (which she always kept handy for her mac and cheese) and set all three on the counter in front of her.

After I rounded up the plates and utensils, I wiggled onto the stool next to Sheryl, and ignored the way she stared at me.

"Just take all my food, why don't you?"

"I cannot drink on an empty stomach. Not when I'm meeting Preston in," I paused and glanced at my watch, "in a little under five hours."

"So," she picked up a cracker and cut into the cheese before I did, "you're gonna keep your conversation with Preston a secret or are you gonna share with me?"

Not even a second passed. "I'm gonna keep it a secret."

She did one of those gangsta leans back and away from me. "Wrong answer."

I took a sip of wine before I said, "He wants to get together to talk."

Grabbing another cracker and a cut of cheese, Sheryl said, "My middle school education gave me enough to deduce that. So what does he want to talk about?"

"Well, my elementary school education gave me enough to deduce that he wants to talk about us."

This time, she chomped on some chips before she said, "So what're you going to tell him?"

I was thoughtful for a moment. "I think I'm going to do more listening than talking."

"Really?" She sucked her teeth as if my words annoyed her. "After a whole week, this is all you were able to come up with? You haven't decided what you want? Who you want?"

"I'll talk, but I really want to listen to Preston since he's the one who called me," I said, thinking about how difficult it had been to not call Preston to see how he was doing. No matter how he'd neglected me over the years, we did speak every day, we did check in to make sure the other was safe. And in this past week, that was what I'd wanted. To know that my husband was safe and that his hurt was at least kinda inching away.

But, I'd followed Sheryl's advice when it came to Preston, giving him the space he needed, knowing he would reach out when his heart said that he could.

"Well, what about Blu?" Sheryl said, taking my thoughts away from my husband.

I shrugged and wondered what Sheryl would think when she found out that I hadn't followed her advice with Blu. What would she say when she found out that I'd already talked to Blu — and hadn't told her? It wasn't that I had planned to keep it away from my best friend, but since she hadn't been home on Wednesday when I'd said goodbye to Blu, and since I'd gone into my bedroom and cried myself to sleep, and since I hadn't seen her until the next morning — by then, there just didn't seem to be a point.

"I cannot believe that you aren't itching to speak to Blu," Sheryl said as if she were intent on breaking up every thought I had this morning. "Aren't you going to call him?"

"You told me not to, remember?" I took another sip to give me more than a moment of reprieve, more than enough time to come up with something profound to tell Sheryl. When

I put the glass down, all I came up with was, "And anyway, I need to speak to my husband."

"Well, that's a good sign. You're still calling Preston your husband."

"No divorce papers have been served."

"Good point." She dumped a couple of chips onto the empty plate in front of her. "So are you prepared to lose Preston? Are you prepared for him to say that he wants a divorce because of what happened with Blu?"

I nodded right away because that had been one of the thoughts that had stayed steady in my mind. "I know that could be one of the things that happens with Preston. I know that he could ask me for a divorce."

"And you're ready?"

"I have to be."

"How do you feel about that? I mean, you were with Blu just once and your marriage may be over. Was that one time worth it?"

I blinked more than a couple of times, trying to gather all of the thoughts I'd had when I asked myself that same question. "Was it worth it?" I repeated her question. "It was just one night, but..." I shook my head wondering how long the memories of that night would remain. I didn't even have to close my eyes, it was still that vivid — I could see him, smell him, taste him, and most of all, I could feel him. I shuddered, hoping that Sheryl didn't notice. "But with Blu," I continued, "I realized all that I'd been missing and with that...then, it was worth it."

Sheryl glanced at me sideways, then said, "You know you're my girl and I love you for life. But you sound crazy right now," she said.

"Why?"

"Because one time with Blu and you know what you've been missing?"

"It wasn't one time with Blu." Before she toppled over with shock, I added, "It may have been only one night with him...in that way. But it was all times with Blu. It was every time we texted, every time we talked on the phone, every time we got together for coffee, drinks, or dinner. Even when we were just playing the game, every time I was with him or had any contact with him, I felt alive. Every time, he made me feel like I was the prize."

Sheryl's lips were pressed together, as if she wanted to be sure that I was done with my soliloquy. "So, are you saying that you want to be with Blu?"

I wish that you were mine.

After a moment, I said, "You know what I want? I want whatever God has for me."

She threw her hands up. "God? Now you want to bring Him into this? 'Cause He wasn't anywhere in the mix when you were sexin' Blu." She sat back as if she'd just dropped the mic.

Her words hurt a bit because she'd asked a good question. There had so many reasons why I'd had to talk to God and ask for forgiveness this week. "Well, if God wasn't there then, He certainly needs to be here now. So, that's what I want."

She gave me a slow smile. "Well, I can't say anything to that." She paused. "But do you wanna know what I think?"

"No."

"I think you should tell Preston everything you just told me. Make him understand how Blu made you feel."

"No man wants to hear what another man did for his wife."

She sighed in a way that made me wonder if she thought I was a little dense on this subject. "Of course, I'm not talking about the physical part, I'm talking about how he got to you emotionally. Preston needs to do his job and connect again with you that way."

I nodded.

"And then," she added, "you need to get on your knees...."

My eyebrows rose to the top of my head.

"And beg and plead that your husband will forgive you, that he will take you back. Tell him you were smoking crack, on that Molly or something, anything that would make you crazy enough to cheat on him."

"Really? And that's your professional opinion?"

She nodded and took a sip. "And I won't even send you a bill."

"This from the woman who encouraged me to do...whatever...with Blu."

"There are three things that are wrong with that statement." She held her hand in the air and began counting off her fingers. "Number one, you know how I am. You know I can be a little crazy," she made a circular motion near her temple, "and number two, I can be out there sometimes. And number three, I was just talking about you having a good time, not committing to a lifetime. I wasn't talking about you making any life changes. I just wanted you to feel good for a moment. I was *never* talking about you and Preston breaking up."

I nodded. Preston and I breaking up. That was something that I had never really considered. Not seriously. Not until I met Blu. And even then, not until last Saturday.

I wish that you were mine.

I'd wished, too. So what did that mean for me and Preston? Was divorce right here in front of my face.

I glanced at my watch. Well, I guessed I would know in about four hours and twenty three minutes. I would know how the next chapter of my life would read.

CHAPTER 27

Angelique

I'd been in search of my happy and now, I was coming home.
I pressed the garage remote, and held my breath for a
moment, wondering if Preston had changed the code. But
when the door lifted, I exhaled. Of course, he would not. My
husband was neglectful, not vindictive.

I eased my car next to his and remembered the last time
I'd done this — a week ago tomorrow. What a difference these
days had made — I'd had to say goodbye to Blu; was this my
goodbye to Preston?

My steps were tentative as I walked toward the door. What
had I been thinking? Why would I agree to meet Preston here?
It felt like I was returning to the scene of my crime and now, I
wished that I'd suggested that we meet somewhere else like
Starbucks.

Well...maybe not Starbucks.

That was the thought before I stepped into our home. That
was the thought before I had no thoughts whatsoever because
it was hard to make sense of what I saw — votive candles that
adorned the floor, setting a pathway. And then what I heard
— Prince:

You own my heart and mind
I truly adore you....

If my steps had been tentative before, now I wasn't certain what to do at all. But I just put one foot in front of the other. And kept moving through the kitchen, following the candle-lit path, until I rounded the corner into our dining room. In there, I stopped.

Here, the music was a bit louder, though still soft. Here, the candles flickered, making the dining room glow. Here, Preston stood, the same way he had on Sunday, holding two glasses of what looked to be champagne.

His face wasn't as hard, nor as stiff as it had been six days ago, though still, he wore no smile. He moved toward me, his steps seemingly as tentative as mine. But by the time he finally stood in front of me, he now wore a semblance of a smile.

My eyes were on his as he handed me my glass. "We started this the other day," he said. "And we never finished...our drink."

He sounded the way he did on the phone, not happy, not sad, no commitment whatsoever. When I took my glass, he brought his glass to his lips and I did the same only because I didn't know what else to do. My mind hadn't quite caught up with my question — what was all of this?

He said, "Here," he moved toward one of the chairs at the side of our dining room table that was set for eight. "Sit down."

It was shock that made me sit, shock that made me look up at Preston and finally ask the question, "What is this?"

He said, "I told you, we never finished our drink."

Still holding my glass, I said, "I thought you wanted to talk."

"I do. But I also wanted us to have dinner together because like you said, we hadn't done that in a long time." He walked toward the other end of the table and lifted a white plastic bag. "And since I didn't have time to cook...."

My first thought — I wondered which delivery guy Preston had hijacked this time. But when he unloaded the Styrofoam cartons onto the table, I couldn't help but laugh.

"What's so funny?" he asked, though I heard the hint of a smile in his voice.

"Really, Preston? The Waffle House?" I looked down at the giant waffle that was surrounded by scramble eggs, sausage and grits.

He chuckled with me, but then, by the time he sat down next to me, there was nothing but sadness in his voice when he said, "You told me this was when you were happiest with me. When we were eating at The Waffle House."

I wanted to reach out and hug him. But although we'd laughed just a moment ago, Preston's pain was so palpable, I was afraid to touch him. I couldn't — not when I was the cause of his pain.

When he looked up and I saw the mist in his eyes, that brought tears to my own. "I'm so sorry, Preston," I said.

He nodded. "You know, I really did want us to eat first. I wanted to chat and laugh the way we used to...and then, talk. But...."

I swallowed, a reflex as I wondered what would come next.

He said, "But we need to talk."

My hand shook as I set down my glass. "I know. "

We sat together, Prince still doing his singing thing in the background and I wondered where this was going? What questions would Preston ask? What answers would I give? It was a rhetorical question in my head because I knew what answers I would give — I would give the truth.

He said, "It's been a tough week for me because I've been trying to figure out what went wrong in our marriage." I opened my mouth but he held up his hand. "No, I heard you. All I could do last Sunday was listen to what you had to say, but," he shook his head, "I don't get it." His tone was filled with the hurt that had been stamped onto his heart by me.

"And I get that you don't."

He tilted his head.

I said, "Because all of this," my hand swept toward the expensive replica of Ellis Wilson's painting on the dining room wall, the four-shelf curio that Preston had designed, and the three-tiered chandelier that sparkled above it all, "this...all of this is your love language. But this," I held up the Styrofoam container, "this right here is mine. Because this means that you paid attention to me, that you heard me, and that you wanted to do something about what I said."

He nodded, but I could tell that he didn't really understand.

"Preston, I get that you work so hard for all of these things. But all of these things have nothing to do with me."

"But, they're all *for* you," he said, his voice filled with astonishment. "I work so hard because I want *you* to have the best of everything."

It was clear that Preston was trying, but it was just as clear that he hadn't comprehended what I'd said on Sunday. "I know what you wanted me to have, but all I wanted was you."

"I heard you," he said, though I wasn't sure that he had. "But don't you realize that I am these things? That all of this and me are one in the same?"

I leaned back. "I never thought you'd have that revelation." Twisting in the chair, I reached for him, then hesitated, but after a moment took his hands into mine. "This week has been hard for me, too. Because I kept asking myself how could I do that to such a good guy as you."

He nodded as if he totally agreed with my assessment of what I'd done. "And did you get an answer?"

"I did." I paused. "First of all, this was all me, and my shortcomings. It had nothing to do with you."

He didn't nod nor did he shake his head.

I continued, "I know it had nothing to do with you because I didn't even think about you."

He flinched.

"I only say that because if I had thought of you, I would have never been able to go through with it. I would have walked away, I think." When he raised his eyebrows, I added, "I hope." That was all I could give him — the truth.

"So why didn't you...why didn't you think about me?"

I knew that he'd have hard questions. "I did start off thinking about you." I didn't add that once Blu's lips touched mine, that was when any kind of memory of Preston ended. "But," I continued, "I think what this was about for me was that I was chasing something."

He gave me a slow nod. "And did you find it?"

That was not the question I expected that he would ask. I thought he would ask what I'd been chasing. That would have been the better question, the easier one to answer.

What was interesting was that it wasn't until this moment that I could answer this question. I guess I had to be in this place surrounded by these candles and the music and this waffle. I had to be in this place that Preston called love for me to be sure.

"Yes," I said as my shoulders rounded. "I found it."

He frowned. "Usually when someone says they found what they were looking for, that makes them happy. You don't sound that way." His tone was just as sad as mine. "Did you find whatever you were chasing…with him?"

I realized then that Preston didn't even know *his* name.

He said, "Did you find it in that…"

My eyes widened in expectation. I'd never heard my husband utter a bad word.   But he skipped over whatever noun he planned to call Blu and asked, "Is that it? Do you want to be with him?"

"No," I shook my head right away, "I don't want to be with Blu," I said his name purposefully. "I didn't find what I was looking for *in* him, I found it *with* him. " I took a breath. "I hate saying this because it sounds so cliché. But I promised myself, I would tell you only the truth. And what I was looking for was me."

Preston frowned like my words totally confused him.

And so, I began my explanation. "From the moment we met, I became lost in you. Everything in my life was about you. About making our home comfortable for you so that you could come home to a safe place after working hard all day. Next, it was what I could do to help you get your Masters. Then it was about making everything work for you while you worked long hours at the firm. And then, the ultimate. I was so excited to do everything I could to help you plan, start and build Wake Forest. But then somehow, I was dropped from that equation. It became all about you, I wasn't included at all anymore. I never put myself first, so why should I have expected you to do it?"

"But it wasn't like you wanted to work with Wake Forest. I thought you had the foundation."

"That you…and sometimes I…treated like it's a hobby. It's not important or else you wouldn't have missed the gala."

262

"It was because..." He stopped as if he caught himself. As if he knew another excuse would not help this conversation. "Okay, so now that we know the reason, where do we go from here?"

I pulled my hands away from him, lowered my head, and licked my lips to prepare to tell Preston all that I needed to say.

But before I could say anything, Preston said, "Because you hurt me, Angelique. You hurt me so much, that at first, I was sure this was beyond repair. I'm talking about my heart and our relationship. I didn't think either one could be fixed."

His words thickened the air with tension.

He continued, "But although it's hard for me to understand what you did, I want us to come back from this." He reached for my hand. "Because if there's one thing that I know for sure, it's that you're my life partner."

Life partner.

He squeezed my hand and it felt as if he'd done the same to my heart.

"It's going to take a lot," he continued. "We'll need counseling because we'll both have to figure out how to put this behind us. We'll have a lot of work to do and we'll have to do it together. But I'm willing to do all of that, whatever it takes to work this out. I want to work past my pain and past all of the pain you've felt because like I said, we belong together."

Life partners.

"So, do you think we can do this? Do you think we can put this back together?" His words were so hopeful and it pained me to think that what I had to say would take that all away.

"Angelique," he called my name as if he wasn't sure that I'd heard his question, "do you want to do this together?"

I gulped in air and a bunch of courage before I said, "Preston, what I want is a divorce."

IF ONLY FOR ONE NIGHT

Epilogue

Nine months later

The salesman handed me the keys and smiled. "Here you are, Mrs. Mason."

I didn't flinch the way I had nine months ago when someone called me by that name. From the moment Preston and I agreed to a divorce, I knew I was going to change back to my maiden name of Angelique Carter. But, I wasn't tripping — since my divorce wasn't final, I still used Mason as my legal name. That was going to change, though, in about four weeks.

Slipping inside the car, I slapped on my designer shades and rolled out of the parking lot with the top down. This car was much older than what I'd been used to while married to Preston. He made sure that I had a new car every two years — another part of his love language that didn't speak to me.

This car was one of the pieces of my new life. Gone was my Lexus SUV and in it's place was this four-year-old convertible red Corvette.

Anyone who knew me would be sure that this car purchase had been inspired by my favorite singer. But this red car had truly been inspired by Blu.

I sighed as I thought about him, and not for the first time. My sigh wasn't a longing for Blu, but rather the regret I felt for Preston. Not that I was sorry about the divorce. There was no doubt that ending my marriage was what was best for me.

But it still hurt because Preston Mason was a good man, just not the good man for me. And because he was so good, because every part of his package was just right, I might have rolled with that marriage the way so many women have done if I hadn't met Blu. Blu Logan opened my eyes. And even though I'd had fleeting thoughts of spending a lifetime with him, they were always just that — fleeting. Because there was one thing I always knew for sure — God wouldn't send me another woman's husband. And except for that one transgression, I was never going back.

So Blu had come into my life for a reason, and Preston had been a very long season. Now, my journey was all about the lifetime — and finding that true soulmate who belonged to only me.

My mind drifted back to this morning, when I'd seen the soulmate who *didn't* belong to me. I'd seen Blu on TV, not in person. We'd really pulled the plug on our connection and hadn't communicated with each other since the day we'd said goodbye. I'm not going to lie, there were so many days I wanted to send a text, call just to check-in, or even start back playing *Words With Friends*. I'd deleted the app so I wouldn't be tempted to reach out to him. At first, staying away was hard. But with each day came a renewed strength - until my heart made peace with the fact that Blu was gone.

When I'd first seen Blu this morning, being interviewed on Fox 26 Morning News - with his wife by his side - I didn't know how I'd feel watching them. The anchor was talking to them about Monica's family foundation, The Taylor Foundation, which was having a big fundraiser next week.

I'd stood in front of the television in shock.

"...and so, we decided to come out of the shadows," Monica said, "to really raise awareness about mental illness. That's what this fundraiser is all about."

She looked nothing like I envisioned. I pictured some pale, scowling woman who looked like she hated life. I don't know why I'd formulated that vision in my head, it's not like Blu ever described her that way. But this woman, looked radiant, full of life. She looked happy. And the way she and Blu kept their hands intertwined, I knew *they* were happy.

"Your family foundation used to have a rich history of funding projects, but over the last few years, it seems you went in a different direction," the red-haired anchor said.

"Oh no," Blu answered, "we were still working with charitable organizations, we just preferred to stay out of the spotlight."

Monica squeezed his hand and turned to the anchor. "My husband's right. Thankfully, when I was sick, he found an amazing organization to help, so we're still active."

My stomach did flip-flops as she continued.

"What organization was that?" the anchor asked.

She smiled, and I could've sworn she looked directly at the camera. But she just turned and grinned at Blu. "That was a donation that we had preferred to stay anonymous on, and since we hadn't cleared it with them, we'll keep it that way."

Blu looked a little uneasy, but he kept his smile as the anchor wrapped up their interview.

"Well, best of luck on the event.....and can I just say, you two are hashtag-love-goals," she chuckled before turning to the camera. "We need to have them back in February to talk about finding your soulmate," she said. "That's it for us this morning, we'll see you back here tomorrow."

As the music came up and the credits began rolling, I'd snapped the TV off and silently wished them all the best.

I pushed aside thoughts of this morning, and turned my attention to this evening, and my new beginning.

I pulled up to my studio apartment, then sat in front of the building looking at my new place. One day — two new sets of keys.

As I stepped out of the car and walked up the stairs to the third floor, I admired the visuals that surrounded my new home. I was going to love this neighborhood. My new place was far from the five thousand square foot home I'd been used to, but it got me out of Cassidy's apartment, which was where I'd been staying since her international flight duties kept her away from home. And while that had been great, it was something about having your own. And this was mine.

Opening the door, I stepped inside and paused after I closed the front door. I wanted a moment to inhale the air, the freedom, I wanted a moment to inhale the new Angelique Carter.

I was looking forward to my new life, committed to throwing myself into Black Girl Magic, earning a great living, and finding my happiness within - until my true soulmate came along.

The End

Want more from

**Victoria Christopher Murray &
ReShonda Tate Billingsley?**

Check out *It Should've Been Me* ...

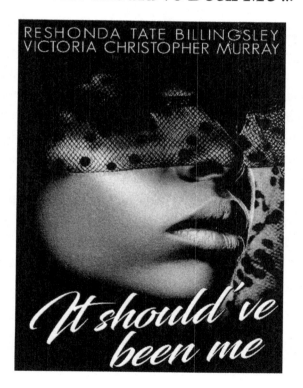

Lights, camera, action…

Tamara Collins is poised to become the next great American actress. The problem is Hollywood doesn't know that just yet…..and since her bills aren't paying themselves, Tamara signs on to star in the new stageplay, It Should've Been Me. Get in, get out, get paid…that's all Tamara wants to do. But her co-stars – including Donovan Dobbs, her ex that left her at the altar and Camille Woods, a young starlet with a serious grudge – could make this the worst decision Tamara's ever made.

Whatever it takes…

Playwright/producer Gwen Tanner Weinstein has decided if her neglectful husband can't give her love, she'll take his money. And use it to make her stageplay dreams come true. She's put together an amazing cast, sold out shows across the country and is ready to take her rightful reign as one of the top play producers in the country. If only she can keep the drama contained to the stage….and that sexy young merchandising guy out of her bed….

From shady crew members, to unscrupulous paparazzi, It Should've Been Me is bound to be turned into real life drama that will rival anything that could ever happen on the stage.

Keep reading for an excerpt…

CHAPTER 1

Tamara Collins

In my last film, I'd played a psychotic woman who stabbed her husband in the stomach thirty-two times with a Swiss Army knife. Now, looking at the man who'd just stepped into this huge conference room made me curl my hand into a fist as if I were holding that knife again.

"This cannot be happening," I mumbled, as I stepped to the other side of the room that had been set up in the Renaissance Hotel for our first rehearsal. I pivoted, so that he wouldn't see me and I could get my face together in a few seconds.

I was already upset because this jacked-up, twenty-degrees warmer than normal Atlanta temperature had turned my Brazilian Blowout into a Philippine Poof. Now I had to deal with this, too?

Clearly, I was being punished for something I had done, maybe in a previous life. I didn't believe in reincarnation, but that was the only way I could explain why I hadn't had a movie role in two years. Or maybe it wasn't punishment. Maybe it was because my name wasn't Cameron Diaz or Jennifer Anniston or that my skin wasn't the color of mashed potatoes.

Yes! That was it. That was the reason why I was in this room, an A actor (okay, maybe an A minus or at worst, a B plus) on the play circuit.

Now, don't get me wrong, I loved theater, always had, always would. Some of the greats -- James Earl Jones, Cicely Tyson, Vanessa Williams, even Denzel Washington -- had all slayed the stage. And August Wilson's "Fences" -- now that Pulitzer Prize winning play was one of my all-time favorites. Having a role in "Fences," on the Great White Way, in the magnificent city of New York, would have been as much of a coup as just about any big screen movie.

But this wasn't "Fences" nor was it "Aida" or "Fela." And this wasn't Broadway. This wasn't even off-Broadway, it wasn't two blocks over from Broadway. This was down the street, around the corner, across the river, and almost nine hundred miles away from Broadway.

And once we began touring, we'd leave Atlanta and go deep into the 'Chitlin Circuit,' probably visiting cities I'd never heard of and towns that sounded like the butt end of jokes.

I did have a little secret, though. One that I would deny if anyone ever asked me - I liked these off, off, off, off, off Broadway plays. Over the years, I'd attended quite a few if I happened to be in the city where one was playing. Of course, I made sure I was unrecognizable, always wearing huge sunglasses, always wearing a hat *and* a scarf, always keeping my head low so that no one would know that, I, Tamara Collins, the classically trained actor, laughed at all the off-center jokes, swayed to all the off-key songs, then stood with the audience at the end, giving all a standing ovation.

So while the title and some of the scenes ruffled my classical Yale University School of Drama sensibilities, I couldn't knock the thousands and thousands of fans who enjoyed these plays and the thousands and thousands of dollars that I was being paid to bring my talents to the stage.

Glancing over my shoulder, I checked to see if I'd been spotted yet. But *he* was still talking to Gwen Tanner, the creator, writer, director and producer of this play. After taking another moment and a deep breath, I sat in one of the chairs lined up against the wall. When I was ready, I raised my eyes and stared. Because him seeing me, and our having to speak to each other, was inevitable.

This made me once again ask myself what was I doing here? It had started just about a month ago. My agent, Maury had received the script from Gwen. I already knew her name. She was new on the play circuit and she was the first female to have massive success. Two plays, two NAACP Image Awards, and lots of buzz for the uplifting messages that followed the slapstick comedy. After I'd read the script, I was even more impressed. Yeah, it had the typical female-on-female hatin', female-on-male drama, but at the end, there was a powerful message of never allowing anyone's voice to be louder than God's.

So with Gwen's reputation, the ten thousand dollars per week they were paying me for the ten-week run, plus two weeks for rehearsals, and the sad fact that I had no other offers, I'd signed on, knowing it was the right thing to do.

That was what I believed when I signed the contract two weeks ago. Heck, that was what I believed yesterday, this morning, five minutes ago. That was what I believed until Donovan had walked into this room.

Donovan Dobbs, the hot R&B singer and a heartthrob who'd been commanding the stage and stealing hearts for twenty years, ever since he was sixteen years old. He could even act a little, but his major talent - he was fine. It was like God decided to toss Michael Ealy, Blair Underwood and Idris Elba into a blender, hit start, and see what came out. Yep. Donovan was the personification of brown and beautiful.

And he was a low down dirty dog.

"Well, well, well..."

My plan had been to keep my eyes on him. But I guess as I'd taken that little jaunt down that lane filled with bad memories, Donovan had spotted me.

"If it isn't the love of my life." His tone sounded like he wasn't surprised to see me.

He was still several feet away when he'd said those words, and I could feel the others in the room pause, then stop and watch as Donovan walked my way with his signature strut; he had swagger before the word had even been invented. He had swagger and that smile. The whole time he kept that smile that I loved. That smile that I hated.

"So, when did you get in?" he asked when he stopped in front of me. He opened his arms, then reached for me as if he was crazy enough to expect some kind of hug.

I wanted to hug him all right. And if I'd had that knife from my last movie, I would have - hugged him and stabbed him straight in his back. Instead, I glared and hoped that my stare was filled with the heat that I felt. I hoped my stare set him on fire, and I swear, if I saw a single flame, I wouldn't even spit on him to save him.

Standing, I didn't part my lips as I moved away. I heard his chuckles as I stomped by, but though I wanted to stop and swing on him, I kept marching until I was right in front of Gwen.

It didn't matter that she was chatting with one of the other actors. We hadn't all been introduced yet, so I had no idea what role the tall, svelte, with a tan that made her one-degree above white, woman was playing. I didn't care. There was only one piece of business on my mind and Gwen needed to handle this now. "I need to speak with you." It was a demand, not a request.

"Yeah, what's up?" Gwen replied, giving me just a quick glance. "Privately," I said.

The actor, who I pegged as a newcomer since I didn't recognize her, gave me a smirk with a little attitude. But before I could roll my neck back at her, Gwen said, "Camille, give us a minute," and the woman did a moonwalk away from us.

As soon as she was out of earshot, I hissed, "What is he doing here?" I jabbed a finger in Donovan's direction.

When Gwen and I looked his way, Donovan winked.

Gwen grinned and I wanted to puke.

By the time she turned back to me, her expression was stiff with seriousness. "Who? Donovan?" She gave a little shrug, and then with a wave of her hand that made the dozen of wooden bangles on her arm jingle, she announced, "He's in the play."

My glance took in the woman who was really quite striking in the floor-length West African print duster that she wore. Her sister locs were swept up on top of her head and wrapped in a matching band. But right now, I didn't care that she stood in front of me like she was some kind of African Queen. I was the star of this play, and she needed to address the problem I had with this.

"I assumed that he was here because he was in the play," I snapped. "What role is he playing?"

I guess that was the question she was waiting for me to ask and the one she wanted to answer. Her grin was back when she said, "He's playing your love interest."

My nostrils flared and my fingers began that search again for that knife. But I stayed calm, remained professional, though not even my Yale training could hide the fury in my voice. "I thought Jamal was my leading man."

Jamal Brown was the R & B singer turned reality star, who didn't have the voice or the looks of Donovan. But what he did have was my approval. Seriously, my contract said that I had approval of the man who would be starring opposite me.

"Oh, yeah. Well, he had to drop out at the last minute," she said as if that fact were not a big deal. "He got a movie deal."

Wait! Stop! What? My thoughts did a little rewind. A movie deal? For a moment, I wanted to keep the button pressed on pause and ask, 'What movie deal?' because this was the problem. This was why actors, like me, couldn't get roles. Singers and reality stars and everyone who couldn't act were landing contracts and taking parts that rightfully belonged to those of us who'd been trained.

But I had to come down from that mental soapbox and stay focused on what was in front of me.

"So, Jamal left and you're telling me that you couldn't find anyone else?"

Gwen tilted her head a little, frowned and stared at me as if my words had put her into a state of confusion.

Clearly, she had no acting training. Or maybe it was just that no matter what she said or did, I knew what this was all about. Everyone in these United States of America knew about my drama with Donovan - it had been covered by every gossip blog, played out in every major tabloid, and dissected on every entertainment show. So Gwen casting Donovan in this role was no mistake. She was trying to take my drama and my pain all the way to her bank.

"Tamara, I'm sorry if you have a problem with Donovan, but the show opens in two weeks." Her tone was saccharine sweet, leaving a bad aftertaste in my ears. "I'm grateful that Donovan was even available on such short notice."

"Well, I'm not about to be in this play with him." I folded my arms and raised an eyebrow. She needed to know I was serious about this.

There was no way Gwen would ever be able to convince me that this was a coincidence. First of all, my mother had always told me there was no such thing as a coincidence. And secondly, I was just supposed to believe that she'd written a script about a woman who'd been left at the altar and now I was to play opposite the man who'd left me right there?

Oh no! I wasn't about to become fodder for the tabloids and the blogs and the shows again.

"Now, Tam," Gwen said, her sweet tone still in place.

"It's Tamara." I snuggled my arms tighter across my chest.

"*Tamara.*" All of that sweetness was gone when she said, "I know you're upset, and I'm sorry I didn't realize this before...."

Yeah, right. She must think I'm BooBoo the fool.

"But I know you wouldn't want Entertainment Tonight, Access Hollywood, Black Voices and every other entertainment outlet to know that your ex ran you off from a professional production, would you?"

I was not impressed because whatever they said about me leaving wouldn't be nearly as bad as what they'd say if I stayed.

I kept my stance and that made Gwen add, "And, if that isn't important to you, just remember, you have a contract."

"And?" I smirked.

"And, you know contracts are binding."

That made me stand up straight, lower my arms, and stare at her as if her brain had just fallen out of her head. Was this heffa threatening to sue me? Over a freakin' stageplay? A Chitlin' Circuit stageplay?

"Look," Gwen said, taking a deep breath before returning to a more natural smile. "I don't want any disgruntled actors, but I have a show to put on and I know you're a professional. You're one of the few talented black actresses out there," she added, I guess believing that flattery never hurt. "I have all the confidence in the world that you'll be able to handle this." Then, she leaned in and lowered her voice as if she were about to share something with me like we were just girls. "Don't let him get to you."

I wanted to tell her first, that true thespians of the female persuasion preferred to be called actors. And then, *don't let him get to me?* How would she handle this situation?

I knew I was trapped, but while I would never admit it, I wanted her to admit one thing. "You did this on purpose, right?"

"Oh, you give me too much credit," Gwen said, making her bangles jingle again.

Yup, she'd never taken an acting lesson a day in her life.

"Look, while this play bears *some* resemblance to your life, trust me, it wasn't done on purpose. Besides if you think about it, it's not really that close to your story. You never made it to the altar, remember?"

My fingers began that clutching thing again.

"Is there a problem, ladies?" Donovan asked over my shoulder. I didn't even turn to face him, not acknowledging him in any manner. Well, at least not on the outside. Inside, I felt a little flutter, and I cursed that right out of me.

But while I tried to do nothing, Gwen flashed a smile. "And why in the world would there be any problem?" she said, her glance settling over my right shoulder. "I was just going over some last-minute script changes with Tamara."

"I'm looking forward to working with you, Tammie-Poo," Donovan said.

I whipped around. No, this fool didn't call me by the pet name he'd given me when we'd first met.

"Whatever," I said, shoving my way past him.

He scurried after me. "Hey, hey, hey, I've been looking forward to this, baby. What's the problem?" he asked, taking my hand and stopping me.

I looked down to where he still held me, then my gaze inched up until I met his eyes. I snatched my hand away and hissed, "You're my problem."

Stepping closer to me, he said, "Please don't be like that. There's a lot you don't know. So much that we have to talk about."

I blinked. Inside his voice, I heard something - like truth, like love.

He moved in what felt like the slowest of motions: His hand raised, he reached toward me, his fingertips grazed my cheek.

And a wave rolled through my center.

Inside, I cursed again. This time I cursed my libido and Donovan. Squeezing my legs together, I wondered why my own body would betray me like this? I hated him and I needed every part of my body to remember that.

His hand lingered on my cheek for too long, and I slapped him away. "Look, Donovan." My tone was as sharp as the edge of steel. "We're both here now, so we'll do our jobs and get this over with."

"Great." He exhaled as if somehow my words had given him relief. As if he'd been concerned that I'd walk out the door. "I was hoping you would stay and now, I hope this means that we can hook up...."

"What?" I exclaimed.

"For a drink. Tonight. I just want to talk."

Hook up? A drink? To talk? After I let the gall of his request settle in my mind, I said, "Donovan, you want to talk?"

He grinned and bobbed his head up and down like a puppy.

This time, I was the one who leaned in closer. "Then go home and talk to your wife."

He blinked.

I added, "Your wife, remember? The woman you left me for."

I did one of those moves that I'd learned in freshman drama - a half-turn pivot, before my arm swooped down into the chair where

I grabbed my hobo, swung it over my shoulder, and then I did a slow, hip swaying strut right out the door.

Read more by getting your copy today!
Available wherever books are sold
www.BrownGirlsBooks.com

CPSIA information can be obtained
at www.ICGtesting.com
Printed in the USA
LVOW03s0407160218
566842LV00009B/139/P